FULL SPEED AHEAD

It was dark, and the two choppers were silent as they skimmed thirty feet over the water. The NEST team had divided into two groups of two members each. One of the team members was holding the wand in the direction of the target boat, while the other watched a tiny screen on what amounted to a small laptop computer. They flew in the dark and in silence—only the faint glow of the heads-up display in the cockpit and the screen of the computer gave off any light at all.

The copilot of the first chopper spoke quietly to his pilot, but all members of the team on board could hear the conversation.

"Radar picks up target at current heading, ten miles out. Time to target, less than four minutes. She is heading straight for us at twenty knots."

Dr. Diane Peters was in the backseat next to Dr. David Tompkins. She nudged him. "Three minutes and we should be lighting up if we've got the right boat."

As they approached their target, warning lights began flashing all over the control panel and heads-up display.

Berkley titles by David M. Salkin

NECESSARY EXTREMES
CRESCENT FIRE

NECESSARY EXTREMES

DAVID M. SALKIN

BERKLEY BOOKS, NEW YORK

THE BERKLEY PUBLISHING GROUP
Published by the Penguin Group
Penguin Group (USA) Inc.
375 Hudson Street, New York, New York 10014, USA

Penguin Group (Canada), 90 Eglinton Avenue East, Suite 700, Toronto, Ontario M4P 2Y3, Canada
(a division of Pearson Penguin Canada Inc.)
Penguin Books Ltd., 80 Strand, London WC2R 0RL, England
Penguin Group Ireland, 25 St. Stephen's Green, Dublin 2, Ireland (a division of Penguin Books Ltd.)
Penguin Group (Australia), 250 Camberwell Road, Camberwell, Victoria 3124, Australia
(a division of Pearson Australia Group Pty. Ltd.)
Penguin Books India Pvt. Ltd., 11 Community Centre, Panchsheel Park, New Delhi—110 017, India
Penguin Group (NZ), 67 Apollo Drive, Rosedale, North Shore 0632, New Zealand
(a division of Pearson New Zealand Ltd.)
Penguin Books (South Africa) (Pty.) Ltd., 24 Sturdee Avenue, Rosebank, Johannesburg 2196,
South Africa

Penguin Books Ltd., Registered Offices: 80 Strand, London WC2R 0RL, England

This is a work of fiction. Names, characters, places, and incidents either are the product of the author's imagination or are used fictitiously, and any resemblance to actual persons, living or dead, business establishments, events, or locales is entirely coincidental.

NECESSARY EXTREMES

A Berkley Book / published by arrangement with the author

PRINTING HISTORY
Berkley edition / October 2007

Copyright © 2007 by David M. Salkin.
Cover design by Steven Ferlauto.
Interior text design by Laura K. Corless.

ISBN: 978-0-425-21791-7

BERKLEY®
Berkley Books are published by The Berkley Publishing Group,
a division of Penguin Group (USA) Inc.,
375 Hudson Street, New York, New York 10014.
BERKLEY® is a registered trademark of Penguin Group (USA) Inc.
The "B" design is a trademark belonging to Penguin Group (USA) Inc.

PRINTED IN THE UNITED STATES OF AMERICA

10 9 8 7 6 5 4 3 2 1

They rest beneath row upon row of neat white markers in Arlington,

In a sea of crosses and Stars of David in places from Normandy to Anzio,

Or in unmarked locations at the bottom of oceans, deep in forgotten jungles or vanished completely, remembered by the eternal flame.

These are the men and women that have given everything to this country.

Their countless tales of heroism are buried with them, most never to be told.

To them, this book is dedicated.

*It's not enough that we do our best;
sometimes we have to do what's required.*

—Sir Winston Churchill

Acknowledgments

The problem with thanking family and friends at the front of a book is that there isn't enough room! To ALL of my family and friends, thank you for the never-ending support and love. I am very blessed.

There *is* a real Mike Skripak and a *real* Chris Cascaes, and after a lifetime of friendship, it gives me great pleasure to immortalize them in my book. While they are nothing at all like the made-up characters in this story, they are two of the greatest guys in the world. If you are my friend and see your name, it just means I love ya. And if you haven't seen your name yet, don't get mad, you'll end up in a novel one of these days, too, so be nice or I'll make you a villain.

To Doug Whiteman, Thomas Colgan, and Sandra Harding at Berkley—my continued thanks for allowing me to "live the dream" of being an author. I am enjoying every minute of it!

To "Team Konig": Stacey and her crew—Missy, Jesse, and Jake—I love you!
   Big Brother Eric: "From the womb to the tomb, my brother . . ."
   Dad and Mom: Still my biggest heroes.
   And to my own little team: Thanks for the smiles every day. Can't wait until my children are old enough to read my books. I hope the world they inherit shows improvement.

And to the real Major General George "Tom" Garrett, Staff Sergeant David Clemenko, Colonel Mark Franklin, Lieutenant Colonel Bill Peace, Sergeant J. J. Vaccaro, and our other men and women in uniform, thank you for all those years of service.

CHAPTER 1

Tehran, Iran

Morning prayers could be heard from the minarets over the mosques, the haunting songs carrying their message to the children of Islam. Most activity had stopped as the faithful knelt on their prayer mats and began their prayers. Imam Ayatollah Kamala could be heard over loudspeakers for many blocks, and his followers hung on every syllable. He had finished with the traditional prayers and went on with this morning's tirade against the West, Israel and the Great Satan. His political commentary was usually as long as his prayers, and his mosque was typically overflowing into the streets with the most radical and violent Islamists in all of Iran.

If they only knew. . . . But how could they? How could the tens of thousands of Islamic fundamentalists who followed the preaching of Imam Ayatollah Kamala, one of Iran's most violent mullahs, possibly contemplate the notion that this man had actually been funneling information to the Americans for over twenty-five years? He was everything an Islamic fundamentalist was supposed to be: devoted to Islam, prepared to use every form of violence to change the world into what the true believers knew it should be, a hater of Jews and Americans, against equal rights for women, against any Western influences, including Western music and art—both guaranteed to turn their youth into whores and drug addicts . . . the list went on and on. How could his followers possibly know that Imam Ayatollah Kamala had actually been born Bijon Mujaharov, a Western-educated intellect who had been present during the sacking of the U.S. embassy some twenty-seven years earlier? Bijon, who had seen his parents killed during the revolution that removed the shah from Iran and changed his country forever. . . .

For the first few months after the revolution, Bijon and his brothers hid, going from place to place with any family members or friends who would help them. They were eventually turned in, and Bijon escaped only moments before his cousins' house was searched, and his cousins and brothers were taken away to some medieval prison to be tortured to death in the name of Islam. It was at that time that Bijon, now alone in the world, decided that his life's purpose was to save his beloved country and avenge the deaths of his entire family.

He wasn't alone. There were other brave souls in Iran who also wanted life to return to "normal." Not that they loved the previous shah of Iran so much, but at least they lived in a comparatively open, modern society. The revolution had set their country's clock back a thousand years, and there was no hope in sight. It would take the bravery of a few citizens who remembered how life *could* be to make a difference. Bijon's life changed forever when he was introduced to an American secret agent named Michael Skripak. Skripak, who had been somewhat unofficially attached to the embassy, had been stuck in Iran after the embassy fell. Four hundred and forty-four days later, the hostages were released, but Skripak stayed behind intentionally, using his contacts and safe houses to move about, finding loyal friends he could count on to move messages about the country.

Skripak had been getting secret messages to and from CIA headquarters in Langley regularly, even during the hostage crisis. He had been "in position" the night the rescue attempt had been made, heavily armed across the street from the embassy, waiting for helicopters that never came because two of them had crashed in the desert. No one had listened to his concerns about the sandstorms, and the celebrations in the streets the next day when the news of the failed rescue attempt became public was heartbreaking. Skripak had been introduced to Bijon shortly after that.

Skripak spent many hours with Bijon over that first month, interviewing him without Bijon realizing he was being interviewed. Every detail was passed back to Langley for verification, and when Skripak was sure Bijon could be trusted, he brought him in one last time.

They sat for hours, talking about the fate of his family and his country. Several times Mike floated out the notion that it would take the individual efforts of everyday men and women if there was to be any hope for the future. He explained to Bijon the need for reliable intelligence, and concocted the idea of reinventing his newly found "agent" into a religious zealot who could attract the most violent and dangerous Islamists in Iran. He would become the magnet, the lightning rod, for these people, who chanted daily about death to the West and to the Jews.

At first Bijon doubted his ability to pull it off. It took several months of study with Mike and a few of Mike's trusted Iranian friends before Bijon realized he could do whatever was needed if he could just summon up the courage. Somehow, Skripak produced a grainy black-and-white photograph from a Tehran prison that showed several dozen naked men, hung and quite grotesquely dead, with their swollen black tongues sticking out of their mouths. One of the men was one of Bijon's brothers. It was that photo that gave him the missing dose of courage. For the next six months, Bijon studied the Koran and read all of the most radical and violent Iranian commentary he could find. He grew his beard and donned the attire of a mullah. When Skripak and his Iranian friends were satisfied that he could answer any question, speak on any subject—religious, political or ideological—they drove him south to a small town west of Kerman, where he was planted as a traveling mullah.

The more violent and radical his views, the more young men flocked to him. It was his dangerous and independent decision to make a public statement that "the Holocaust never happened" that made him famous and catapulted him to fame and country-wide respect. At first, Skripak had been horrified when he read the comment in the state-run newspaper. Then, when he saw the public reaction, he recognized the brilliance of his new agent. The bigger the lie, the more it was believed. This was classic spy craft. Skripak had found a natural. Within two years, Imam Ayatollah Kamala was known all over Iran. Arab news agencies throughout the Middle East, some of which were not particularly fond of Persian Iran, recognized the great power and wisdom of this up-and-coming star in the Islamic world. Imam Ayatollah Kamala could change the fate of the Arab world just as easily as he could for the Persian world, and Al Jazeera and the rest of the Arab media listened to every word. The more vile and hateful, the closer it was placed to the front page. This man had potential. Within a few weeks, Syria, Lebanon and Egypt all had devout followers of this Iranian sword rattler.

Imam Ayatollah Kamala was a very brave man. Not because of the vile speeches he made to thousands of hysterical followers, but because once each week or so, he would send a burst transmission from his bedroom, identifying new thugs, murderers, planners and terrorists to CIA headquarters in Virginia. There were certain coded phrases he would use during his speeches—which of course were monitored by the CIA—which would alert the chief of Middle East Intelligence that a burst transmission was coming that night.

Imam Ayatollah Kamala, who only a few years ago had been a humble Bijon Mujaharov, could never have guessed how successful he would become. Before long, he was being invited to Tehran to speak with the clerics, the president, and even some of the conservative Majlis. Bijon had been a scholar as a young man, and harbored no ill will against the Jews, the Americans or the West in general. It had been his dream to one day live in America, and in fact, a professor whom he had corresponded with at Princeton University was a Jew. To be speaking such contemptuous and hateful ramblings about the Jews and infidels left a bad taste in his mouth, and he was only able to be believable by overacting and "going over the top" in his speeches. The irony was that the more he lied and made up history, the more he was believed. He had questioned his handler, Skripak, about this many months before, and was told to keep doing what he was doing since it was working much better than they had planned. The fact that it *was* working so well was what was troubling Bijon. Just how far could he go before he was either caught as an impostor, or incited World War Three?

It was this last transmission that changed everything at Langley. After his third trip to Tehran, where he was treated as a national hero, including an invitation to a private lunch with the president and several clerics, he went home and sent this:

"Situation Urgent. Verified with highest levels of Iranian authority. Iranian nuclear facility producing weapon-grade material with aid from Russia. Weapons being developed. Syria connection. All being done with 'end game' in mind. Israel most likely target, but can't rule out any Western nation. Estimated time to completion of weapons system less than six months. Cannot confirm site of facility yet, but will attempt soon. Advise highest priority be given to this situation. Check following: Muhammad Ali Basri, Ali bin-Oman and Kumani Mustafa Awadi. All were present at meeting and apparently have more information on this subject. Awadi link to Syria. Do not believe anyone suspects surveillance yet. No contact with Mike S. for two weeks, advise his health. Out."

CHAPTER 2

CIA Headquarters, Langley, Virginia, Middle East Desk

"Oh crap," mumbled Dex.

Dexter "Dex" Murphy had been Middle East assistant chief for three years. It had been the longest three years of his life, costing him his girlfriend, most of his "regular" friends, and possibly his health. He typically worked seventy-hour weeks, weekends and nights, whatever. Only forty-three years old, Dexter's hair was already graying from his "Irish Red," and his ruddy complexion was giving way to more lines than a street map of New York City. After being around the block a few times, including two wars in Iraq and an invasion of Afghanistan before making assistant chief, very few things fazed him. This latest message from Bijon gave him heartburn.

He printed the message on his secure personal printer and grabbed the phone to call the chief's desk. Darren Davis picked up on the first ring.

"Davis," he grumbled, obviously as tired as Murphy.

"Chief, you got a minute? I need to show you something, *pronto.*"

"Come down right away," came the reply, followed by a click.

Thirty seconds later, Murphy was knocking on his glass door. Davis had a "tight room," meaning it was a secure cube that couldn't be eavesdropped on or interfered with from anywhere inside or outside of Langley. Aside from the heavy glass door, the room was a vault, with its own air-filtration system and redundant systems for everything from secure encrypted cable to satellite imaging and links to hundreds of secret places around the Middle East. Unlike Murphy, Davis had a direct phone to the director of the CIA himself, Wallace R. Holstrum.

Murphy entered the office and waited as Davis finished scribbling on a yellow legal pad.

"Jesus H. Christ. You been watching the news lately? NSA is catching a ration of shit about this wiretapping. The Hill ever gets wind of the crap *we* do, and we'll all end up in front of a Senate subcommittee for the next four years. Do these pencil-pushing bureaucrats believe *any* of the shit coming out of their own mouths?"

Murphy started to respond, but Davis continued talking over him, "They *very much* don't want to get letters full of anthrax or watch planes fly into their buildings, but they expect us to ask permission to do surveillance on scumbags that want to blow up kindergartens and shopping malls. Unbelievable. Just another day in paradise here in Virginia. What's up?" He sounded particularly foul this morning.

"Just received a message from Iran. It's Bijon, but this is something you need to read yourself, Chief." He handed Davis the message, hot off his secure printer.

Davis read it quietly, rubbed his face, obviously tired and now even more stressed out than he was two minutes ago, then reread it slowly.

"Verified with highest levels? You think he got in to see the president again? Jesus Christ. This operation has developed a life of its own. He says the Russkies are giving the nuke intel to the Iranians. Are they out of their fucking minds? I know they are hurting for cash—but Jesus, the Iranians? Why not just sell nukes to Hamas and Hezbollah outright? First the Russians said they would build the nuke facility in Russia to make the low-grade uranium for power only. How the hell did they go from *that* to helping these fanatics build rockets? Six months? That's just great. I'll have to tell Director Holstrum about this right away. I want you sitting in on the meeting— you have more insight into Bijon than the rest of us. You run these three names yet—'Muhammad Ali Basri,' 'Ali bin-Oman' and 'Kumani Mustafa Awadi'?"

"Not yet, sir. This came in literally one minute ago. He also says there has been no word from Mike for two weeks. That's unlike Mike. I haven't heard anything out of him directly for months, which is pretty normal, but Bijon speaks to him regularly. Should I start sending feelers out? You think he's okay?"

"Skripak is resourceful as hell. I wouldn't worry about him just yet. Get me Intel on those three names, *pronto*. We'll meet with the director within the hour, and he'll want something to chew on."

"Yes, sir, I'm on it," he replied and took off back to his office where he called his staff together to start gathering whatever they could on the three names from Bijon.

CHAPTER 3

Duce

Anthony "Duce" Cory was a lifer. At thirty years old, he had already spent twelve years in the Army, and held the rank of first sergeant. It hadn't really been his plan to stay in the Army for life when he enlisted. Originally, it was just a ticket out of the projects in New York City. A recruiter had spoken to him and some of his classmates when he was a senior in high school. Duce wasn't exactly college material, and certainly wasn't getting any scholarships. That being the case, he sure didn't have an extra fifty or sixty grand lying around to pay his own way, and his mother was making just enough money to keep them in the disgusting apartment in which they lived. His choices were fairly limited: stay with the crew he ran with and commit petty crimes, sell drugs, jack cars and eventually end up dead or in prison, or get a dead-end job making minimum wage for the next sixty years or so, and then end up dead or in prison.

When the Army recruiter walked into Duce's school, he raised quite a stir. He was an Army Ranger master sergeant with enough ribbons and commendations to cover his entire chest. The high school girls, many of them already with children from assorted fathers, whistled and catcalled the soldier as he walked down the hall, jump boots spit-shined until they glowed. He smiled at the girls to be polite, but he was all business. He headed straight to the guidance office, where he met the school's principal and was given a small desk to sit at and chat with the seniors. There had been some dissention and comments about having a recruiter in uniform at the school, but the principal was a product of the GI Bill himself, and put those fires out relatively quickly.

Over fifty students met with the master sergeant over the course of the day. They represented mostly kids who weren't going to have any chance at college, although there were three pretty bright prospects looking for financial aid through the ROTC programs. Mostly though, they were poor, tough kids from one of the roughest parts of the city. Going into a war zone wouldn't be much different than walking home from school every day.

When he sat down with the master sergeant, Duce was quiet. He was looking at all of the ribbons and decorations, and then saw the patch that read "Ranger."

"Ranger? That like Smokey the Bear?" said Duce, trying to look unimpressed.

"Not exactly," said the master sergeant. Like Duce, he was African-American, although he looked to be about forty years old. His head was almost completely shaved, except for a slight shadow on the very top. He sat rifle-straight in the chair, facing Duce, who slouched back, one arm hanging off the back of the chair, a toothpick hanging from his lips. The master sergeant didn't speak. They sat there for what seemed like a long time until Duce couldn't take it anymore.

"Well? Aren't you gonna try and sign me up or something?" he finally asked.

"Not exactly." He smiled back.

"What? You think I ain't good enough for the Army?"

"I didn't say that. I don't know anything about you. Why don't we start with your name?"

"What's *your* name?" he snapped back.

"I am Master Sergeant Reginald Thompson," he said dryly. "And you are?"

"Duce. Real name is Anthony Cory, but only my mama calls me Anthony."

"I see. And where did 'Duce' come from?" asked the master sergeant.

"I have an older brother. Everybody used to call him Aces. When I got old enough to hang out with him and his friends, they joked that I must be the duce, since I was next. He's in jail now. Busted a couple of times for jackin' cars. Ain't seen him in a few months now." He rolled up his sleeve to show his "Duce" tattoo. The master sergeant smiled at the misspelling of "Deuce."

"And what about you? You want to hang with your friends on the street until you get busted for something stupid, or do you want to serve your country and maybe learn some skills that can land you a job when you get out?"

"See? I knew you was here to sign us up. Get the brothers to fight for the man so whitey can stay home."

"Whitey, huh? Would that be the president of the United States, or Major General Tate . . . Oh wait, Major General Tate is black, you can't mean him."

"They got black generals?" Duce asked suspiciously.

"Yup. Even had a black chairman of the Joint Chiefs of Staff. You mean to tell me you never heard of Colin Powell?"

"I heard of him."

"Yeah, right," laughed the master sergeant. "Let me ask you something, Anthony—what do you want to do with your life? You want to go to college? You want a good job? Make some money to take care of your family? What are you going to do? Graduation is only a couple of months away. Then the party is over—time to get a job. What are you going to do?"

"I don't know. Guess that's why I'm talkin' to you. How come you a ranger instead of a soldier?"

"I am a soldier. Every ranger is a soldier. Not every soldier is a ranger."

"So what do you do if you're a ranger?"

"Soldiers who qualify for ranger school learn the skills needed for special missions and tactics. You might end up jumping out of a plane, fast-roping down out of a helicopter, climbing a mountain—all kinds of things you've never imagined. You also get schooled in computers, mechanics, languages, lots of things that can help you get a good-paying job when you leave the service. Or, you might just stay, like me, and be a lifer." He smiled.

"Lifer? Like you stay for life?"

"Well, twenty-five years. Maybe longer. The Army is a good home. It's been good to me. Took me out of the slum in Los Angeles and sent me all over the world. I have seen and done things that you've never dreamed about. I have served my country, and I feel pretty good when I put on this uniform."

"They let you keep it when you leave?"

It took a second for the ranger to understand what he meant. "The uniform?" He laughed. "Yeah, it's mine. I earned it. You gotta earn your own stripes, though."

They talked for almost an hour, much longer than any of the other interviews. By the time they were finished, the master sergeant realized that Duce Cory had a brain, and a desire to escape the projects. They made an appointment to speak again, and the master sergeant invited Duce, whom he intentionally referred to as Anthony, to bring his mother to his office.

Duce walked home that afternoon instead of riding with his friends. He used the time to think, and mostly to really look around at where he lived. He had been to other parts of the city, but never other parts of the country. From what he had seen on TV, almost anyplace would be better than where he was now. By the time he got home, he had made up his mind.

Duce wasn't sure how his mom would take it when he broke the news. There was just the two of them at home now, with his brother upstate in prison. His mom had brought home a sack of White Castle hamburgers from work for them to share for dinner, and she unloaded them on the kitchen table, along with some fries, while Duce grabbed a bottle of Pepsi out of the refrigerator. She sat down with a heavy sigh, obviously tired from another lousy day at work.

"How was work?" Anthony asked, trying to break the ice.

"It was just great, Anthony. They gave me a check for a million dollars for working really hard all week, but I told them I didn't need it. I said I just wanted some of the delicious little hamburgers instead."

"They are pretty damn good." He laughed.

"Watch your mouth," she snapped.

"Sorry," he said quietly. On the street, Duce was a fearless wiseass. At home, Anthony Cory was quiet and respectful of the only person he feared on the planet. She was also the only person he really loved, other than his brother, but he hadn't been around much when Duce was little, and now wouldn't be around for at least three more years. He had never met his father.

"A recruiter came to school today, Mom," he said after a few greasy bites.

"Oh yeah? From what company?" she asked.

"The Army, Mom," he said as he looked up to see her reaction.

"Oh child, please!" she exclaimed. "The Army? I don't think so."

"Why you say that?" he asked.

"The *Army*? Child, you can't be serious. You want to go fight halfway around the world and get killed for nothing? I don't think so. Nuh-uh. I already lost one child and I will not lose another."

"Mom, the sergeant said I could learn stuff and get a good job when I get out—"

She cut him off. "Yeah, that's right, he say all *kinds* of garbage till you sign on the dotted line. Oh *God*! You didn't sign anything, did you?"

"No, Mom. I didn't sign anything, but I want you to come with me and talk to him. I been doin' a lot of thinkin'—"

She cut him off again. "Child! You *ain't* been thinking! The *Army*? *Puh-leeeze* . . ."

They went around and around for almost an hour, until she relented and agreed to meet with the master sergeant at his recruiting office. That was twelve years ago.

Army Ranger Sergeant Cory had been in Kosovo when he was wounded the first time. He had only been in the Army for three and a half years at that time and had just made sergeant. A grenade had exploded nearby and shrapnel had gone whizzing by in a hot cloud of murder. The squad leader next to him had taken the brunt of the blast in his back as he faced Cory, yelling instructions. That didn't stop several superheated fragments from hitting Cory in the face and arm, though. His Kevlar helmet and vest had protected him from being mortally wounded—not so for the staff sergeant in front of him.

In the movies when a soldier is wounded he sometimes gets a scar. When that occurs, it is always something dashing and symmetrical, adding a macho accent to a chiseled face. When Sergeant Cory's bandages came off in an Army hospital in Germany, he had no such luck. The pieces of near-molten metal that hit his face almost removed his cheek and ear. It was at that moment that Anthony Cory decided he would be a lifer. In his uniform, he would look like a warrior. In his bathrobe in the hospital, he looked like a creature out of a horror movie. The scarring was a mess. It extended from his left ear to his mouth and chin. It was not the neat line on a GI Joe doll's face; it was a raw-looking blob of scars that *looked* like they had been made by superheated, jagged metal.

Sergeant Cory was out of the hospital within a month; he was given light duty, and was allowed to return to his unit, which had been rotated back to the States. He was awarded a Purple Heart, the first of many awards he would receive in his life, although one he would have rather not have qualified for. No one in his squad commented on his new face, but he could always see the eyes darting back and forth between his eyes and his cheek when he spoke to someone. Shaving was a torturous assignment each day, and took twice as long as it had before. He was crushed when he learned that the staff sergeant with him that day had died in the firefight. He had never even had a chance to say good-bye or pay his respects. He had been unconscious after he was wounded; a pressure bandage was shoved over his still-burning face, and he was shot up with morphine. The truth was, he didn't remember much of anything other than waking up in Germany several days later with an Army doctor explaining how lucky he was to have his vision. Looking in the mirror at his own face, he often wondered.

Back at Fort Benning in Georgia, Duce spent the next few years continuing with his ranger training. He was naturally athletic, fearless and level-headed under stress. This made him popular with his superiors and his squad mates. By the time he finished specialized weaponry training, advanced escape and evasion courses, urban warfare techniques and specialized night operations, he had already been promoted to staff sergeant and was now being recommended for promotion to sergeant first class. The promotion, of course, would come with another five-year commitment to the rangers. For some soldiers, it is the ultimate career decision: Do you stay and follow the path for a lifetime in the military, or do you leave while you are still young enough to use your Army resume to try and land a job in corporate America? For Duce, the decision was easy. The only time he felt comfortable with his shrapnel-modified face was when he was in uniform.

Duce was able to work a week of vacation into the beginning of his new contract with Uncle Sam, and he used the time to go visit his mother in New York City. He flew from Georgia to Newark Liberty Airport in his dress uniform. He already had several ribbons on his chest besides the Purple Heart, and with his ranger beret, scarred face and new sergeant stripes, he looked like every child's image of Sergeant Rock from the comics. When he walked onto the plane, a pretty young stewardess took him by the arm and brought him to first class. She whispered that they had an extra seat and he was nothing short of amazed when he sat in the oversized leather chair. Two minutes into the flight, he was given a glass of champagne—a first for him. Even though it was cheap champagne, he enjoyed it immensely.

The stewardess flirted with him every time she was nearby, and he drank a beer with his lunch. Overall, it was the most enjoyable experience he ever had on an aircraft. Most importantly, at no point during the flight was he expected to jump out of the moving aircraft, something he had done countless times but was not particularly fond of (although he would admit that to no human on the planet). The highlight of the trip actually came at the end in the most unexpected form. As Duce pulled his duffel bag out of the overhead compartment and turned to exit, an old man with white hair touched his shoulder and whispered, "Rangers lead the way," with a wink and a smile. He held up two fingers and with his hoarse whisper said, "Second Rangers." He patted the young man's arm and walked away. It took a second to sink in, then Duce smiled. The Second Rangers had climbed the cliffs of Point-Du-Hoc during the Normandy invasion and made the rangers an American legend. No doubt, the old man was one of those warriors, still alive to remember that fateful day.

Duce called his very excited mother from the airport and took a bus back into the city. When he arrived at his old apartment, the door flew open and his mother just about smothered him. She hadn't seen him since his injury the year before and squeezed him so hard he broke into loud laughter.

"Damn, Mama, you're gonna break my back!" He laughed.

She playfully smacked him and snapped back, "You ain't too old to wash your mouth out with soap, child. Watch your mouth!" She laughed and hugged him again like she would never let go, then pulled him into the apartment. The apartment smelled amazing, with the greasy aromas of Mom's homemade fried chicken. She pulled him into the kitchen and made him sit down right away, taking his duffel bag from him.

"Mercy, child, you are a fine-looking man," she said, smiling as she patted his muscular arms. Then she made a pouty face, "But what they been feeding you, Anthony? You look so skinny."

"I eat plenty, Mom." He smiled. "We just run it off. But

your chicken smells so good. There ain't nothing in the Army like Mama's home cooking!" She was beaming, and she filled his plate with enough food for three men. Duce ate every bite on his plate as his mother caught him up on everything and everybody in the old neighborhood. Births, deaths, divorces, weddings and arrests were all covered in great detail. She finished with an update on Duce's brother, Ace, who was still in jail but might be getting out in the next two months. He didn't write as often as he used to, and she was worried that jail had hardened her oldest boy past fixing. Talking about her disappointment with her Ace brought her back to Anthony, who looked so striking in his dress uniform.

"And, child," she said, "you send me so much money! They pay that good in the Army? You ain't doing nothing illegal, are you, Anthony?"

"Please, Mom." He smiled. "I'm only sending you three hundred a month. It's not that much."

"But what you livin' on, Anthony?"

"Mom, the Army gives me food, shelter and my gear. I've got money saved up, too. It was a good decision, Mom."

She frowned and touched his scar. "But, baby, you got hurt so bad. You coulda been killed. When you gonna leave the Army and come home?"

Anthony took a deep breath and held his mother's hand. "Well, Mom, that's why I came home. I wanted to tell you. See these stripes?" he asked, showing her his new sergeant stripes. "I made Sergeant First Class, Mom. That's a big deal for me. It means more money, and means a lot more responsibility. I've gotten a lot of new training and I really like it, Mom. I signed up for another five years."

He waited for that to sink in before he continued. He could see her eyes welling up with tears. "Don't be sad, Mom. What was I gonna do here? End up with Ace in jail?"

"God forbid!" she exclaimed.

"Mom, I miss talking to you every day. And I know it's hard being here by yourself, but I have a chance to make something of myself. I like the Army, Mom. I wasn't sure what to think when I went in. Wasn't sure if I would hate it.

Didn't know if it was the right thing to do—but it was, Mom. I want you to be happy for me and stop worrying all the time."

She got up and walked around the table and hugged him, and started crying. "Anthony, you're all I got, baby. Your brother, he ain't never gonna amount to nothing. He'll probably never come home. You—you are the one from this family gonna do something great. I'm so proud of you, son. You grew up fine—just look at you." She held his face and looked at him, her eyes full of pride, and gave him another hug and kiss. "There ain't nothing around here for you anymore, Anthony. You go and learn whatever you can. Make a good life for yourself and stay safe. You just come home and visit your Mama once in a while." She forced a smile, even though Anthony knew her heart hurt to think he would be leaving again soon for who knew where or for how long. "And don't you worry about me. With the money you been sending and my work, I'm actually saving some in the bank for the first time in my life. I'm gonna be just fine, Anthony."

They cleaned the kitchen together, and then went and sat on the couch, where Duce amazed his mother with stories of travel, intense training and cultures from all over the world. He sounded different. He wasn't a tough thug from the neighborhood anymore—he was a professional soldier who spoke like an educated man. He even spoke to her in Arabic for a few sentences, just to show off some of his language skills. By the time they both went to bed, her chest was so full of pride she thought she would burst.

The next day brought some visitors from around the apartment complex, but Duce was a different person now, with very little to talk about with his old friends. They were doing exactly the same things they had been doing when he left, except for two locals who were now living upstate in the same facility as his brother. By the end of the second day, Duce couldn't wait to get back to what he now considered home at Fort Benning, Georgia. He had no idea what would be waiting for him when he returned.

CHAPTER 4

Langley, Virginia

By the time Middle East Desk Chief Darren Davis and Middle East Assistant Chief Dex Murphy met with Director Wallace Holstrum, they had a small file to bring to the meeting. While one of the names, Ali bin-Oman, was completely unknown, a search for information on both Muhammad Ali Basri and Kumani Mustafa Awadi had resulted in small biographies. Basri was a direct link between the president of Iran and Hamas, although he was careful to avoid any direct public connection to Hamas. Awadi's name had been floating around since 9-11, in circles with Al Qaeda, Hamas, Hezbollah and both Iran and Syria. Very little was known about him other than the fact that he never traveled without a lot of security, and he was often seen with the highest levels of both governments. He had no official title, but the smart money was betting that he was making deals between terrorist organizations and the two countries that sponsored them.

Wallace Holstrum walked in with two of his assistants, something he didn't usually do for high-level meetings involving deep cover agents, but this was urgent, and his two assistants had the highest security clearances. Chief Davis had informed Holstrum of the topic of the meeting, and Holstrum and his team arrived with lots of files. After a very brief handshaking and greeting session, everyone sat and began pulling out files.

"Tell me what you have so far," began Holstrum. Davis chucked his chin at Murphy, who cleared his throat and began.

"Our best asset in Iran has sent us this coded message via burst transmission," he began as he gave his only copy to the director of the CIA. "We believe, based on our man's previous history of direct contact with the president of Iran himself, that this information is accurate. It might be worth checking with Russian assets to follow up on the nuke story. We all know the Iranians have been working on their nuclear reactor against the Nuclear Regulatory Commission's sanctions, and they are pretty blatant about not giving a rat's ass. Russian president Putin and the Chinese are arguing for 'nonbiased' nuclear energy capabilities to all countries interested, but that's just for some quick cash. Neither one of them wants the Iranians getting nukes, so it's hard to know what they are really thinking long term."

The director cleared his throat, a sign that he only wanted raw data and not advice from an assistant desk director.

Murphy fumbled a bit, and then went on. "We have only just started looking at the three men mentioned in the transmission over the past hour or so. There is nothing on Ali bin-Oman, but we had hits on both Muhammad Ali Basri and Kumani Mustafa Awadi. Basri is linked to the president of Iran as well as Hamas, and Awadi's name shows up all over the place. Awadi has been seen in Iran, Syria and Lebanon, and was rumored to have traveled to both Afghanistan and Sudan. He may be an arms dealer, a money mover or just coordinating terror plans among the world's nastiest bunch of citizens. We'll continue to work on those names, and I'm sure our man in Tehran will also."

Murphy's reference to Bijon simply as his man in Iran was no accident. Only four people in the world knew who he was, and three of them were in the room. The fourth, Skripak, was wandering around in Tehran somewhere, maybe even running for his life. In this case, due to the high degree of importance of their star agent, the director didn't share this name with even his trusted assistants.

"Where are we with their nuclear facility?" Davis asked, looking at the director.

Holstrum exhaled slowly and rubbed his temples. He looked as tired as the rest of them. He sat back in his chair and loosened his tie. "I met with the president and the joint chiefs yesterday. We discussed options for taking out the facility, but quite frankly, that will be an act of war that brings the Russians precariously close to siding with the Iranians. The Chinese will protest loudly in the UN, but our China folks don't believe they would do much more than that. Not so sure about that with the Russians. The president spoke with Putin several times this month, and their stance hasn't changed. They still say 'nukes for everybody,' as long as they are doing the selling. It's quite a pickle."

Holstrum leaned forward and sipped his coffee. "The Israelis have offered to do the job for us. They absolutely will not allow the Iranians to get a nuke, and the president understands their position. The prime minister says he would rather just fight them outright now than deal with a nuclear missile strike next year, which doesn't seem so unlikely, given the Iranian president's recent speeches about the 'Holocaust never happening' and his belief that 'Israel needs to be wiped off the face of the earth.' Those are quotes, gentlemen, and lady," he said, turning to female assistant, Undersecretary Renee White.

"The last time Israel hit the Iranians, it was with four F-16 fighters flying four feet below the belly of a commercial airliner. Israel may be leaning toward a missile strike this time rather than risk their pilots. They hinted at that when the prime minister spoke with the president last week. The president, of course, asked the Israelis to stand down, but I am not so sure it isn't the best play. Someone has to take that facility out. The question is, simply, who."

Murphy spoke so quietly that at first, no one heard him.

"I have an idea."

The *second* time he said it, all eyes went to him.

"Go on," said Holstrum.

"What if we could take it out from the inside?"

"Inside Iran? You mean use your man to try and sabotage a facility *that* secure and *that* large? No offense, Dex, but that isn't in his training, nor would he have any reason to be anywhere near that place. He'd have no chance."

"I actually wasn't thinking of him, directly, sir. I was thinking of something on a much larger scale."

Everyone's forehead crinkled.

"I was thinking, maybe it's time for another revolution."

CHAPTER 5

Bob Still and William Hollahan had only returned from their assignment with the Mediterranean operation three weeks prior. They had been on loan, outside the Bureau, for almost a month doing some of the most dangerous work of their careers. Working with a secret team of agents on loan from the CIA, NSA, FBI and the military, they had intercepted a Scud missile aboard an oil tanker destined for Washington, D.C. The mission had just about gotten them and their team killed. Hollahan was talking about retiring now that they had "saved the world" and somehow lived through the experience. Still was more pumped up than ever and was looking for more work at the same intensity level. They were sitting in Still's small office, which amounted to a desk, a phone, a safe, filing cabinets, a computer and one fairly dead plant. Hollahan was sitting in the only extra chair in Still's office, while Still leaned back in his larger swivel chair.

"I can't believe you're just gonna hang it up, man. You'll be bored silly. Whatcha gonna do, fish for the next twenty years? Come on, man, you're way too young to retire. Besides, you'll miss me too much. And the next time I save the world without you, you'll be embarrassed as hell," Still said with a smile.

"I told you before we did that last gig that it was going to be my last. I've already spoken to HR about my pension."

"You shittin' me, man? You put your papers in already and you didn't even tell me first?"

"Why? I have to ask your permission or something? You'd just try to talk me out of it, like you're doing right now."

"You're damn right." Still sat up straight in his chair and pointed his big meaty finger at Hollahan. "That's bullshit, man. After twenty-five years working with me, you're gonna make me read about it in the paper?"

"I'm here now telling you, aren't I? Jesus, we sound like an old married couple. I'm telling you, Bob, save your breath. I am D-O-N-E."

"All right. Fine. If that's how it is, I won't waste my breath. When is your last day?"

"I have enough vacation time saved up that I can leave now. Today if I wanted. I'll clean up my office, and I'll be out of here by the end of this week. Cheer up. You'll probably get a new partner about twenty-five years old with great big hooters who loves big black macho types who just saved the world. You'll probably bang her on this very desk."

"Thanks, man. You're all heart. My luck, the boss will walk in and I'll lose my pension."

Hollahan smiled and stood up. He looked serious for a moment and extended his hand to his old friend. Still half smiled and stood up. He shook Hollahan's hand with a slow, firm handshake and said quietly, "I'll miss you, man."

"We'll stay in touch. I want a few months to decompress, maybe go someplace warm and do nothing for a while. It must be ten degrees outside. I want to have bare feet in the sand somewhere, maybe drink a cold beer or two."

Still laughed quietly. "Sounds like a good plan. Wouldn't mind a little sun and sand myself." When he said it, he wasn't picturing himself in the Middle East.

CHAPTER 6

Fort Benning

When Duce arrived back at Benning, he was happy and focused. He had been stressed out about his decision to become a "lifer," and then having to tell his mom. He worried about her, all alone in that crummy apartment. He hadn't told her, but with his signing bonus he was planning on moving her out of that neighborhood to someplace safer, someplace where he wouldn't be constantly worried about her being mugged or her apartment being ransacked. He would save that surprise for later, when the cash was in the bank and he had time to find a place for her. For now, he was light on his feet, happy with his life and ready for whatever the Army would give him.

Being home that couple of days had given him perfect clarity about his life. He had been given a chance to do something for himself, his country, his Mom—all honorable and far away from the criminals he had grown up with. Seeing them back there, on the street, doing the same stupid-ass things they were doing four years ago, solidified his place in life. He would have a career, learn languages, computers and whatever skills he could, and maybe one day he would make sergeant major. He had plans, and they all included pushing himself to "be all he could be."

When he arrived back at his small apartment on base, which he shared with a staff sergeant named Whittaker Jones, he had a surprise waiting. He walked in just in time for lunch—Jones was in the kitchen making a cheeseburger—and he got an interesting reception.

"*Ohhhhhh, man* . . . What did you do on leave, my man?" asked Jones, laughing.

"Huh?" was all Duce could muster.

"What happened? You get busted by the MPs or something? This must be good. Come on, man, don't hold out on your roommate. What did you go and do?"

"What the hell are you talking about?" Duce asked, incredulous.

"You ain't gonna fess up?" Jones waited, and then realized that maybe Duce really didn't know anything. "General Garrett himself knocked on the door looking for you, man! The general! No phone call, no nothing, he just showed up in his civvies, like you was old buds or something. What's up?"

"You're shitting me," dismissed Duce.

They both stood staring at each other for a long moment.

"You're not shitting me?" Duce asked, feeling his calm demeanor turning to nerves.

"Hell no, man. I wouldn't mess you with you about this. General Garrett—oh, wait, he left something for you." Jones pulled the hot burger off the griddle with his hand and threw it on his plate, turned off the stove and ran off to another room. He was back in an instant with a letter for Duce.

"He handed this to me and told me to give it to you. The general, man. In our apartment. This is some interesting shit, Sergeant First Class Cory."

Duce took the letter from Jones and looked at it. His rank and name were handwritten on the envelope—the general's return address in the upper left corner. So Jones wasn't kidding after all. The general had come looking for him. Duce's heart sank and he walked over to the kitchen table. Jones followed him and plopped down in a seat across from him.

"You want me to make you a burger before you read that? It might kill your appetite."

"Too late," said Duce, trying to smile. What he hell would the general want with *him*?

Duce slid his finger under the flap and tore open the envelope. He slid out a letter, handwritten by the general.

Dear Anthony,

Every now and then, an opportunity comes along which, if acted upon, will change a man's life. I am offering you one such opportunity. Be at the O Club at 18:30 hours. The doorman will be expecting you. Dress Uniform, and I am buying you dinner.

It was signed by the general. Duce sat there and reread it a second and third time, then sat back in his chair and started laughing at Jones.

"Oh *shit*, man—you *had* me!"

"What are you talking about?" Jones asked.

"Come on, man. Enough's enough. You had me cold, Whit. How'd you get his stationery and all?"

"I am not messing with you, Duce. The general gave that to me. He was here, at our apartment, in person, like you were his old buddy. I am not shitting you."

The two of them sat there for another moment, until Jones took the note from Duce's open hand. He read it, then reread it.

"Holy shit, Duce," was all he could muster.

After a few more minutes had gone by, Jones finally spoke. "Damn, man. How the hell you do that?"

"Whittaker, I have no idea."

Officer's Club
18:30

Duce had all day to prepare for his dinner with the general. He had no idea what the general would want with *him*. He had never even met the man, much less been invited over for a personal dinner. To calm his nerves, he had gone for an eight-mile run, and he had run hard. He showered and headed over to the barber to get "high and tight" for his dinner. When he got dressed later that day, he had Jones inspect him and his uniform very closely. He rarely wore his dress uniform with all his ribbons, but even Jones had to admit he looked like a poster boy for the Army. Duce had mumbled back that the only poster he would be on would be for wearing a seat belt or for plastic surgery.

Duce had Jones drive him over to the O Club, since he didn't own a car. Jones gave him a high five and wished him good luck, and left him in the parking lot. Duce was less nervous in combat. He approached the door, where another sergeant shook his hand and said, "Good evening, Sergeant Cory. The general is in the back right of the dining room."

Duce started to walk in, hesitated and turned back around. He looked around and no one was within earshot. "You know General Garrett?" he asked the sergeant.

The sergeant smiled and whispered back, "Oh, sure, we go out to the titty bars every night together." Cory just stared at him. "No, Sergeant, not really. He just said you'd be coming, to point you in his direction. Look for the gray flattop on a big white dude—that'll be the general."

Duce patted his arm and hustled off into the dining room. Sure enough, the general was easy to spot. Duce was surprised to see another man seated with him, wearing civilian clothes. He walked to the table and saluted, not sure exactly what to do in this situation. The general gave him a casual salute and told him to sit.

"At ease, Sergeant." The general smiled. He extended his hand and they shook, then he introduced the sergeant first class to his "associate," Ben Adams.

"Ben used to work with me a while ago," he began. "He was AC of S, G2 coupla years back."

Sergeant Cory was trying to translate the acronyms in his head, and the general saw him struggling to keep up.

"That's assistant chief of staff, Army Intelligence. He was

over at INSCOM—Intelligence and Security Command—before he moved along to other assignments. Ben and I spent some time together in Vietnam just as the whole thing turned to shit. Ben's intelligence work has now shifted to another agency. It's what we are here to talk about."

The waiter came over to the table and took a drink order—two scotches, and a light beer for the sergeant. He dropped off menus and the general told the sergeant he should try the steak. Since anything out of the general's mouth was an order as far as Duce was concerned, he didn't bother opening his menu.

The general continued speaking. "You see, Anthony, the Army has close ties with outside agencies. You just reenlisted, which I think was a great move on your part. You are a decorated combat soldier, and you didn't turn tail after you were wounded. Your commanding officers think highly of you. You aren't married, no kids on record—the world's your oyster, son. Ben wanted to speak to you about the possibilities."

They were interrupted when the waiter brought drinks and took their dinner orders. Amazing how fast the service was when you had a general at your table. They all ordered the steak with baked potatoes. (The general ordered first, followed by two "I'll have the same"s.)

When they had privacy again, Ben leaned closer and spoke quietly, somewhat monotone. "Anthony 'Duce' Cory, born in New York's shithole, served with distinction in Kosovo, made Sergeant First Class in nine years, totally clean record, well thought of by your men, and you just reenlisted, which shows your commitment. How would you like to do some more exciting work?"

They all sat quietly while Duce tried to keep up. "Exciting, how, sir?"

"My name is Ben. You can call me by my first name. The outfit you'd be working with is all first names, no ranks. No one in the unit is less than a staff sergeant, but all are combat veterans with specialized skills. I am told you have an ear for languages, Anthony?"

Duce smiled broadly.

"That a yes?"

"Actually, sir, no one except my mama calls me Anthony. Everyone calls me Duce. But, yes, sir, I seem to pick up on languages pretty fast. I forget them fast, though. Don't remember much from Kosovo. Been practicing some Arabic in case I go back to Iraq. I was only there for a short tour. Our company was pulled early to go to Afghanistan, and then we ended up in Germany instead. Not sure what that was all about exactly."

The general cleared his throat. "Occasionally, situations occur which require strength to be set aside for events that don't occur. Your company was going to Africa, actually, to help with a small revolution. The decision was made higher up the food chain to balk at getting involved in the Africa situation, so you were sent to Germany to wait, and it never panned out. 'Hurry up and wait, son.'" He smiled.

"In any case, Duce, if you were to consider joining our little operation, you would be 'on loan' so to speak. You would be immediately promoted to E-8, Master Sergeant, but would also receive a *second* salary at *E-9* combat rate. You would most likely be with us for three years, tops, at which time you would return to the Army, keeping the rank of E-9. You would be a very young sergeant major with an entire career still ahead of you."

Duce was speechless. He had made sergeant first class in almost record time, due in part to his combat time and commendation medals. He had commanded soldiers in combat as a staff sergeant, and when enlistments slowed after the Iraq war started, he accelerated through the ranks. Duce was still a young man. He couldn't think of a sergeant major he had ever met who wasn't at least forty years old. He thought about his mom and getting her out of the city.

"Sir, did you say I would get both pay grades at the *same time*?"

"That got your attention, huh? Yes. You are on loan, but still officially in the Army and will receive all pay and benefits. *We* would just be paying you *in addition*, and we always pay one grade higher than your current grade as an added incentive. By the way, you'll be back in combat, and earning every penny. That said, our mortality rate is lower than Army and Marine combat units. Our people are specially trained and work in unique situations. The downside is the secrecy element. No one will know what you do or where. Your communication will be censored and restricted. And it will be the busiest three years of your life."

The steaks came and they ate quietly, Duce thinking as fast as he could. He would be making enough money to move his mom not only out of the lousy neighborhood, but out of the city altogether, and still have money for himself in the bank. He wanted to know more.

"What kind of assignment?" he finally asked.

The general leaned forward and spoke quietly. "The kind we don't discuss in the O Club, son. There is a reason Ben doesn't wear a uniform anymore. No uniforms, first names without ranks, lots of money—you getting the picture here, son?"

Duce felt a little uneasy. He just blurted it out quietly. "But it's all *legal*, right?"

The general and Ben laughed. Ben smiled and said, "Of course it's *legal*, it's just secret. No one will know what you do outside your unit and your command chain. You'll be in and out of places before anyone knew you were there."

"And you get to blow shit up and kill bad guys." The general smiled.

Duce shook on it before the coffee arrived.

CHAPTER 7

Iran-Iraq Border

Skripak had left Tehran by car and traveled for two days straight on lousy roads, stopping only for fuel, nature calls and snacks until he was in Khorramabad, an ancient city of brown buildings built into a small valley of the Lorestan Mountains. Once there, he ate dinner and stayed overnight. It was cooler in the mountains, but not freezing. At least he was out of the city. Tehran smelled like ancient car exhaust. And besides, when he was there, he was constantly "on duty." It was an angry city of political dialogue that never seemed to calm down. At least here it was quiet. If someone killed him out here, at least it would be personal, like a tribal turf war, and not because the secret police had tracked him down.

The next morning, Skripak awoke to the sounds of a market and crowing roosters. He had a simple breakfast and then continued on in his ancient heap of a car through the mountains, the transmission whining in protest at the grade changes. What would have taken twenty minutes on the New Jersey Turnpike took four hours of bouncing and honking as he tried to keep his piece of junk from sliding off a cliff.

When he had reached a tiny village on the western side of

the mountain range, he was almost within sight of the Iran-Iraq border. He traded his car to a bunch of Lur tribesmen, who would in turn sell it to someone else, since most of them had never driven a car. For the car and a small sum of cash, he bought traditional Qashqai tribesman clothes—as comfortable as they were colorful—and a sturdy camel. The tribesman packed some dates and dried snacks in a bag that they gave him as a "gift" along with the smelly beast, convinced that they would be rich when they sold the car.

Dressed as a tribesman, he moved westward, unnoticed, in the mostly barren countryside. When he got closer to the border, it became more dangerous, with Iranian Army patrols occasionally within sight. The nomadic tribes in western Iran did not care much about international borders, and moved their herds of sheep back and forth between countries to wherever the grazing was better. Armies from all countries had taken to ignoring them most of the time, unless there were large numbers of them in trouble spots. One man traveling by camel in the middle of nowhere did not raise much interest from anyone.

When Skripak came to a crest that overlooked a grassy plain, he knew he was there. A few ancient rusted tank frames still lay half buried in the dirt, remnants from the Iran-Iraq war that left hundreds of thousands dead on both sides. This was the actual border, although no fence or sign acknowledged that particular fact. Skripak carefully raised his binoculars, making sure that no reflection from a lens would alert anyone to his possession of them. He scanned in every direction for a quite a while, and only when he was sure he was very much alone in this wasteland did he kick his nasty, smelly camel to move west.

Army patrols were one concern—landmines were another. The borders tended to have large minefields that were often not marked and shifted with each sand storm. He wasn't happy about crossing into Iraq, but he had his orders.

Before the emergency message, he had been lying low near Tehran for a few weeks, feeling paranoid. After living there so long, it was rare for him to worry. But something was brewing, and he was concerned that he might compromise Bijon, who was doing such amazing work. Evidently, Bijon had become concerned when he hadn't heard from Skripak for a couple of weeks, and must have alerted Langley. Langley's reaction was very strange. They had given him the coded message for bugging out immediately, with coordinates in Iraq. This had all been in their bag of tricks for years in the event he was discovered, but he was completely unaware of any immediate threat. He was paranoid, yes, but wasn't sure what exactly was going on. The message was the message though, and he was in the wind immediately following the transmission.

Now he sat on top of this nasty beast, looking across a wide open plain of scrub and nothingness that turned steeper and nastier as it became the mountains that separated the two countries. The camel took long strides toward the border and Skripak pulled his red and white hood and scarf tighter around his neck. He bounced along in rhythm with the angry camel, awaiting the sound of a landmine that, thank God, never came. He traveled along one of the few fairly flat areas along the border, in a small valley among the many mountains. There were Iranian Army patrols in this part of Iran because of the fact that it was easier terrain. Small groups would move through the mountain passes, but a large army would use this valley, as had happened in the Iran-Iraq war when hundreds of thousands of soldiers had flooded those valleys.

It took another four hours by smelly, nasty, human-hating camel before he was at the actual formal border. Within an hour he was in Iraq. He passed ancient bunkers and concrete battlements that had been shelled, covered with sand, uncovered by wind and used by passing nomads. It was a lonely place that still had a scent of death and sadness. He slowed his pace and started watching more carefully. What was left of a metal fence and barbed wire formed a border, with a few Iranian guards camped nearby. Skripak coaxed his camel into the low hills and wound through the same passes that insurgents and goatherds used every day, with the same lack of resistance from either Iraq or Iran. As long as it wasn't a large-scale army, no one seemed to really care. When he was inside of Iraq, he began to relax a bit. Although dressed as he was presently he wasn't much safer there than in Iran, at least the Iranian Army wouldn't be shooting at him. He traveled through more destroyed bunkers and rusted out artillery pieces, wondering about how many soldiers had disappeared into the ground beneath him. The Iranians had made up for poor equipment by fighting in huge human waves, like the Chinese during the Korean War, and the results were as would be expected. The grass and plants grew better here for a reason.

A mirror flashed from a hilltop in front of him. He didn't change his stride at all, and almost imperceptibly aimed his camel at the flash. It was another five minutes before he saw it again from the same place. He smiled inside his hood. He was starved for the English language. He wanted so badly just to talk to another American! About anything! Who won the Super Bowl? Hell, who was *in* the Super Bowl? In another lifetime, Skripak had been a Vikings fan. Now he lived with people who lived and acted like them.

He quickened his pace and continued straight for the mirror signal. Every five minutes, on the button, there it was. He approached what looked like an old village, abandoned long ago, perhaps during the war. So many missiles had been fired along the borders that many border towns simply disappeared. When he was clearly on a hard road, although covered by sand in most spots, the mirror began flashing quickly. He stopped his camel and hopped down, walking the beast with the reins in his hand. He almost jumped out of his skin when a Bradley Fighting Vehicle seemed to appear out of thin air. It had been hidden in an old building, no more than a shell, really. Now it roared down the street, straight at him, a gunner standing in the turret.

Skripak smiled and removed his headscarf, raising his hands. The vehicle continued straight for him, slowing when it got close, and finally stopping a few yards in front of him. The doors opened and two soldiers hopped out in battle dress uniforms. One of them held the door open as another man emerged from the vehicle in native civilian clothing. This man, a hard-looking sort with a white crew cut, walked briskly to him and extended his hand.

"Name's Woodcrest, Jerry Woodcrest. And you are an ugly, hairy, skinny-ass, smelly version of Michael Skripak. The pictures I have of you look a damn sight better than *you* do, mister." He smiled.

Skripak shook his hand with a huge smile on his face. Woodcrest had a slight southern accent. It was even better than just an American voice—it was an American voice with a twang. They didn't teach that in English schools in Iran. He hadn't heard a twang in so many years he wanted to hug the guy. "It's nice to hear an American," Skripak managed to say, his own voice with an Iranian accent now.

Jerry smiled and smacked his arm. "Come on back to the truck. We're going for a ride. Jesus man, I have seen POWs that were in better shape than you are."

"Up that hill?" Skripak asked, referring to the mirror signals.

"Yeah, we have a forward observation post up there. A few Army Rangers mostly. I'm not Army, but you probably figured that. These guys are, but we'll wait to have our chat till later on. For now, relax and enjoy the ride. I have something very, very special for you for the trip up the hill." With that, he reached under his seat and produced two red and white cans of Budweiser. They were a little dented and battered looking, but Skripak almost cried when he saw them. Jerry popped the top on one of them and the white foam bubbled out. The inside of the truck smelled like beer, and Skripak's smile was blinding.

"Holy shit," was all he could muster. "Jerry, you are the man," he said as he tilted the beer to his mouth and tasted the nectar that hadn't crossed his lips in over three years, since the last time he was out of Iran. He drank it straight back without stopping and enjoyed a loud beer burp that cracked up the soldiers who were all jealously watching him chug it. Skripak wiped his mouth with the back of his hand and then smelled his hands . . . Beer. God, how could it be so good? He leaned back and closed his eyes, and within five minutes was sound asleep.

When Skripak awoke, the Bradley was bouncing along at a wicked incline.

"Welcome back," said Jerry. "Beer go to your head?" He laughed.

"Yeah, probably. That and not sleeping for a week straight. We getting close?"

"Close as we're gonna get in this baby. We'll have to get out and hump it pretty soon, but it's not far. Just a short walk through the goat trails and we have a very warm, dry cave that we call home."

Five minutes later the Bradley stopped, and the sergeant driving called back, "This is the end of the road, gents."

Gears crunched to a halt, and the driver killed the engine. All five of them got out of the vehicle and started walking up a tiny rocky trail that seemed to go straight up. Skripak huffed and puffed, not used to mountain hiking. The other soldiers, some carrying sixty pounds of equipment, didn't even change their breathing pattern. A soldier stepped out from the side of the trail wearing a sniper's gilly suit. They silently acknowledged each other, and the men followed him back into the brush to the mouth of a small cave.

Once inside, the group continued into a large cavern. There was a generator inside, running heat, lights, and several laptops and satellite phones. It was a secret base in the middle of nowhere, and even Skripak was impressed. There were at least a dozen men inside, some at the computers, some sleeping, some cleaning weapons or arranging packs. They quietly eyed their Arab stranger, not quite sure what to make of him. Jerry led Mike all the way to the back of the cavern. There was a bedroll on a small portable cot, luxurious conditions for rangers. A small meal of MREs had been prepared for their honored guest, who still carried the other Budweiser.

Jerry motioned for him to sit on the cot.

"Eat, sleep and chill out for a bit. I'm sure you are beat. Tomorrow we'll have a long talk. That's it for now. I'll go tell Big Brother that you are safe and sound."

Although Mike was dying to know what was going on, he was exhausted, and for the first time in many months, he was totally relaxed and feeling safe, surrounded by a squad of rangers in a cave in the middle of nowhere. No one was going to crash through his door and pull him out of bed tonight, something that he never took for granted in Iran. Tomorrow would be a new day. For now, he did as he was told. He ate enough rations for two days, drank the other beer and passed out on the cot where he slept like a hibernating bear for almost twelve hours.

CHAPTER 8

CIA Headquarters

Darren Davis and Dex Murphy had been at it for almost twelve hours, stopping only twice—once for some cold pizza, and the other time for a half-hour power nap to clear their heads. Both of them had gotten into the habit of working insane hours, and occasional power naps would recharge them and buy them more time without real sleep. It was a habit Murphy had picked up in the Marine Corps many years ago—he could sleep anywhere at the drop of a dime.

Davis had two other people helping them out, running names and places and keeping up with intel reports from the Russia desk, the China desk and Syrian and Jordanian intel. Connie Wu was the first back with information about one of their names. She knocked on the door to Davis's office, where he and Dex had been working together. Davis waved her in, and she sat down and began pulling out papers and photos.

"This is Muhammad Ali Basri," she began, pulling out a grainy black and white photograph. "Basri is the direct link between the president of Iran and Hamas. This photo was supplied to us by the Israelis, who are working very hard on killing him. The picture was taken after a speech in which

Hamas claimed responsibility for a bus bombing in Tel Aviv that killed thirty-four civilians. The confidential informant works for the Israelis, but isn't an operative that could have put a hit on Ali Basri. Basri was seen in Iran, Gaza, the West Bank, Libya, Syria and Iraq before the war. Anywhere there are violence, guns and fanaticism, he shows up. We think he is a weapons dealer, trainer and organizer all in one. No known address, other than staying in the presidential palace in Tehran. He's about as nasty as they come."

She pulled out another photo. "This charmer is Kumani Mustafa Awadi. We're pretty sure he was connected with the Crescent Comet missile plot that was intercepted a few months back. He is thought to have arranged the Scud being moved with Syrian assistance to the tanker that was supposed to deliver it to our backyard. Unfortunately, he wasn't on board the ship when our people turned it into fish food. He was last seen back in the Sudan, most likely supplying weapons to the Gangaweed rebels, although that isn't confirmed. We currently have no assets on the ground in Sudan."

She paused, and no one spoke, remembering Peter McAllister, who had been killed the previous year while posing as a Canadian reporter to gather information on what was going on in the Sudan. The Agency hadn't tried again since his death, and considered the entire country a complete disaster beyond any hope at the moment. Any monitoring was currently being done from border countries.

"Awadi hasn't been seen in a few months. He could be anywhere. One bit of good news—I got a call from Amy Lang. She has connections with the Israelis. They aren't talking much, but they have confirmed that they have a few agents in Iran. That could be huge later on, especially if they are in eastern Iran where the action is on the nuke facility. Anyone we could get in would have to come from the west through Iraq."

Connie had no idea that Skripak or Bijon existed, and wasn't about to be told.

"We are still waiting on more intel on Ali bin-Oman. So far we have nothing, but we are still shaking the trees."

"Good work, Connie, thanks. Anything else?"

"Yeah." She smiled. "You guys need to go home and take a shower. Your office is starting to smell like a gymnasium." She laughed and walked out. Dex and Darren looked at each other and both smelled their armpits at the same time. They simultaneously said, "It's not *me*!"

Darren's phone rang. He picked it up to hear the boss's voice calling them in, and he hung up and straightened his tie.

"Showtime," he said to Dex.

The two of them put their jackets back on and headed down to Director Wallace R. Holstrum's office. They went right in and sat in his situation room. They were extremely surprised to find the chairman of the Joint Chiefs of Staff in the office with several other high-ranking officers. It was not so uncommon to have meetings with the J-2 military personnel, but they had never met in this office before.

Holstrum waved them to two empty seats. "General Braddock, Lieutenant General Stanley, Major General Booker and Colonels Pierce and Taylor, this is Darren Davis, Middle East Desk Chief, and Dexter Murphy, Middle East Assistant Chief." All of the men shook hands and sat back down.

"Gentlemen," Holstrum began, addressing the officers, "the options being discussed at this time are very preliminary in nature. Suffice it to say, there are many scenarios in the bag we can pull out, as well as military options, but Assistant Chief Murphy may have an interesting idea. It will require a brief history of what we have going in Iran, which is all Classified Top Secret."

He paused to let that sink in, and then continued. "We have had an asset in Iran for almost three decades. He is a well-known religious leader who has been preaching hate and violence for many years, and has quite a following of nasty thugs that love everything he says. And he works for us." He paused again, and watched the little smiles across the desk. "Our man over there has regular visits with the Iranian president, the top clerics, and the most important people in that country. His handler just slipped out of Iran and is currently, as of yesterday, in Iraq with a small team of rangers that are operating a forward observation post on the Iranian border. Dex will present this scenario to you now for you to consider. You are in the loop on this from the ground up, in the event that the president decides on military action instead. Personally, in discussing over the past few days what you are about to hear, I believe this is a better option than having to start another war in the Gulf, for a myriad of reasons. Dexter, the floor is yours."

Dex was totally unprepared for the meeting, but knew the material inside out anyway. He couldn't help but wonder why he hadn't been told ahead of time so that he might have been able to put together a full briefing with slides and photos. He took a deep breath and began. "Thank you, Director Holstrum. Gentlemen, what I am proposing may sound like a wild idea, but I think it is an idea whose time has come. Our asset in Iran was recruited after the fall of the shah. His entire family had been killed by the new government, and he didn't take a lot of convincing to turn. He is like hundreds of thousands of moderate Iranians—the silent majority, who would be much happier with a different government.

"Our man poses as a religious fanatic in a country where the most vocal and the most violent rule, but they are *not* the majority. The silent majority is an oppressed people lacking leadership to take on the government. The Iranians are not short on bravery, just organization and leadership. In the Iran-Iraq War, they were outgunned in terms of military strength, but made up for it by human waves of infantry attacks. They paid a heavy price for their lack of tactics and weaponry, but did manage to drive the Iraqis out of Iran. Point is, they are willing to fight. They just need a push."

Dex stood up and started pacing as he spoke. He had found his stride in his pitch and was getting excited about his idea. Holstrum just sat back and let him go.

"I believe that our man in Iran can get close enough to take out the president and a majority of the ruling party. He can make it look like someone else did it. We can use other assets to mobilize the people at the same time the news comes out about the hit. A coup, gentlemen. The beginning of a revolution. A more moderate government gets welcomed into the world community and 'gives up' the program as a goodwill gesture in return for aid and food. We avoid World War Three, get rid of the government of Iran, bring another Middle Eastern country into the twenty-first century and add stability to the region in the post-theocracy Iran."

He sat back down and took a drink of water, waiting for someone to speak.

General Braddock sat back, a scowl on his face. "Interesting concept. Let's talk about it. First, how does your man take them out? Second, how confident are you that he can actually get it done, and what happens if it doesn't work? Third, what makes you think the government that replaces them will be any better than the lunatics they have in there now? Fourth, how far along are they on their nuclear program, and what kind of missiles do they have? That's just for starters." He gave a fake smile, crossed his arms over his chest and waited.

Dex glanced at Holstrum and began. "As far as taking them out. We have a few ideas so far. The plan I like best is to have our man supplied with some high-density explosives. He can wire his mosque and invite special guests for an event of some kind. Get them all in one place at one time and have our guy slip out the back as the roof comes down. When our man resurfaces, he can be repentant—a message from God to change his ways . . . let him see the light and start preaching about Western ideas."

"Good God, man," groaned General Braddock. "You really think anyone would believe he wasn't involved? You think he's just going to turn over a new leaf and get away with it?"

"Actually, sir, I do. These people look up to him with great respect. I think he can pull it off. Of course, I gave you the simplified version."

"You said high-density explosives. You mean C-4? How are you going to get that much C-4 to him to take out the whole place and guarantee your kill zone?"

Dex looked to Holstrum and waited.

Holstrum cleared his throat. "General, the high density explosive is not C-4. It is not available yet to the military. Our agents just call it silly putty. It's gooier than C-4, but very stable. Very heavy stuff. Kicks about ten times the intensity of C-4. A little bit goes a long way."

The generals were all obviously pissed. They hated it when they didn't have the latest toys. Holstrum could sense it, and kept speaking. "When the stuff is studied a little further, I'm sure it will become available to the military, General Braddock. As it is right now, the stuff is expensive as hell, and packs such a wallop that it's considered too dangerous for general military use." He regretted that last sentence as soon as it left his mouth.

"Too dangerous for us soldiers, huh? Better leave it to your professionals." He wasn't smiling. "Continue, Mr. Murphy."

Dex quickly jumped in to cover the rough spot. "Yes, sir. The silly putty could be carried by our man all by himself. The switches are smaller than conventional. It's actually very easy to set. The only downside to the stuff is the size of explosion. They tend to vary somewhat. That's why it isn't quite ready yet for general use. You have to give the stuff a wide berth, otherwise you end up a casualty by your own hand. Anyway, placed correctly around the mosque, we can turn the place into a big smoldering crater."

One of the other generals said, "I like the sound of that." They all grunted in unison.

Braddock pushed him to continue. "Okay, so your guy manages to take out the upper echelon and get out alive. Then what?"

"We will have our other folks in-country working with the silent majority to begin the revolution. There are a handful of men already waiting for the opportunity. We have had some limited contact with them. All they need is the chance."

The general sat back, looking pissed again. "Son," he began in a condescending voice, "does the Bay of Pigs ring a bell with you? That was another little coup attempt that came out of this office that got a lot of friendlies annihilated."

"I understand your reluctance, sir, but these people are fighters. They are combat hardened from the Iraq war. All they need is leadership and an opportunity. We anticipate most of the Army putting their weapons down without a major war. The president and his cronies are hugely unpopular with all but the oldest hard-liners. The young people, soldiering age, they want reform. They want tits and ass, sir."

"Now *that* I believe. Go on," said Braddock.

"So the rebellion begins, helped by us. If it gets a little bigger than anticipated, we do have a hundred and fifty thousand troops across the border."

"With their hands full," interrupted the general.

"Understood, sir. But it is an option."

"A shitty one. What else have you got?"

"Well, like I said earlier, our Holy Man starts preaching reform—a new vision of Iran, et cetera. He can pick our people to support from the inside. His blessing will appease the hard-liners, but, once in, they can slowly open the door to the West."

The generals looked at each other. Braddock wrinkled his brow. "I don't love it, but I like it better than sending in jets and declaring war. In the end, that option is always there." He turned to the other soldiers in the room. "Gentlemen? Comments?"

The other generals looked at each other, waiting for someone to comment. Finally, Major General Booker spoke. "This whole plan rests on one man being able to pull this off. You think he has the balls?"

"It's *his* country, Major General. He has been waiting for a long time. He will get it done. These people are ready for a change."

General Braddock stood up, signaling the meeting was over. "Gentlemen, thank you for bringing us in early. There is a joint chiefs meeting tomorrow, oh-nine hundred hours. You are all invited. The president will be there. Unless someone comes up with something better, this may be the best suggestion. Good work, Murphy. Thank you, Director Holstrum." With that, the generals stood up, shook hands and made their exit.

Holstrum smiled at Dex. "Sorry to do that to you. It happened fast. I was actually happy to sit back and hear you explain it so I could give it a fresh listen. I like it, Dex. Much better now than the first hundred times we discussed it. This all comes down to Bijon. I spoke with Ben Adams yesterday. He is putting together a small team to bring the silly putty in and sit on the border in case Bijon and Skripak need to get out of Dodge. My guess is, Bijon won't be going anywhere. This is his chance to rebuild his country, but Skripak was burnt out two years ago. We need to get him home and de-iced for a year or so."

"Roger that, boss."

"Okay, that's it for now boys. Go home and catch up on your sleep."

"Yeah, and maybe even take a shower," smiled Murphy.

CHAPTER 9

FBI Building, Washington, D.C.

Bob Still had arrived a few minutes late, uncharacteristic of him, but he was slightly hung over from Hollahan's retirement party. Hollahan had specifically said he didn't want a party, but of course Bob ignored him and surprised him with lots of old FBI friends, including a couple of friends from the Crescent Comet case who were in D.C. on other business. It was serendipity that Bob had e-mailed invitations to Chris Mackey and Anthony "Tee" Cicero when he did, because normally they wouldn't have been in D.C. The fact that they *were* meant two things: they got to see William Hollahan off into the sunset, and Bob got his chance at more action on an even larger mission than the last one.

Over drinks the night before, Tee had hinted that they were there "on business." Still had asked if he could join them, and Tee was very receptive to the idea, having been through the fire with Still and surviving once before. They promised they would put in a good word for him at their meeting, and Still said he would ask his boss, Special Agent in Charge Walker, if he could go out "on loan" again. He really was addicted to the adrenaline rush of action. He called Walker's secretary and asked for an appointment, and was surprised to have her tell him to "come right down."

Bob was there in his office a minute later. He went right in and sat down, waiting for Walker to get off the phone.

Walker hung up and smiled at Still. "I was going to say 'welcome back,' but apparently you have other ideas?"

Still chuckled softly. "Man, there are no secrets in this building, huh?"

"Apparently not. You spoke to Cicero and Mackey yesterday about going back out. You just got back, and I might add 'barely.' You sure you want to do this, Bob? I'm asking you as a friend. I can get you back on their team, but you have to ask yourself if you really want to push your luck. You almost ended up fish food that last mission. You're getting a little long in the tooth for this kind of work. Hell, you're almost ready to retire yourself."

"Boss, I appreciate your concern, really. But I'll be honest with you. I haven't been this fired up about work since I was a rookie. That last mission—I have to admit, some parts were absolutely terrifying. But it was also the greatest thing I have ever done in my career. William 'bailed' last night, and that's his right—but I'm not ready to hang it up yet. I still have a few solid years left, boss. Let me back out there."

"Bob, frankly, the decision isn't mine. Your friends Mackey and Cicero have some pull at the top of the chain. You want in, you're in. You'll be back out on loan again. This time you will officially be on loan to the CIA. After you go inside over there, it's up to them what they do with you. Your desk here is yours whenever you want it back."

Walker stood up, signaling the meeting was over. "Good luck, Bob. I mean that. I admire your grit. I know I wouldn't be chomping at the bit for these kinds of jobs anymore, but then again, I have a wife and kids. Changes your career."

"No shame in that, boss. I appreciate your help."

Walker looked at his watch. "Go get your stuff together. Your phone is going to ring within the next twenty minutes. Your buddies already put things in motion for you."

Still smiled and shook hands with Walker, then walked

back to his office with long, energetic strides. He was smiling broadly, feeling energized like a twenty-year-old instead of a fifty-six-year-old. He was only in his office for a minute when his phone rang. It was Tee's big, deep voice laughing on the other end.

"Welcome back, old man. Me and Mack are downstairs with the motor running."

Still was downstairs in a couple of minutes, his gym bag filled a bunch of clutter from his desk. He hadn't even gotten new case files yet, and now he was leaving again. The trio exchanged hugs and back slaps outside, and questioned each other about their collective hangovers. Still hopped in the backseat of Tee's rented car, his knees almost at his chin in the small rental. Tee and Mackey didn't have much more room up front.

"You guys spared no expense, huh? Why not just get a bicycle for us? I could have sat on the handlebars," mumbled Still from the backseat.

"We'd just better hope we don't have to go uphill in this jalopy with you two fat bastards," replied Mackey.

"All muscle, baby," Tee said with a smile. He wasn't really kidding either. Like Still, he had lost a few pounds during the last go-round, and was hard as a rock.

They drove from the FBI building into Langley. On the drive, Mackey, the pilot who had saved their asses on the last mission, debriefed Still on what they knew thus far.

"We had only been in D.C. for one day when we got your e-mail. Total luck I checked my e-mail when I did, or you would have missed us. We were working in Afghanistan when we got called back. We're both still dragging from the time change. Anyway, the skinny is we are heading back to the Middle East pronto, but we don't have details yet. I know a guy in the company who's working in Iraq right now with some rangers. He's one of the few guys that I keep in touch with all the time. We kind of watch each other's backs. We don't officially work together, but we have been in so many of the same places over the years that we constantly bump into each other. His name is Jerry Woodcrest. A southern boy. You'll like him, he's as sarcastic as you are, and not much younger."

Still interrupted him with a "fuck you" for the age comment. Mackey just laughed. "Hey, man, I'm not any younger than you are. Anyway, Jerry was vague when I ran into him in Germany. I was headed to Afghanistan, and he was heading to eastern Iraq with a small squad of rangers. He didn't say, but I think they are sitting right on the Iranian border. Everybody has been holding their breath with the Iranian nuke issue, so I think El Presidente is starting to ramp up on the border to keep his muscle close by just in case. Jerry speaks some Persian and Arabic, so my guess is he is in the middle of whatever they have planned. He's a solid guy with a lot of experience under his belt. He makes the Comet intercept look like child's play. That man has seen some shit in his career."

Still asked, "You said he told you he was heading to eastern Iraq. Isn't all this stuff classified? How is it you tell each other what you are up to?"

"Like I said, we watch each other's backs. Most of the time, no one knows where anybody is or what they're doing, which translates to, 'if you get caught in some shit you are on your own.' Jerry and I have been through a lot of shit together, some of it way too close for our own good. We always promised each other we'd never leave each other out in the field. This isn't supposed to sound like macho bullshit, but spooks work alone a lot. Sometimes guys go missing and no one goes looking for them. A few could have been saved over the years if someone had bothered to try, and Jerry and I always said we'd try, that's all. We try and let each other know what's going on without compromising too much information. Yeah—it's against the rules, but fuck it. Most of what we do is against the rules anyway."

Still nodded quietly. Mackey turned around and faced him from the front seat. "Understand that what I just said, I never said. I am entrusting you with this because you are going to be part of our team, and we watch out for each other, rules or not.

Most of our lives are spent under the radar. HQ doesn't really care what or how we do what we do as long as they get results. This is *not* the FBI. You guys go out of your way to stick to the rules. We don't operate quite the same way."

Still quietly said, "I read you loud and clear," and Mackey turned back around. They rode in silence for a while and then made some small talk as they pulled into CIA headquarters in Langley. Still was beaming in the back seat at the sight of the immaculate grounds and architecture.

"This place still cracks me up." He chuckled. "You have the nicest government office I've ever seen."

"You should see the Oval Office," said Mackey with a smile.

"Bullshit," said Still.

Tee chimed in, "No, man, really. Mackey over here has been there a bunch of times. He'd be almost famous if he wasn't a spook!"

They all laughed and Tee parked the small car. All of them groaned as they got out, which led to more laughing as they tried to stretch. Mackey was the smallest by far, and even he was six feet tall. Tee and Still looked nothing short of comical getting out of the compact car, like clowns at the circus. They cleared the foyer and took a secure elevator to a conference room where they waited for a minute until two men they didn't know walked into the room.

The first of the two, a fortyish man with dark circles under his eyes, extended his hand and introduced himself as Darren Davis. They all knew his name as Director of the Middle East Desk in the CIA, but none of them had ever met him in person or seen his face before. He, in turn, introduced them to Dex Murphy, his assistant at the Middle East Desk. What they referred to as a desk was actually a department of almost a hundred people, and that number didn't include almost two hundred field agents from Syria to Iran. The Middle East was a busy place.

They sat down and Dex produced a standard folder that contained Top Secret Clearance papers, which they simply referred to as "contracts." It was something new since 9-11 and the Patriot Act that simply put on paper rules that needed to be followed pertaining to all top secret information. The bottom line, as the agents all said, was the "keep your mouth shut and eyes open or get shot document." Mackey and Tee both scribbled their signatures, and Still, having no idea what he was signing, followed suit.

With that out of the way, Dex pulled out files and photos and maps and began spreading things out all over the table, while Darren began the briefing.

"Welcome back, gentlemen. First of all, congratulations on your last assignment—I know the last bit was a little hairy. I actually spoke to a few other folks involved. Mackey, you are a helluva pilot."

Tee spoke up. "Amen to that. He saved our asses that day." Mackey didn't comment, and Darren went on.

"The reason you were called home was because this briefing is extensive and no one was comfortable trying to do this over a phone or computer. What you are about to hear is *beyond* Top Secret. There are only five people in the world who know the whole story, and you three are about to get the lion's share of that story. As you are well aware, the Iranians have thrown out the nuclear inspectors, and the Russians have been supplying equipment and information. Originally, the Russians were going to build the plant on their side of the border and simply sell the energy to the Iranians, but that wasn't good enough for the Iranians. They want their own plant. It's pretty obvious why. And we have disturbing news about just how close they are to their bomb.

"We have a man inside Iran. Deep inside. His latest report says they are close to building a bomb and putting together a longer-range rocket. The Israelis want to hit them now, but the president has been asking them to stand down. In the meantime, we don't want them getting a nuke any more than the Israelis do. Dex here has some ideas that have been reviewed and cleared as a go. That's where you come in. You will be making a delivery to a forward observation post in eastern Iraq."

Still did his best not to grin. Son of a gun, Mackey did

know his stuff after all. Mackey glanced at Still, but Still kept his eyes averted to avoid smiling.

"Our man in Iran is going to attempt the beginning of a regime change." He paused and let than sink in. "Our contact in Iran uses the name Imam Grand Ayatollah Kamala."

Mackey interrupted. "You're *shittin'* me . . . *The* Grand Ayatollah Kamala? Are we talking about the same guy?"

Tee and Still were silent because they hadn't heard the name before.

"If you mean the Imam Ayatollah Kamala, the hawkish, fanatical, Jew-hating, Western-hating, American-hating Islamic fundamentalist, then yes. The same guy. He was born Bijon Mujaharov, a regular guy. A very Western-minded Persian whose family was wiped out after the shah fell. He wants his country back. He has been set up for years as an Iranian cleric and has worked his way up the Iranian world to become a very well-known hardliner. He meets with the president and the clerics regularly. And he hates their guts. He doesn't know it yet, but it's payback time. You will be delivering special explosives to him via Iraq. Another agent will be bringing them back to Tehran and handing them off to Bijon, who will invite everyone over for a little barbeque." He smiled at his own joke.

"Holy shit," mumbled Still under his breath.

"Yeah, holy shit about sums it up. This whole operation is very sketchy at best. I wish we had another six months to plan and get our people inside Iran organizing, but we don't. If Bijon is correct, they will be arming that missile with a nuclear warhead very soon. Or, if they don't feel like nuking Israel themselves, they'll simply sell the bomb, or, hell, *give* the bomb to Hamas and let them nuke Israel. Either way, they get what they want—a smoldering mess where Israel used to be. The U.S. jumps in with the Israelis, maybe the Russians back the Iranians—and we have the beginning of World War Three or another cold war. Not to mention the Chinese jumping in someplace, who knows where. Bottom line, we don't want Israel making a first strike with things so messy in the Middle East right now. The Arab nations would see it as more

American interference in their backyard, and we will have a real war on our hands. Dex's plan has a lot of unknowns, but it's the best we have right now. At the very worst, we'll get a new government as bad as what they have now. It can't be any worse."

"So all we are doing is delivering the explosives? That's it? You could have had anyone do that," said Tee.

"Well, not exactly. First of all, the explosives are classified. We call it silly putty. It's about ten times more explosive than C-4. It's very gooey, heavy stuff that is somewhat unpredictable. It is easy to set and detonate, but the problem is how much to *use*. The lab boys make it the same way every time, but it never explodes the same way twice, maybe because it is such a gooey mess. In any case, they are trying to make it better, but in the meantime it's the best we have to take out a large building without being spotted. A vest full of the stuff will knock down a very large building. I mean very large. We don't want this stuff ending up in the wrong hands, either. I don't need Al Qaeda finding a way to copy the stuff."

"So are we supposed to deliver this to Tehran?" asked Tee.

"Actually, we aren't sure just how far you will be going. We are sending the three of you with a couple of rangers to our forward observation post in eastern Iraq. You will link up with our team there and another agent from inside Iraq. His name is Mike Skripak. That's the second name I just divulged to you that very few people know about. Skripak has been in and out of Iran for almost thirty years. The guy is invaluable, but he's also burnt out. Creating the Grand Ayatollah has been his life's work.

"If he thinks he can make it back by himself, that may be the play, but you will have to assess things on the ground. It is a long way from Iraq to Tehran. If you aren't comfortable with him making it alone, someone is going to have to babysit. The rangers at the FOP are off-limits, but the three who are going with you from D.C. are on loan to us. I will give you dossiers on them to review before you leave. All three are qualified combat veterans. They will help you get through the mountains to find the FOP and get into Iran if you need to go."

Still was smiling. He could feel the adrenaline pumping again. Mackey and Tee had been around long enough to know not to get excited so early on.

Mackey spoke first. "Is it your intention that we travel by ground, regular means, to Tehran? That's a long way in Injun country."

"It's almost three hundred miles, actually, from the forward observation post to Tehran. But Skripak made it out just fine. Getting back will be a little hairier, plus he'll have the explosives. But like I said, they are extremely compact, which is why we are using them despite their imperfection."

"When would we be going?" asked Tee.

"As soon as we can get you to the range to show you how to use the silly putty and get you geared up. Most of your weapons and supplies are already packed and waiting with your rangers at the plane. You'll be in the air before tomorrow night. We don't have much time to screw around."

They spent the next three hours discussing maps, terrain, the ranger personnel and equipment needs. When everyone was comfortable with what they needed, they went by bus over to a closed weapons range deep in the Virginia woods.

CHAPTER 10

Tehran

Imam Grand Ayatollah Kamala had just finished morning prayers, followed by his usual speech about keeping Iran free from Western influences. He went on his usual tirade about the Jews and the Americans, and had thousands of his followers protesting against the West in the streets of Tehran when he was finished. Nothing like a good American flag burning to get a party started in Tehran.

One of his assistants, Bopal, appeared after his speech, smiling. "Imam, you are the chosen voice of the people. The president himself has called to tell you that he watched and listened to you this morning. He calls you the Prophet's Instrument, Imam. You have been invited back to the presidential palace for dinner tomorrow. Only the most important people in all of Iran have been invited. You are deserving of this great honor."

Imam Grand Ayatollah Kamala smiled at the young man, a boy, really, and told him to make whatever arrangements would be necessary. When the boy left, he went to his room and locked the door. Once inside, he carefully inspected everything to make sure the room was clean, which of course it was—after all, he was inside his own mosque—and then he pushed his bed a few feet and lifted the rug. He uncovered a small hole in the floor and pulled out a small computer with a burst transmitter inside. He checked to see if there was mail from Skripak, and gave a long exhale of relief when he saw there was a message. He opened the mail and waited as the computer de-scrambled the message after he had used the proper codes. It was a short message:

Bijon, I am safe across the border but will be returning with plans to make your father and brothers smile.

That was all it said. Bijon felt his heart beating faster in his chest and he typed out a quick message:

I have dinner at the presidential palace tomorrow. Awaiting your return.

He sent the message and quickly put everything away under the bed, fixed the rug and pushed the bed back where it belonged. Every time Bijon sent a message, he waited for his door to come crashing down with secret police, but the truth was the Iranians had nothing sophisticated enough to detect the special burst transmissions that he had been using for years. He lay on his bed and stared at the ceiling. Something big was brewing. Skripak rarely left Iran, and when he did, it was planned weeks ahead of time, usually just for some R and R, and he told Bijon way ahead of time. This was different. Bijon smiled. Perhaps the years of waiting were over.

CHAPTER 11

CIA Weapons Training Facility, Virginia

The small bus rolled through the checkpoint, where all of the men in the bus were required to give their clearance papers. A man named Clark Cheney had accompanied Tee, Still and Mackey to the weapons training facility deep in the Virginia woods. Cheney had been introduced by Darren Davis as a weapons and explosives expert, and then they were sent on their way. Cheney wasn't a big talker, but ran down the basics of the explosive that the lab boys called CX-10, but was more commonly known as silly putty. The stuff simply wasn't ready yet for practical use by the military because they were afraid that soldiers might blow themselves up before they could be properly trained, and they couldn't be properly trained because the stuff wasn't consistent yet.

As the bus rumbled along, Cheney stood in the aisle, facing the trio in the back of the bus, going on and on about the history and development of this new high-explosive. They sat quietly and listened, but basically just wanted to watch something get blown up. They were the only ones on the bus other than the driver, who had a shotgun locked next to him. Evidently, no one was getting on the bus without an invitation.

When the bus bounced to a stop, they looked outside to find themselves in the middle of a huge artillery range. There was a makeshift town in the center of an open field, and there were craters everywhere. Evidently things were being blown up here on a regular basis. They got off the bus, and the driver pulled away back toward where they had just come from. Cheney carried a small duffel bag; the rest of them had nothing but binoculars.

Cheney began, sounding like a drill instructor. "Gentlemen," he said as he pulled out a foil-covered block, "this is CX-10, the most powerful conventional explosive, pound for pound, in the world. It is twenty times more powerful than C-4, and is perfectly safe until detonated." With that, he peeled opened the foil to reveal a tan, soft-looking clay. He pulled off a chunk, rolled it into a ball and threw it on the ground as hard as he could. Then he stomped on it with his foot. Then he picked it up and held it in his hand while he flicked his Zippo lighter and held it over the flame.

"You cannot detonate CX-10 with anything other than these high-intensity fuses. The timers range from one minute to twelve hours, and are easily installed." He pulled out another small bag and unzipped it, revealing small plastic timers about the size of a silver dollar, with three prongs sticking out the back. He pulled off a piece of putty about the size of a nickel, flattened it to the back of the timer and squished it down until it was all mashed into place, then walked over to one of the buildings with the men following behind. Cheney bent down and pushed it into the lower corner of the outer doorway of the small building, which was about the size of a small ranch house. He turned the timer to ten minutes, pressed a button on the side and turned to the other three men.

"Try and keep up," he said with an evil grin, and started running. At first the other three just looked at each other, but Cheney wasn't slowing down, so they ran after him. They ran for what seemed like five minutes, with Still huffing and puffing in last place. When they were almost a mile away, Cheney stopped and turned around, taking a knee.

"Jesus Christ, man—you think we ran far enough?" said

Still sarcastically. "If you have to blow a door, it's nice to be able to be close enough to run into the doorway *afterward*."

"Who said anything about blowing the door?" asked Cheney calmly.

After that, no one spoke for almost five minutes, at which time Cheney flopped to his chest, his head up, facing the house. The other three thought it was a little dramatic, but did the same thing just as the explosion blew the entire house to pieces. The ground seemed to vibrate under them, and as soon as the explosion occurred, Cheney yelled, "Faces to the ground!" They all covered their heads with their arms and could feel heat and dust travel over them a second later. They stayed on the ground for a few more seconds, waiting for any tiny debris to finish hitting the ground before they sat up.

After a collective "holy shit" from all three of them, they stood up and started walking back to where the house had been. As they got closer, Tee was the first to speak. "You have to be shittin' me, man. That piece was tiny—the house is *gone!*" They continued walking until they got to where they guessed the house had been. There was a hole in the ground almost two feet deep and five feet across, and no sign of the foundation. The remaining pieces of the house were no bigger than firewood.

"That's unbelievable," said Mackey. "That piece was nothing. It was smaller than the friggin' fuse. This house is just *gone . . . totally gone*."

"Like I said," Cheney said, "a little bit goes along way. The brick I have here is enough to take down a large skyscraper, hence the tight security. In the wrong hands, this stuff would be a nightmare. In the right hands, you have a serious tool here, gentlemen. Now, one thing you need to remember is that this stuff gets gooey fast, especially when it's warm. In a hot environment, you need to really get the fuse in there so it doesn't fall off. The other problem is that the explosion size varies when the stuff runs, so you might want to leave it in the foil if you can. It will still detonate in there as long as the timer is good. Easy as hell to use. It's so powerful that you don't need careful placement on the structure—you can put it anywhere and the building is coming down. I just stuck this on the doorjamb, and the house is gone. If I had used the whole brick, we probably weren't far enough away. Make sure you leave yourselves plenty of time to get out the way. Any other questions?"

"Waterproof?" asked Still.

"Yup, one-hundred percent. You can detonate underwater as well. We sank an old destroyer with half a brick like the one I have here. Split the hull right in two."

The trio was shaking their heads.

"Age matter?"

"We aren't really sure. The stuff is so new that we can't really be sure about the shelf life. I can tell you that it's good for over a year, and you are getting a fairly new batch, so it shouldn't be an issue. Anything else?"

The three of them looked at each other and shrugged.

"Okay, I guess we're done here, boys," he said and pulled a phone from his pocket, calling the bus back to their location.

They hopped on the bus and headed out to Andrews Air Force Base, where they would begin their journey.

CHAPTER 12

Andrews Air Force Base

Still, Tee and Mackey arrived at Andrews by that same bus, with Cheney there to see them off. He gave them a small vest that was very heavy, but very slim. "There is the equivalent of two bricks of CX-10 in this vest. I understand you will need to transport it easily, and this should do the trick. There are timers in the inside pockets. You can jam timers directly into the vest or cut the vest open and use small pieces. Even if a bullet hit this vest, it would not detonate. Any questions?"

No one had any questions, so Cheney just wished them all luck and saw them off the bus in front of a large hangar.

They were met in the hangar by three hard-looking men wearing Army style pants and jackets, but not actual uniforms. The cargo pants and jackets looked like typical Army BDUs, but all insignias, ranks and identifiers were missing. Even with the rumpled, nonstandard clothes, there was no mistaking these men for anything but trained soldiers. One of the men was slightly older, maybe late forties; the other two were late twenties, early thirties, tops. Their heads were newly cropped, faces closely shaved, and they were sitting on top of their duffel bags when the trio walked in from their bus ride carrying their own duffel bags.

The three men jumped to their feet when the trio walked in. The oldest of the three approached Mackey and extended his hand, smiling broadly. "Good to see you again, Mack," he said as they hugged each other. Mack stepped back and extended his arm toward Tee and Still.

"This here is my team—Bob Still and Anthony Cicero. Just call him Tee. Boys, meet Sergeant Major Don Rogers—we go back a ways."

The sergeant major shook hands with Tee and Still and introduced his companions. "This here is Master Sergeant Duce Cory, and this is Staff Sergeant Ramon Sanchez. They are both Army Rangers, on loan for a while."

They all shook hands and had started to ask each other questions when Dexter Murphy walked into the hangar.

"Afternoon fellas," he called from across the hangar. He was smiling and carrying a large rifle case. The six men turned and faced their surprise guest. "You didn't think I'd send you off without a good-bye, did ya? I even brought you some going away presents." He walked over and took a knee, then opened the large case. Packed in foam was an unassembled M40A1 sniper rifle with one hundred rounds, two pairs of night vision binoculars and six throat-mic, voice-activated communications systems.

"Master Sergeant Cory, I understand you are quite the sharpshooter. This M40A1 sniper rifle will be your wet dream. If you're any good, you'll be lethal from over a mile out. Standing record is from Afghanistan, almost two miles." Murphy smiled. "The voice-activated commo equipment is the latest and greatest, with extended range for mountain use. You can even call out to air support with these on different channels. A couple of night viz goggles in there, too. What did you all think of the silly putty?"

Tee spoke up first. "Unbelievable stuff."

"Yeah, I think so, too. Let's hope our boy gets a chance to use it. There are satellite phones and laptops on board your plane, along with your weapon kits and supplies. You're hitching a ride on a B-52 heading over to Afghanistan. The crew doesn't know your mission, and doesn't need to know. They are merely dropping you off in Baghdad on their way to Afghanistan. You will have Marine transport waiting for you when you arrive. The Marines will take you out toward the border. Contact info is in the commo kit on the plane. You can open it when you get to Baghdad. Skripak is at the FOP waiting for you with a guy named Jerry Woodcrest—Mackey knows him. You'll be on your own at that point and will have to decide how to proceed from there. The government of the United States does not authorize you to be in Iran and will not recognize any U.S. personnel on Iranian soil. That said, good luck, gentlemen."

Murphy shook hands with each man and walked them out of the hangar to the huge B-52 sitting on the runway, its crew standing outside having a cigarette and stretching their legs before the long flight. They made their quick intros to the crew and walked up the steps, waving good-bye to Murphy and the United States.

CHAPTER 13

Tehran

Bijon, in his most ornate cleric robe and headdress, was picked up by limousine with his assistant at his mosque. He had been invited to a small dinner at the presidential palace and was always nervous at those state events. This was a more personal event than usual, and Bijon, coming as Imam Grand Ayatollah Kamala, was one of the honored guests. He would be starting the dinner by leading them all in prayer, ending dinner with another prayer, and at some point during the evening would most likely be called upon to give his religious views on the problems in the Middle East. To keep his hosts entertained, these speeches required new slants on old topics, so Imam Grand Ayatollah Kamala always studied the Koran to find some obscure passage he could point out and distort to work for his own purposes. The president and the clerics never grew tired of his outrageous lies about the Americans, the Israelis or the problems with other Arab states that were inferior to their Persian homeland.

The president, Mowad Asmunjaniwal, was convinced that constant saber rattling with foreign governments would distract from the fact that his country's economy was a complete mess. He continued to push for an atomic weapon, but even his closest ministers couldn't tell if it was so they would have something to exchange for economic gain, or if Asmunjaniwal was really going to fire a nuclear warhead at Israel. President Asmunjaniwal was only the second noncleric president since the revolution, but he was even more conservative than most of the clerics. Since his presidency began, women had started wearing traditional clothing that covered them from head to toe, and college education for women was becoming increasingly difficult. Men were required to grow beards and wear long sleeves, and all Western music had been banned immediately after he took office.

Many European companies that had started to make inroads during the previous administration were thrown out without warning, losing millions of dollars in the process. This, of course, only served to worsen the economy, but President Asmunjaniwal did not want outside influences corrupting his Persian people. Radical fundamentalists were becoming more vocal since his regime took office, and they were partly the reason Imam Grand Ayatollah Kamala had become so wildly popular. The president continuously funneled hundreds of thousands of dollars to Hezbollah and Hamas fighters for continued acts of terrorism against Israel. Several terrorist groups had gone to Imam Grand Ayatollah Kamala for prayers and blessings before heading out on various terror missions. Their success rate, however, was very poor due to the fact that Imam Grand Ayatollah Kamala radioed whatever intelligence he had immediately to Skripak. Kamala could personally take credit for stopping over twenty-five attacks around the globe by "blessing" the martyrs before they reached their destination. They had no way of knowing his blessings were, in fact, a kiss of death.

Imam Grand Ayatollah Kamala sat back in the stretch limousine as the car followed a black SUV with flashing lights that led them at high speed through the heavy traffic of Tehran. He looked up at the mountains surrounding Tehran. Such a beautiful country—he wondered when it could be taken back by the people. A modern Iran could compete with any country in the world, he thought to himself. We have oil, we have a rich culture and hard-working people—the possibilities were endless. He would avenge his family very soon, and it made him smile.

Their little convoy pulled up in front of the presidential palace after clearing the gate security, and guards opened the door for their honored guest. The presidential guards were carefully chosen, and these hardliners were all big fans of Imam Grand Ayatollah Kamala. They saluted smartly and treated him with the greatest of respect. The imam was guided through the hallways of the palace to a large room, where, once he was seated, servants brought him coffee. Other guests arrived about the same time, and each one bowed deeply before Imam Grand Ayatollah Kamala, expressing great blessings upon him and thanks for his great wisdom and spiritual guidance.

The imam smiled like a king holding court from his royal chair, until President Mowad Asmunjaniwal himself entered the room with his entourage. They all rose, including the imam, and each exchanged greetings with their president and his ministers. President Asmunjaniwal took extra care to properly greet Imam Kamala, treating him like an old friend. He kissed both cheeks and then turned to his guests, holding up the Imam's hand to show his closeness with this man of God. There were smiles all around, and the group followed the president into a very large, ornate dining room.

The room was, as one might expect, beyond opulent. The chandeliers were as large as small homes, hanging from fifty-foot domed ceilings with gold-gilt beams and intricate murals. They sat at a long wooden table, heavily carved and inlaid with mother of pearl, lapis and gold. The imam sat only a few seats away from the president, near his minister of defense, a position of honor at the large table. With only thirty or so guests, this was considered a very personal meeting. The president stood and rambled on about their great country and their fight against the infidels and outside influences. He finished with great compliments to those loyal servants of Islam seated at his table, and called upon the imam for a blessing before dinner.

Imam Kamala didn't disappoint anyone with his fire and brimstone preaching from his seat, and finished by blessing the president and those who served him. Everyone was beaming, especially the president, at having such religious power at their table. The dinner began, taking several hours. When fruits and nuts were served with coffee and pastries for dessert, the staff was dismissed—it was time for the president to speak on more important matters. The president introduced two quiet guests at the far end of the table, Muhammad Ali Basri and Kumani Mustafa Awadi, who both stood and bowed to the president, then sat again quietly.

"My friends, tonight you meet Muhammad Ali Basri and Kumani Mustafa Awadi, two heroes of the Islamic people who are helping to change the world. The United States of America, protector of the Jews, denies us the right to have our own nuclear program while at the same time they build bomb after bomb and give them to Israel in our backyard. The time has come to make things right in the world. Muhammad and Kumani have helped our friends from the Ezzedeen al-Qassam grow stronger and carry on the work of the Prophet Mohammed, blessed be his name, in all parts of the world. Very shortly we will have our *own* nuclear weapon, and no one will dictate terms to Iran!"

Polite applause followed, and then another ten minutes of political rhetoric about Hezbollah, Ezzedeen al-Qassam and Hamas in general. The message was clear enough: Muhammad Ali Basri and Kumani Mustafa Awadi were the president's links to Hamas and Hezbollah, and were linked to the nuclear weapons program as well. The president had called the meetings to take a slightly more overt stance with Hezbollah and Hamas, perhaps to send signals that he was a hardliner to his own countrymen as well as the rest of the world. Imam Kamala listened quietly, growing nervous as the president worked himself into a tirade. Muhammad and Kumani sat quietly, but were obviously surprised when the president called them to his seat at the head of the table.

They rose and walked to the president, where they both bowed. The president rose and opened an ornate wooden box on a small table near his chair. Inside were two ancient swords, hand-engraved in solid gold scabbards inlaid with jewels. The president presented the swords to the men, and asked the imam to bless them. The ceremonial swords were given as a testament to the work of these fine warriors, and the president pledged more support for their work in the future. The imam made a beautiful speech and gave a great blessing, all the while trying to remember every detail about the two men.

The night went late and eventually guests began leaving. The president made it a point to thank the imam several times and hinted at him becoming more involved with the president's domestic cultural agenda. Imam Kamala humbly thanked the president and said he was at his service whenever he was called upon. Both of them had plans for the other, but with quite different agendas.

CHAPTER 14

Baghdad Airport, Iraq

The B-52 landed smoothly and rolled to a stop near a small hangar. Dozens of American military aircraft were scattered about, with hundreds of military personnel from almost every branch scurrying about like worker bees. The six men from Langley packed up their gear and waited for the airman to open the door as the stairway was brought to the aircraft. The open door flooded the aircraft with hot sunshine like a blast-furnace. It took three trips for them to bring down all the gear, with the help of the airmen on the plane, and they piled it neatly on the hot, dusty runway. They were all perspiring heavily in their clothes, already miserable in their new surroundings.

A Unites States Marine MP approached the group and addressed them. "Would any of you be Chris Mackey or Sergeant Major Rogers?"

The sergeant major, used to being in charge, barked back, "I'm Sergeant Major Rogers!"

The MP saluted, even though the sergeant major was out of uniform, and asked the men to sit tight for a minute. He started speaking quickly into a radio, and within a few minutes a small convoy of Bradley Fighting Vehicles and M-151 jeeps, some with .50-caliber machine guns mounted in the back, sped across the runway to their position with a LAVC-2 light armored vehicle in the lead.

The convoy came to a stop and a hatch on top of the LAVC-2 opened. A Marine major popped his head out of the top and lifted his goggles. "Good morning, gentlemen." He smiled. "Or is it evening where you are?"

The group was, no doubt, jet-lagged and tired, but they were about to start a busy day. The sergeant major walked over to the vehicle and looked up at the major.

"You going my way, Marine?" he joked.

"Well, if your way is out in the middle of fucking nowhere, that would be a roger." The Marine barked a few orders into his radio, and one of the jeeps pulled around his vehicle. Two grunts hopped out of the jeep and started grabbing gear from the pile. They filled the back of one of the vehicles, then pulled up the second jeep for the other half of their gear.

"You boys are traveling heavy," said the major from his perch. "I was told you only needed one vehicle."

"Yeah, well, I wanted to make sure I had the right shoes for every outfit," said the sergeant major with a smile.

"Alright, Sergeant Major, we'll get you squared away, but you're gonna have to sign for the extra truck. It's not coming out of my pay."

The six men, who had been nicknamed "wrecking ball" by a very self-entertained Dex Murphy, assembled and got ready to hop into two of the jeeps with their equipment. The major was watching them and started screaming at them.

"Whoa there! Hold up! You people are riding in the Bradleys."

He climbed up out of the hatch, weighed down by thirty pounds of Kevlar, his helmet, a Colt .45 and a radio. He maneuvered himself down onto the hot tarmac and walked over to the sergeant major.

"You in charge?" he asked the sergeant major, who in turn pointed with his thumb at Mackey. The major walked over to Chris Mackey and said, "Listen, sir. I have strict orders to deliver you to an obscure map reference point in one piece. We are heading way out of our normal AO. You're gonna be in Injun country. I need you and your men riding in the armored Bradleys. Any of you get hurt on my watch, and it's my ass. That was a direct quote from Lieutenant General Thatcher. We hit a few dozen IEDs a week here, and those jeeps tend to disintegrate when that happens." He walked toward an M2 Bradley Fighting Vehicle and spoke into his mic. The rear doors opened and the commander, an overheated lieutenant, got out.

"Welcome to Iraq, gentlemen." He smiled. "This vehicle carries six infantrymen plus the crew, so you can all fit no problem. A little tight and a little warm, but we do pack a 25-mm chain gun and a machine gun, along with a TOW missile launcher, so the bad guys tend to boogie when they see us coming. I understand we have quite a ride, so get comfy and find your seats."

The six men took off some of their gear and worked their way inside the Bradley. It was about eighty degrees inside the cooled vehicle, which was better than the triple digits outside on the tarmac. The lieutenant saw one of the older men—"Still," a very large African-American, obviously older than most of the others—wiping his face with the back of his hand. He looked miserable.

The major spoke to him. "Sir, you need to keep hydrated out here—minimum one liter per hour when it's like this. If you forget, you'll end up feeling like shit and go down hard. Tell your buddies, too. You'll adjust fast enough, but trust me, drink lots of water. Oh, and only *our* water. Don't eat or drink *nothing* out here unless you know it's GI approved. Some of the friendlies out here give you food sometimes, but until your body adjusts, I'd pass on that. Some of the spices and shit they use will give you the Mexican Two-Step for *days*. And since you're riding in *my* Bradley, I'd just as soon not have you shitting yourself." With that he smiled, patted Still on the arm and hopped up on the Bradley.

The six of them were seated tightly in the infantry section, and the three-man crew mounted up. The vehicle took off with a jolt, and was surprisingly fast for a fifty-thousand-pound armored vehicle. Chris Mackey had been given a headset to speak with the commander of the vehicle, Lieutenant Bruce Simmons. The driver and gunner were both sergeants who also wore headsets to speak to the commander and each other only. Tee leaned over and tapped the gunner on the shoulder.

"This thing is pretty fast," he yelled over the engine.

The sergeant smiled and yelled back, "We can do over forty-five on a paved road. Feels faster when you're bouncing around in here. At least the AC is working—these things are unbearable when it goes out. Get cozy . . . it's going to get a little claustrophobic in here in about five hours." With that he smiled, pulled his headset back down and sat back, looking into his periscope.

The six men in the back passed around a plastic bottle of water and broke out a map. Chris Mackey was senior man. Although his main function was typically as a "pilot," he had done so many secret missions that he was considered by the folks at Langley to be an all-around agent. He would be leading the team in terms of general operations, but the sergeant major was in charge of any combat operations and the two other rangers answered to him. Tee and Still were tagalongs on this mission, there in support roles and for brainpower once they were on station at the forward observation post on the Iranian border. Decisions would have to be made about the mission itself on location, without any help from Langley. They were operating on their own, or, as Dex Murphy had put it so nicely in Langley, "walking the wire without a net."

With the map unfolded in their collective laps (their knees were touching inside the tight quarters of the Bradley), they began to look over the terrain. Mackey used a grease pencil on the laminated map surface.

"This here is the approximate location of the forward observation post. Skripak is already there, waiting for us." Mackey pointed to the area on the Iranian side of the border and said, "This area here is all mountainous. It's where Skripak exited from Iran, and where he'll be heading back. The question is going to be, is he going back alone? And if not, how far does he get escorted? We cannot allow the CX-10 to fall into Iranian hands—I can't even imagine Hamas with a vest full of this stuff. We also need to increase Skripak's chances of getting it back to our man in Tehran."

"What kind of support do we have at the FOP?" asked Staff Sergeant Ramon Sanchez.

"There is a light platoon of Army Rangers there—that's it. The area has had its share of insurgents coming through into Iraq to cause problems, and the rangers use that FOP to spot them crossing the border. They have several snipers up there who have over fifteen confirmed insurgent kills. All of the insurgents were carrying explosive vests, mortar tubes and rounds, AKs or IEDs. Two were confirmed to be Saudis, one Yemeni and five Iranians. The others are unknowns. Most crossings occur at night. Fortunately, we've been tipped off a few times from our man in Tehran, so we sometimes know when and where to look. The rest is just good soldiering— along with some good shooting." He smiled.

"Sorta takes the 'fun' out of 'fun'damentalism, doesn't it, Skipper?" asked Duce.

The men chuckled. Still thought for a second, then asked, "So Skripak would not only have to worry about running into Iranian Army at the border, but also potentially coming across insurgents heading the other way?"

"Exactly," said Mackey. "There is the dilemma. There are only a couple of passes through the mountains to cross back into Iran without losing lots of time. Not to mention the fact that Skripak crossed by camel—it's not the fastest way to travel."

"Jesus Christ," mumbled Still. "And I was gonna bitch about the inside of this death trap."

Duce patted his thigh. "Hey man, this machine is primo. I've been in these puppies in combat, and let me tell you, they make a big statement in the battle space. These suckers knocked out more tanks in Gulf One than the Abrams tanks did."

"Bullshit," said Still.

Duce yelled over the drone to the commander. "Hey, Lieutenant! In Gulf One, didn't these Bradleys beat the dog shit out of the Iraqi tanks?"

The commander turned and smiled back. "That's a big roger! The TOW missile launcher has a range of almost four kilometers and is dead on. We don't miss, son. We can kill anything with this vehicle—you name it: tanks, infantry, bunkers, any armored vehicle. That's day or night. In Gulf One, it was so dark with the oil fires burning, we used night vision during the daytime. We were taking out enemy tanks that couldn't even see us. Do not fuck with a Bradley."

That was followed by two simultaneous *hoooaaa*s from the driver and gunner.

"I told you, man, not to worry. This machine kicks ass." Duce smiled. When he smiled, only part of his face moved on his bad side, and he saw Still's eyes move to the bad scar—a mess of skin that looked like brown melted wax. Duce touched his own face without thinking about it.

"Nasty scratch," said Still, trying to smile.

"Yeah. Lucky to be sitting here, I guess."

The commander yelled back to the infantry hold. "We'll be leaving Baghdad in a couple of minutes, fellas. About three hours on good roads, then we stop to refuel before we get out into Injun country. We'll be on rougher roads once we get to Kifri. It is a bumpy road to Halabja, and if we are going to have any problems along the way, that's where it'll be. Still plenty of bad guys running around between Halabja and the Iranian border."

Duce looked over at the commander and asked, "LT, that name, Halabja, it rings a bell. Big battle out there or something during Gulf One or Two?"

The sergeant major piped up. "It wasn't a battle, it was a massacre. March of eighty-eight. The Iranians held the town, along with some Kurdish rebels who sided with the Iranians against Saddam during the Iran-Iraq War. The Iraqis dropped chemical weapons on the town—everything from mustard gas to VX, sarin to tabun to who knows what else. Three quarters of the victims were women and children—over five thousand killed in a day or two. Some people say maybe ten thousand or more, no one knows. But I saw pictures in chemical weapons training classes. You ever see gas coming in on you and you don't have a chemical suit to put on, just blow your brains out as fast as you can."

Everyone was quiet for a moment, letting that sink in. Finally, the commander cleared his throat and continued. "Yeah, well, that is correct, and that's where we're headed. Good news is, it's a Kurdish area. They like seeing us around and give us pretty good intel when they see anything fishy coming from the east. They hate the insurgents as much as they hated Saddam, and they consider us liberators and take care of us. We will camp overnight in Halabja, one last refuel, and then head northeast into the hills to the FOP. Once I get you guys there, you will be met by other friendlies and we are out of here. I'm not sure if we are picking you up or if someone else is, but that's all the info I was given. I bring you there in one piece, and then get our asses back to Baghdad. I guess I don't have to tell you that you need to watch your asses up in the mountains. It's the wild west out there."

The men in the back went back to studying their map and marking the towns that the lieutenant had just given them to show their route. When they were finished, they leaned back as best they could and tried to close their eyes, letting the rumbling and bouncing of the Bradley rock them to sleep after two very long days.

CHAPTER 15

Forward Observation Post,
Iraqi Border

Skripak woke up in the dark. He sat up in his creaky cot and looked around. Two other men were sleeping in the same cavern, but on the floor in bedrolls. He looked at his watch; it was almost five in the morning. He had been sleeping for over twelve hours, something he hadn't done since his last R and R about three years ago. He sat up and tried to get his bearings. He stretched his back and stood, realizing he had to relieve his bladder. Mike carefully walked toward the light at the mouth of the cavern, where the sun was barely peaking over the mountains. He walked outside where a ranger stepped in front of him with his finger over his lip to quiet him. Skripak froze and moved back into the mouth of the cavern. The ranger was whispering quietly into his radio, and then paused to listen. When he was satisfied, he went back to Skripak.

"Sorry about that, sir. Some movement on the trail. We have a team watching them. Might be insurgents; they're watching."

His radio squawked and he picked it up and whispered into it. "Yup, couple of bad guys heading west to cause trouble. Won't cause trouble for anyone now." With that, he smiled and went back into the mouth of the cave where he had a very small piece of Sterno heating up a metal cup of coffee that was starting to smell pretty good.

"Need a morning jolt?" he asked.

"Need a morning piss, then a morning jolt," he mumbled back.

"Well, for pissing, may I suggest any one of the lovely trees and bushes around here. For serious business, we have a portable lavatory to the back left of the cavern. The cave opens up a bit on the left and is pretty big in there. Excellent acoustics in there as well—you can listen to your ass echo. Oh, and let me shake your hand *before* you piss. Name's Reynolds, Tim Reynolds."

Skripak just said his name was Mike and shook hands, then headed off into the bushes to urinate. When he got back, Tim was kind enough to have coffee for him. Mike realized the kid was interested in his new mystery guest, and mumbled a thanks for the coffee.

"So you came out of Iran, huh?" he asked.

Skripak looked at the ranger, who looked to be all of twenty years old and a hundred and forty pounds soaking wet.

"Sorry, bud, classified. Good coffee, though, thanks." He started to walk back into the cave when Jerry Woodcrest walked out of the bushes with two rangers who were wearing gilly suits and carrying sniper rifles.

"Morning there, Sleeping Beauty," said Jerry. "Well, the 'sleeping' part, anyway. Man, you were snoring so loud I thought you were gonna give up our position. Feeling any better?"

"Yeah, much, thanks. Your man Tim here just hooked me up with a cup of joe."

"Excellent. We'll make some chow in a couple of minutes. Sergeant Ruiz over here bagged a goat yesterday, so we have fresh meat. We also bagged two bad guys this morning, one of them carrying a bunch of crap to make IEDs."

"We won't eat *them*, though," said Ruiz.

"Meat's too stringy," his companion said with a smile.

Jerry smacked Mike's arm and told him to follow him inside. They wound their way through a gravel path inside the large cave to an anteroom off to the right. There was a small space heater and lights, and it was actually comfortable, bright and dry inside.

"I received word last night when you were sleeping; the cavalry is on the way." It went over Mike's head; he was still a little groggy. "Your team is en route. A Marine convoy is bringing them up through Halabja. Should be here day after tomorrow at the latest. Don't have any other instructions other than to wait here with you, so that's it. If you are interested, you can sit in on briefings up here and we can show you what we have been doing, otherwise, you can eat, sleep and do nothing until your boys get here. Up to you."

"Guess I'll tag along a bit, if it's okay with you. Doing nothing for three days in a row might make me nuts. Besides, if you and your men know these mountains well, I'd like to get as much intel as I can about the terrain out here. I can trace my same steps back, but if I run into problems, it would be nice to know alternate routes."

"Roger that. There aren't too many options across the border up here, which makes the hunting good for us, but makes crossing back hairier for you. The Lur disguise was a good move. Plenty of sheepherders around here back and forth across the border. If we see folks moving without animals, we usually assume the worst. In fact, you might want to rustle up some goats or sheep or something to take back with you when you go. A lot less likely to raise suspicions."

Skripak nodded his head. "Good idea, Jerry, thanks. Just not sure how much that'll slow me down, but I'll think about it. Maybe I'll bring them across the border, and then sell them to the first tribe I come across. Guess I'll see what these guys have to say when they get here. I still don't know why I was scrambled out of Tehran. No one said anything to you? Any news on the political scene in Iran I don't know about?"

"I probably know a lot less about the political scene than you do, bud. We don't get Fox News or CNN out here, in case you hadn't noticed. My job is simply to kill bad guys and keep my men safe. Four more months of living like a goat and I rotate back to the world for a while. You're the one who's supposed to know what's going on in Iran."

"Yeah, well, I thought I did until a few days ago. I guess we'll both find out soon enough. In the meantime, I'll tag along with you and your men and figure out which is the easiest way back across the mountains. I tell ya, I am getting way too old for this shit. The camel ride here almost killed me."

CHAPTER 16

First Marines Convoy

The convoy moved along what they called Highway 7, heading northeast. They stopped at a Marine base near a tiny village called Ul Ajed a few miles outside of Kifri to refuel and stretch their legs. When the two jeeps pulled up along side the Bradley, two Marines in the jeep started pulling out their gear.

"What are you doing there, Corporal?" asked Sanchez.

"Time to lock and load, sir. We are out of the city and will be off the good road in a mile or two. Convoy got hit here yesterday and another last week. I'm told we are supposed to keep moving and get north ASAP, but if we hit a snag, everyone is going to want their weapon."

The first lieutenant, commander of the Bradley, walked over as the corporal was explaining. "He's right." He turned to the rest of the team. "All of you people need to get your Kevlar on, and get yourselves combat ready. Weapons are empty inside the Bradley, understand? You keep your clips handy, but not loaded. I don't need rounds bouncing around inside our vehicle."

The roar of the LAVC-2 pulling up made them all turn

around. The hatch popped open and the major stood up from inside. "You all have twenty minutes to refuel and hit the head, then we are gonna make double time to Kifri. A small patrol got hit between here and Kifri about an hour ago. Engineers are still finding IEDs along our route. When we get refueled, I want everyone buttoned up tight and moving fast. I have orders to get you to your destination ASAP and unharmed, and I intend to get that done. It is fourteen hundred twenty hours—fourteen forty we are on the move! Eat, drink, piss, get your weapons inspected and load up!" He smacked his hand twice on the top of his vehicle and it bounced forward, with the major disappearing into the hatch as it sped off to the front of the small column.

The first lieutenant squinted at Mackey. "Who the hell *are* you guys?"

Chris smiled and took a swig from his water. "What do you mean?"

"The major is a cool customer. How come you boys make him so nervous?"

Chris just laughed and walked over to the jeep to grab his M4 rifle. He shoved a few clips of ammo into his web belt and cargo pant pockets. Tee and Still were wrestling with their new Kevlar vests and were bitching about the heat. The three soldiers were already squared away and adding water to their foil pouches for a quick "lunch." Twenty minutes later the trucks were refueled and everyone loaded up just as the first lieutenant started yelling back into the infantry hold to prepare to move out. The doors were shut and the column started up again. With the extra equipment on, the quarters were even tighter and much warmer for the occupants.

Still leaned back against the side of the Bradley, his head vibrating inside his Kevlar helmet. Sweat was dripping down his face. He was mumbling to himself that he should have listened to Hollahan back in the bureau and gone fishing.

The three soldiers of the group were in the best physical shape and didn't complain, although it would take a few days to adjust to the heat. The sergeant major handed Still a canteen and Still drank it back in a couple of gulps. Everyone else got the message, and drank another liter of water. It was the desert—you drank lots of water or died, simple as that.

The sergeant major leaned forward. "Last time I was here I was running around this fucking desert with eighty pounds of crap on me in one hundred and ten degrees. One liter per hour, minimum, or you drop. The rag heads have been here so many generations they do better out here than we do—but you'd better stay hydrated or you are gonna be miserable, my friend."

Their convoy was moving steadily at almost forty-five miles per hour when they heard a muffled explosion. Still's eyes opened and he sat forward. Their vehicle bounced and threw them around a bit as the driver flared out to the right flank, the commander speaking quickly into his radio. "No visual here!" he was yelling as another muffled explosion could be heard.

The Bradley was bouncing hard now, as the vehicle left the road and sped across open desert. A voice was yelling over the Bradley's radio. "Three hundred yards, right flank! I can see flashes! Get some fire on those mortars!"

Another mortar round impacted, this time followed by a secondary explosion and then two quick but loud blasts nearby.

"God damn it! Get a medivac on station. One of our jeeps just took a hit," screamed a voice over the radio.

The Bradley came to an abrupt stop and the gunner was speaking quickly to the commander, who cleared him to fire. The 25-mm Bushmaster chain gun started firing like a buzz saw. A large *whump* rocked the Bradley as one of its TOW rockets fired off the left tube rack. A huge explosion was followed by several secondary explosions a moment later.

The sergeant major was cursing, "There's a fucking war going on out there and we're stuck inside this heat box!"

The crew was too busy to hear him, and the others were just sitting and waiting for something else to happen. Their Bradley took off again, and then cut a hard turn that had them all hanging on to each other. The chain gun fired a few more bursts then went silent. The commander of the Bradley was speaking to the major more calmly now, and instructed the driver to head back toward their injured Marines. Two minutes later, they came to an abrupt stop and the commander yelled that they could open the rear doors.

Doors and hatches popped open, and the crew and passengers jumped out, slapping clips into the M4 rifles as they fanned out in the scrubby countryside. The acrid odor of burning fuel filled the air, along with the smell of gunpowder. One of the jeeps was upside down and burning. A mortar round had landed nearby and sent them fanning out into a makeshift minefield where the insurgents had set off two improvised explosive devices, one of which took out the jeep. After the IEDs went off, the insurgents tried to shell the area with mortars, but the Bradleys had made short work of their position. The bad guys still underestimated the range of the Bradleys. The bottom line was, if they could see a Bradley, no matter how far away it was, the Bradley could hit them dead-on every time. So far, they hadn't figured that out.

Four Navy corpsmen, two of whom were female, were hitting the jeep with fire extinguishers and trying to get the two wounded men out from underneath. Sergeant Major Don Rogers, First Sergeant Duce Cory, and Staff Sergeant Ramon Sanchez were running at full speed toward the burning jeep as two other Bradleys and another jeep pulled up to the scene. Don, Duce and Ramon grabbed extra fire extinguishers from the corpsmen's truck and helped put out the fire while one of the corpsmen got on her belly and started crawling under the still-burning jeep. She yelled back that she had one, and her comrades grabbed her ankles and started dragging her out while she pulled an unconscious Marine out from inside the jeep. As soon as he cleared the wreckage, another corpsman had him up on his shoulder and ran away from the burning vehicle in case it exploded. Ramon, seeing what had been done on one side of the jeep, belly-crawled under the other side until he was close enough to reach the other Marine.

"He's pinned!" he yelled from under the vehicle. Flames reappeared from the rear of the jeep and the others quickly adjusted the aim of their fire extinguishers. Other Marines were running over with more, and the empty extinguishers were tossed away every couple of minutes.

The first lieutenant was at the jeep and started yelling orders. "You men get on that side and rock it slightly this way. Go slow, it's sitting on our man in there!"

A half dozen men ran to Ramon's side and pushed and lifted, rolling the jeep slightly. Ramon was yelling from inside, "A little more! A little more!" When the jeep was lifted enough, Ramon yelled to pull him out, and he, like the corpsman, held on to the injured Marine while others pulled his legs. The Marine they pulled out was a bloody mess and was unconscious like the first. Two medics had arrived with a stretcher and slid a board under the wounded man, then lifted him to the stretcher and quickly got him up and away from the still-burning vehicle.

While the medics popped an airway into the Marine and tried CPR, the first wounded Marine started screaming.

"That's a good sign," mumbled the sergeant major. "You gotta be alive to feel pain."

A helicopter could be heard inbound. Everyone looked up, thinking it was a medivac, but it was two Apache gunships coming in low and fast over their position, scouting ahead to where the enemy had been. They circled three times, and then headed out again, after they had radioed the all-clear to the major. Two Bradleys and the LAVC-2 had raced ahead and their infantrymen jumped out to find the insurgents. They located three bodies, and what might have been a fourth, but there was really no way to tell. The TOW had been a direct hit on their position. The squads fanned out and searched through the rocks and bushes, but apparently the fight was over and the enemy was all dead.

While they searched the area and set up a perimeter, the medivac helicopter appeared and landed near the ambulance. The first stretcher was loaded, with a corpsman straddling over the Marine on her knees, still performing CPR, as the litter was lifted aboard with her on it. The injured Marine had pressure bandages on his legs that were soaked through with blood. The second litter was loaded quickly, this Marine's head wrapped in bandages and his arm immobilized for an obvious break, but he was stable and awake. The chopper was up and out within seconds, the female corpsman still with her patient aboard the helicopter.

Several Marines knelt and said a quick prayer as the chopper took off. The major pulled up in his LAVC-2 and hopped down from his vehicle. He walked over to the corpsmen and got a personnel report on the injured. He was obviously pissed off at being attacked and having men injured, losing a vehicle and being on a mission that he shouldn't have had to be on if it weren't for these uninvited guests. Mackey saw the major's expression after he spoke with the corpsmen and hustled over to him.

"Major, a word, please?"

"I'm a little busy right now," he answered gruffly.

"Sir, just one minute."

The major turned around and faced him, his hands on his hips and his eyes showing rage.

"Sir, those were good men, and I know they wouldn't be on this mission if it weren't for us, but let me tell you that this mission is vital to national security. We aren't a bunch of bureaucrats doing an efficiency study."

The major took a deep breath and leaned closer. "Chris Mackey, is it?" Mackey nodded. "I apologize if I am taking this out on you. I just lost one of my men on that chopper—he was nineteen years old. This is not how I like to start my day. I just damn well hope you are doing something important wherever the hell you are going."

"Roger that, sir. We may just change world history."

The major grunted and smacked Chris's arm in an attempt to bury the hatchet, and then hustled off to his vehicle. Platoon leaders started barking out orders to reassemble, and the team got back into their Bradley. The convoy reassembled itself, less one jeep and two Marines, and pulled back onto the road to Kifri.

CHAPTER 17

Tehran

Imam Grand Ayatollah Kamala had two surprise visitors: Muhammad Ali Basri and Kumani Mustafa Awadi had been shown to his private chamber in the rear of the mosque. His assistant had been very excited when he knocked on the imam's door and told him about his guests. The imam faked a smile and walked to meet the two men, who were seated and had been given coffee. They rose when the imam walked in, bowed and kissed his hand.

"Good morning. You honor me with your visit. To what do I owe the pleasure?"

Muhammad Ali Basri spoke first. "It is we who are honored, Imam Ayatollah. The president speaks so highly of you, and your mosque is becoming one of the most popular in all of Iran. We have listened to you regularly, and we believe we can help each other."

The imam sat, as did his guests, and the imam motioned for him to continue. "I believe our philosophies about the future of the Middle East and Iran are similar. We are constantly pressured from the Americans and the 'United Nations of Infidels' as to how we should govern our own people. The Americans

honestly believe that only they should be allowed to own nuclear weapons and keep a stranglehold on the Middle East.
Who are they to determine the future of countries halfway
around the world? They plant Jews in our backyard, and keep
the Faithful out of lands that belong to us. In the meantime,
their country is full of drug addicts and whores. The time has
come to change the maps."

The imam smiled and sipped his coffee. "And how do you
propose to 'change the maps,' as you say?"

"The president is a brave leader. He understands that
Hamas, Hezbollah and other fighters for Mohammed, blessed
be his name, can only do so much. We bleed the Israelis a little at a time, but our martyrs have only limited success. At this
present state of war against the infidels, the Holy Lands won't
be freed for generations. We need one swift, decisive battle to
clear the Holy Lands for good."

"And you think that Iran should start an open war with
Israel? By ourselves? With the Americans in Iraq and
Afghanistan? What chance do you think we would have
against the Americans?"

"Openly declared war? No. But Kumani and I have been
working quietly for over a year with supporters from all over
the Middle East—the Syrians, the Palestinians, our supporters
in Lebanon, Saudi Arabia and others. We have reached out to
every organization we could find to help free the Middle East
from the interference of the infidels, God willing. Iran will not
officially participate in any act of aggression against anyone,
and the president will be as surprised as everyone else when a
nuclear warhead detonates in Israel. But *after*, when chaos en-
sues and the Israelis are reeling, we will help launch simultaneous attacks all over the country. The Palestinians will move
as an army and take the major cities with our help. We have
thousands of fighters ready to become martyrs if need be, and
they will be everywhere. The Israelis would never be able to
stand simultaneous attacks all over the country after a nuclear
explosion."

Mustafa smiled as he listened to his comrade speak, envisioning Israel's population incinerated once and for all.

The imam stroked his beard as he listened, quietly horrified but not showing it. "This is a very big undertaking. And very dangerous. If Iran is implicated in an atomic attack, the Americans will invade here like they did in Iraq—or worse, hit us with nuclear weapons. It could mean the end of Persian rule in Iran. What does our president say about all of this?"

"The president has been very supportive. In the past two years, he has financed almost fifty million dollars to Hamas, Hezbollah, Islamic Jihad and other fighters. And most importantly, the atomic weapon is finished."

That hung in the air for a moment.

"Finished? I thought that our nuclear weapons program was still years away from completion?"

The two men across from the imam smiled and leaned closer. "Because that is what we *want* the world to think," Muhammad whispered. "The president has been building an energy facility openly in Halileh near the Turkmenistan border with the help of the Russians. Everyone knows it and has been watching it. What the Americans don't know is that we have also been building in the west—underground. We have tunnels under Halileh that are two miles long, and we have been removing highly enriched uranium for almost a year. It has been transported secretly across Iran and moved to our nuclear facility in the west where our first atomic bomb has been completed. While originally intended for a missile, we have changed plans and will detonate it on the ground. The missile will be detonated by martyrs who have already been selected for this great honor."

"You have already selected people for this plan? Do you infer that the plan has been approved by the president already?" asked the imam, trying to hide the rising panic.

"As I said, the president does not need to know every detail. In fact, it is better that he doesn't. He has provided the necessary transportation—a ship to move the bomb."

"Ah, by ship then. And where will the bomb be detonated?"

"The bomb will be loaded aboard ship in the south, and we will travel along the coast to the Red Sea and through the Suez Canal to Israel. It is our plan to offload a large vehicle in Israel and travel inland to our primary target by truck. If we are detected, or transportation is impossible, we will detonate in the port."

"Which port?" asked the imam, still stroking his beard and trying to ignore the butterflies in his stomach.

"It would be better if you didn't know, with all due respect. I am sure you understand the complexity of such a large operation. I can promise you that we will not destroy Jerusalem with the bomb, if that is your concern. The city will be taken back intact, and all of the land around the Dome of the Rock will be in the hands of the True Believers, God willing."

"Blessed be Allah," said Mustafa quietly.

"Ah," mumbled the imam, trying to cover for himself. "Of course it is only the protection of our holy sites that I am concerned about. You must also consider the proximity to other nations. Jordan, Egypt, Lebanon or Syria will not appreciate nuclear fallout on their lands."

"Of course, Imam, we agree. The winds will no doubt bring some of the cloud over Egypt, but we will allow Egypt to expand into southwestern Israel without protest—it is a good trade for them."

"A good trade? So the Egyptian government is aware of your plans already?"

Muhammad smiled. "We do not act officially in any government capacity, as you are aware, but we have been in constant contact with our Arab neighbors. Let us just say that other governments will turn a blind eye to our activities. They do not know about the bomb, but they are comfortable with a more aggressive campaign to free the Holy Lands of Jewish presence. Al Qaeda groups in Saudi Arabia and Yemen are also eager to assist. Once Israel has been returned to Moslem hands, the Saudi family will be next. They have been servants to the Americans for far too long. It will take a long time to return the Middle East to proper governments that embrace traditional values, but we will see it done in our lifetimes. The only things holding us back are the Israelis and Americans. With Israel gone, the Americans will go away as well."

The imam had a million thoughts running through his

head. "The president is not concerned with an Israeli counter-attack? The have several bombs of their own. What if they strike inside Iran?"

"They will have no reason to believe the bomb came from Iran. By the time they launch an investigation it will be too late for Israel, blessed be Allah. There will be chaos all over Israel as our groups coordinate with the Palestinians and Hezbollah in open warfare. Who would the Israelis strike? The Palestinians? They couldn't use an atomic weapon without killing their own people. They won't risk that. The entire world will scream and condemn and protest and no one will do anything to help the Jews. The Americans will offer military assistance perhaps, but aimed at whom? By the time they could mobilize, it will be all over. Hezbollah has built an organized army in southern Lebanon, ready to invade the instant the fighting begins. With such political unrest in Israel, the cities burning, open war—Egypt, Jordan and Syria will be *forced* to enter Israel to help."

Muhammad smiled after he said that, and then continued. "The area must have *stability*. Who better to provide it than the neighboring Arab communities? We could not allow the Palestinians to detonate a second bomb—it would be too large a crime against humanity." He laughed openly after he said that.

"The Palestinians?" asked the imam, slow to follow.

"Of course the Palestinians!" laughed Muhammad. "The world will blame them, and in the end, who cares what happens to them? So maybe the UN carves out a small piece of the West Bank for them—so what? Egypt, Syria and Jordan will divide Israel. Why would Iran want any land there anyway? No one will suspect Iran when Iran stays out of the fight after the war begins. In fact, our president will call for peace and order, and will help broker the peace agreement between all of the parties that will take over Israel. And that is where you will come in, Imam Kamala."

The imam cocked his head. "Oh?"

Muhammad gestured toward Kumani to continue. Kumani leaned forward and spoke softer than Muhammad. He was a thin, wiry man and wore round spectacles, like a mad scientist. His humble manner hid the sociopath below the calm exterior. "We have given great thought to this, Imam. Iran will be seen as a world leader when we help broker a peace accord amongst the Arab countries that take Israel. The Arab world will look to Iran, and they will look to *you*. Spiritual guidance will be needed in the unrest following the destruction of Israel. A man like yourself will reach out beyond the Iranian borders. You will be the glue that holds the Arab world together. Bin Laden could have done that, but the non-Moslem world will not accept him. You, on the other hand, will be seen as a holy man interested only in peace and the rebuilding of the Middle East."

"You make this sound so simple. Do you really think the Israelis will just lay down their weapons, even after a nuclear attack? You would have to kill every last one of them."

"We intend to, your eminence. We have enough tabun, VX and other chemical weapons placed all over the Israeli borders so that, when the time comes, our martyrs will simultaneously deliver large-scale chemical attacks all over Israel and make them defenseless. By the time the UN or the Americans can intercede, there won't be a Jew breathing in Israel." He sat back and smiled, so proud of his months of planning.

"Chemical weapons? Nuclear weapons? This is very dangerous ground you are treading on. The world will call the True Believers animals."

"They do *now*, your holiness. What do we care? After we have restored the Middle East to Moslem control, followers all over the world will rally to our side. After 9-11, did you not see the outpouring of support for Al Qaeda and Osama bin Laden? That will be *nothing* compared to what the world's Moslems will do after we annihilate the Israelis. The Chosen People of the Koran will rise up all over the world and begin to cleanse the earth of the infidels."

The imam sat back and stroked his beard again, feeling slightly dizzy. He needed to remain calm and focused. This was almost too much to comprehend—a fanatic's fantasy potentially coming to life.

"Have you consulted with any of our military regarding the attack plans? This is a huge undertaking, and a tremendous opportunity. There won't be a second chance if this goes poorly."

"We have been planning for months, Imam. We have looked at the battlefield results of the Arab-Israeli Wars since the 1960s. We have looked at satellite intelligence provided by our allies. We have had many generals from different countries discuss various elements of the planning. It will work. We will be everywhere at once following the atomic blast. The Israelis will want to scramble their fighters, but to attack whom? The battle will be raging inside their *own* country. Only their ground forces will be able to fight, but they will be gassed before they know what hits them."

Muhammad leaned forward and put his hand on the holy man's shoulder. "It is a new beginning for the True Believers, Imam. You will be the new religious leader to millions of Believers all over the world. Your mosque will become the new center of the world."

The imam put on his best smile. "I admire your courage, gentlemen—I just hope that you can succeed. If Israel were to survive the attack, there will be full-blown war all over the Middle East—possibly nuclear war. If it comes to that, we will all lose."

"Imam, there are almost five million Palestinians living inside Israel, Gaza and the West Bank. They will all rise up when the fighting starts. We have thousands of key people spread throughout Israel, ready for the moment of liberation. With over five hundred of our faithful equipped with gas, the attack will be so overwhelming, the Israelis will have no time to counterattack. There will be a revolution in the streets, and our people will take no prisoners. The fighting will stop when the Jews are all dead, and not before. With the Jews out of Palestine, the Arab nations will move in to divide it. With Iran brokering the peace as an outsider, a peace that is acceptable to all of the Arab nations involved, it is perfect."

"Have you thought about how long such a war will last?" asked the imam.

Muhammad smiled. "Yes, holy one. Less than one week.

The atomic bomb and gas will start everything on the first day. The largest population centers and military targets will be annihilated the first twenty-four hours. The Palestinians will fight house to house throughout the cities while Hezbollah forces sweep into northern Israel out of Lebanon. Our martyr brigades are spread throughout key areas to destroy communications, government buildings, hospitals, artillery and other military targets to keep the Israeli Army from organizing. By the third day, Egypt, Syria and Jordan will all move in to help calm the situation. Their soldiers will be given orders to kill any looters. Of course, *anyone* out in the streets could be a looter." He smiled again.

Kumani interjected. "For that matter, anyone hiding inside their *house* could potentially be a looter as well. They will *all* be dealt with."

Muhammad continued, speaking slightly faster as he became more excited. "By day number five, the world community will be demanding answers and either the UN or the Americans will be arriving on the scene. We will scale back by the end of the week, but by then Israel will no longer exist. Palestine will be returned to Moslem rule for the rest of time."

The imam sat back and crossed his arms. "I see you have taken great pains to make this work. I congratulate you on your plans. When will this happen?"

"Your holiness, it is better if you don't know exactly—you understand how these things are. You will need to be a little patient, but we will return Palestine to the Moslem people. We will need more help from you, though."

"And what is it that you need from me?"

"We will need you to appear more in the coming weeks. You need to continue to build a larger audience. The traditionalists love you, and more flock to you every day. We need to get you on television every day. The president has agreed. He will give you an hour each day, if that is enough. If you want more you need only ask. You will speak to the people daily and remind them of their duty. You will make them ready for the coming war. Al Jazeera will pick up your message and send it all over the Arab world until every Moslem knows your name. And it will be *you* they all turn to when the war has started. You will call them to action all over the world—soldiers of Islam—and they will listen to you, great one."

"There may be another issue though," the imam countered. "Grand Ayatollah Seyed Ali Mustafa Bin Azed may not appreciate my emergence as the Supreme Grand Ayatollah of Iran. He is still the number two man in Iran after the president, and our supreme religious leader. I have heard comments from others that there may be a growing resentment coming from him and his followers." The imam was testing new waters, curious about how he could use these people to help secure a spot in rebuilding his country when the time came.

"Imam, the president thinks very highly of you," Muhammed said. "He is not in a position to remove Grand Ayatollah Seyed Ali Mustafa Bin Azed right now. However, after a major change in the Middle East, the president will be stronger than ever. He will be able to replace the Supreme Grand Ayatollah—one way or another."

And so there it was, on the table. Help the president annihilate Israel, strengthen the president's position within his own country, and be appointed the new Supreme Grand Ayatollah in exchange. The imam sat back and stroked his beard thoughtfully. These men did not know they were the fish on the line, and not the other way around. Imam Kamala smiled. "Blessed be Allah," he said quietly to the smiling faces of the men in front of him.

CHAPTER 18

Langley

Dexter Murphy had read the message, then reread it, then reread it a third time, more slowly. Impossible. They were bluffing. There was no way the Iranians had a bomb already finished in some secret nuclear facility. CIA satellites passed over Iran regularly, as well as high-altitude supersonic aircraft. The country of Iran had been photographed with high-resolution images, infrared cameras, radiation detecting equipment, computer modeling geologic imagery to detect underground activity, and more. It was impossible. They had that country covered wall to wall. But what if it wasn't? What if those sneaky bastards got better at hiding their activities? Damn it.

Dex slammed his hand on his desk and picked up the phone to Darren Davis's office. It was barely six in the morning, and they had both been in the office for two hours already trying to catch up with their group's movements in Iraq. The time zones were a killer when you had to be on top of Iran while still trying to function on East Coast time in America. Sleep was a luxury that was getting harder to come by these days. Darren answered in his usual tired voice.

"Davis," he mumbled after the first ring.

"Boss, it's Dex. I just got a burst message from Bijon. This is totally off the charts. I'm on my way over." And he hung up and headed out.

Davis was standing in his office pouring two coffees when Dex walked in. He handed one to Dex, and took a sip from his. Black, strong and nasty as hell—but it did keep you moving.

"You'd better sit down for this one, Darren," he said. Dex rarely called his boss by his first name, so Darren knew this would be a whopper. He sat and read the message slowly, occasionally looking up at Dex, then back to the paper.

"Jesus fuckin' Christ. This sound plausible to you?"

Dex shrugged. "Sounds like a fuckin' nightmare is what it sounds like to me. This is not what we had planned for. Our team is there to deliver the CX to Bijon and take out their leadership. They are not equipped to try and track down this bomb. We are going to need the military on this one. Navy, Air Force—somebody. If this bomb makes it to a ship, we need fast intel and a sub or ship . . ."

Davis put his hand up to cut him off and picked up his phone to Director Wallace R. Holstrum. Holstrum answered his own phone; he, too, was already at his desk before sunup.

"Director, we have an emergency. We need to see you immediately."

Holstrum told them to come over and they went immediately, message in hand. They were in Holstrum's situation room within a minute. They skipped the usual pleasantries such as "hello" and "good morning" and "drop dead" and just handed him the message from Bijon. It was the longest message they had ever received from him, and the most incredible. Holstrum's reaction was exactly the same as Dexter's: "Jesus fuckin' Christ."

"Alright, we're going to need the secretary and the joint chiefs on this one. God damn it." He sat back in his chair. "You think Bijon has another agenda?"

"Sir?" asked Dex.

"Like maybe he's not quite ready to take out his buddy the president, and he'd rather have us do it for him?"

"Sir, Bijon has lived this assignment on and off for almost thirty years. He wants his pound of flesh. He has been reliable every step of the way."

The director sighed, then took off his glasses and rubbed his eyes. "I know," he mumbled. "But a nuke? For Christ's sake, this is a lot to swallow. I wouldn't have given the bastards credit for a bait and switch like this. Make a big show with the Russians about a nuke facility, and the whole time they have another facility underground somewhere else? This makes us look like total morons. Wonder if the Russians built that one for them, too?"

"I have news on our team as well," added Darren. "They are with the First Marines headed northeast toward their rendezvous with Skripak. They had an incident along the way. One Marine was killed and another injured. That was yesterday afternoon, their time. They have continued north since then and should be in Halabja anytime now. They will contact us when they get there. After that, it gets a little dicier into the mountains. A chopper would speed things up, but might also give away the location of our forward observation post out there, so they have to proceed on the ground. Roads are almost nonexistent, so Lord knows how long it will take to get to the FOP. The message makes it sound like we have a minimum of a few weeks, plus a couple of days of transport time via ship. We need to have Skripak back in Tehran within the week to be on the safe side. It's cutting it a little close. Should we reach out to the Israelis with the intel on the nuke?"

"That's above our pay grade. The president will make that call himself. I'll contact the Secretary of Defense and set up a meeting with the joint chiefs ASAP. This plan was risky enough without this monkey wrench. Damn." Director Holstrum picked up the phone and had *his* secretary contact the secretary to the Secretary of Defense. She rang them back a moment later and told them they were on for seven sharp. This was going to be a long day, and the sun wasn't even up yet.

Within the hour, there were over a dozen people crammed

in the director's situation room, going over pictures, discussing Ali bin-Oman, Muhammad Ali Basri and Kumani Mustafa Awadi, Hamas, nukes, shipping lanes, the whole gambit. By the time it was quarter of seven, they had no less than a dozen possible scenarios to present to the joint chiefs and Secretary of Defense, none of which was particularly pleasant.

Holstrum, Davis and Murphy hopped out of the small sedan with the government plates and double-timed it to the White House situation room. The joints chiefs were arriving at the same time, along with the Secretary, and the room was buzzing. Once everyone was seated, the Secretary of Defense started the briefing.

"Director Holstrum has called an emergency meeting based on new information out of Iran. While our current operation, code name Wrecking Ball, is already underway, there has been a major new development. It may or may not change the course of what we have already started. Mr. Director . . ." The Secretary handed off the morning's meeting to Director Holstrum.

"Thank you, Mr. Secretary. The following information is Classified Top Secret. You are about to be given further details on Wrecking Ball as it pertains to a new problem in Iran. As you know, the Iranians have finished their nuclear facility in Halileh. It has been our assumption that they would be a few years away from a weapon. Latest intel says they have a bomb *now* and are ready to use it on Israel."

That got several comments from the crowd, and many exchanged glances and frowns, but Holstrum ignored them and kept going.

"It seems that the three stooges we have been trying to track the last week are completely immersed with the president as well as Hezbollah, Hamas and the underworld, all working together for the common cause—that being the total destruction of Israel and a new fundamentalist power play in the entire region. Our man in Iran tells us that he has been contacted directly by Muhammad Ali Basri and Kumani Mustafa Awadi, with the full support of the Iranian president, to get ready for a strike on Israel with a nuclear bomb, followed by simultaneous chemical attacks. He mentioned taban and VX, specifically, which we all know they have, and have used in the past. Scarier yet is that the chemical weapons are supposedly already on site, or at least nearby, awaiting the bomb to start this little massacre.

"Our man in Iran is a well-known religious leader. He is supposed to start stirring the pot from now till D-Day over there and then call upon all Moslems to join the attack at the proper time. We are only talking a matter of a couple of weeks now. The bomb is supposed to be delivered via ship through the Suez Canal and offloaded by truck inland into Israel for detonation. That's when the chemical attacks start all over Israel, with the Palestinians being called upon to start World War Three."

Dex interjected. "If I might add, sir, the Palestinians being blamed for the atomic weapon seems to be part of the plan as well. The Iranians are removing themselves from the attack. They are supplying the weapons and funding, but will sit back and watch until Egypt, Jordan and Syria intervene, at which time they will offer to broker a peace and divide up whatever is left of Israel."

That was the last straw for Lieutenant General Wilson. "Oh come *on* now people, this is ridiculous. First of all, these people don't *have* a nuke according to *you*. Second, Egypt and Jordan aren't going to attack Israel even if the Syrians are crazy enough to do it . . ."

"General, Jordan and Egypt are not going to *attack*, they are going to *intervene* and help stabilize the situation in Israel. In other words, make sure that the Israelis are all killed, then carve it up for themselves."

The lieutenant general wasn't moved. "Son, you mean to tell me that the Egyptians and Jordanians know about this whole plan and are just sitting back doing nothing waiting for Hamas or Iran or whatever nut job to blow a nuke in their backyard? I think this is the biggest load of horseshit I've ever heard, pardon the expression." He sat back and crossed his arms, covering thirty years' worth of combat and campaign ribbons on his uniform.

"Sir, prior to 9-11, if someone told me that four planes were going to be successfully used simultaneously against targets here in the U.S., I am not sure how fast I would have believed that either."

"Yeah, well evidently, you people didn't believe it," sneered the lieutenant general, an obvious nasty dig at the CIA.

The director stepped in to stop the arguing, he himself turning red with the last comment. "Ladies and gentlemen, the information we have received comes from one of the most reliable sources in the agency. The question is, if it *is* true, and these people aren't just manipulating him for some other reason, then we need to ask ourselves if it changes our current operation in Iran. Do we still want to destabilize the government and start a civil war if they do in fact have a bomb ready for use?"

The Secretary chimed in. "And what about Israel? They need to be prepared for an all-out attack. We need the president on this."

Another general, this time Air Force General Witcolm, spoke up. "If we tell the Israelis, they will strike immediately, and there goes our plan to avoid another war."

"Sir, they don't know *where* to strike any more than we do. The weapon isn't in Halileh, it's in western Iran, or so our contact was told. The weapon will be transported south and put aboard ship. Ideally, we could sink it off the Iranian coast before they can get too far, but we don't have any names or leads on which port."

"Well then let's just carpet bomb the whole damn country," mumbled Lieutenant General Wilson, obviously frustrated.

"We were trying to avoid an all-out war, remember?" said Dexter.

The Secretary was getting annoyed. "Director Holstrum, do you have a recommendation for the president?"

Dex, Darren and the director looked at each other. They had discussed it in the car on the way over. The director began. "At this time, we suggest going on with Wrecking Ball and monitoring the situation as closely as possible. If we can change governments, or at least start a small civil war, it may distract the Iranians enough to avoid moving the bomb while they are fighting in their own streets. Our team should be on location tomorrow or the next day at the latest. They will get the explosives to our men in Iran. If they have more to work with by tomorrow, maybe they can get inside and snoop around for a nuke themselves, but that is extremely risky, with low odds of success. I don't want a team of Americans being grabbed up inside of Iran."

Darren added, "One of the obvious problems with the Iranian nuke situation is that when we exert pressure from the outside, it solidifies the Iranian people. They'd prefer a sociopathic mullah dictator to outside intervention on their soil. The more the U.S. or UN protests, the better their president looks to their people. The average Iranian wants reform and a more relaxed social stance in their country, but they will not take the side of the U.S. against their own president. Wrecking Ball may be blamed on the U.S., Israel, internal coup, who knows? But it doesn't matter. When our man, a staunch conservative religious leader, starts telling the people—*his* people—that it is time to change, it will have a tremendous impact, much more than a B-52 strike by us, which will only have the masses protesting against the U.S. in the streets."

The generals discussed military scenarios for the next hour, not particularly happy to have CIA running the operation outside of the Pentagon. In the end, however, the general consensus was to follow the recommendation of the director, while the joint chiefs, in the meantime, started making plans for moving troops near Iran and Israel. If the CIA's plan fell flat on its face, the joint chiefs would not be caught with their pants down. The Secretary would brief the president, who would make the decision on whether or not to inform Israel, and whether or not to check in on the Egyptians and Jordanians to emphasize the importance of stability in the Middle East, and to remind them of the position of the United States—that Israel was an ally not to be messed with. Apparently, nobody would be sleeping much again this week.

CHAPTER 19

Marine Convoy, Near Kifri

The convoy rumbled in the heat and dust of the Iraqi scrublands until they reached Marine Corps Base Reliant, a small refueling and supply depot guarded by a company of Marines, with a few Navy personnel such as Seabees and corpsmen. The convoy stopped inside the compound and everyone unloaded and stretched while all of the vehicles were refueled. Nearby, the city of Kifri bustled with inhabitants who were living without the fear of Saddam for the first time in decades. The farther east they headed, the better they seemed to be received by the locals. It took three hours for all of the vehicles to be refueled and resupplied with ammunition that was used during the earlier insurgent incident. Many months ago, the young Marines were always happy to be under fire—they all wanted their first combat experience. It was different now. The big battles in the John Wayne movies weren't going to happen. The war was over, and now it was just a daily grind of heat and boredom, punctuated with occasional IEDs that killed or maimed them or their friends. There was nothing macho, heroic or exciting about driving over an improvised landmine. It wasn't the type of "action" they had signed up for.

When they were ready to roll, they saddled up again, and rumbled out toward Halabja. As they passed through Kifri, gunners sat in their turrets, ever ready for something to explode, but instead waved and smiled at children as they passed through, occasionally throwing candy bars from their vehicles. Duce commented on the open hatches and more relaxed atmosphere here in the city, and the commander hopped down and leaned over to speak to the men. The driver assumed temporary command of the vehicle as the lieutenant spoke.

"I'll tell y'all a true story, happened about six months ago right here. We had been on a humanitarian run here in Kifri. The place hadn't been too beat up during the war, but still, things were rough on the kids, so we spent some time delivering food, first aid and toys and shit. The corpsmen did immunizations and helped the locals, some of whom had never seen a real doctor in their lives. This one little girl sort of adopted us. Cutest little kid you could imagine—big brown eyes like saucers of coffee. Anyway, we had given her this blue teddy bear that she fell in love with, and she followed us around all day. Her mother was nearby, and kept an eye on her, but pretty much let the kid hang out with us all day. Anyway, a week later our convoy is back up here to set up a water treatment facility for the locals, and as we drive into town, this kid is sitting in the road with her blue bear, and she won't move. The whole damn convoy has to stop. Guys are yelling at her to move, but this little kid will *not* move out of the way. Had it been a guy, maybe somebody would have fired a round over his head or something, but it was this cute kid that I remembered, so I got out and walked over to her. When I got closer to her, she stood up and held up her hand like she wanted me to stop. Then she stands a foot to the left and points to the ground where she had been sitting. There was a damn wire sticking up out of the road to trip the biggest improvised explosive device we'd ever seen. Took a whole team of engineers a long time to decide to blow it in place. That little kid had saved the friggin' convoy because we gave her a teddy bear. I picked her up and hugged her and she gave me a smile that renewed my faith in humanity. That's the shit that doesn't make it to the evening news at home, but let me tell ya, these people are happy we are here, and things are changing for the better."

Duce nodded and smiled his crooked grin. The commander hopped back up to his station and they passed through Kifri without incident. As soon as they passed east of Kifri, the road changed. The smooth highway became a bumpy, potholed mess, which after another two hours passed, gave way to a dirt and stone road. The men in the back jostled and bumped into each other, trying to sleep in the rocking drone of the vehicle. After an hour of rocking, they were all fast asleep, the jet lag having finally caught up to them. The jolt of a complete stop and gears shifting finally woke them up. The three rangers in the back instinctively grabbed for their M4s. Still was only half awake, and Mackey and Tee were making fun of him.

The commander yelled back to the group. "Welcome to Halabja, gentlemen. The folks here are friendly and like Americans, but we are close to the border, so keep your eyes peeled. These folks will usually tell the town elders if they see anything suspicious, and they'll come tell us, but stay sharp anyway. There is a field outside the town where we will set up camp using the vehicles as a perimeter. It gets a little brisk up here at night, so grab your jackets out of your rucks. My Marines will take watch so y'all can get your beauty sleep, then tomorrow morning, you boys will be on your own. I have a couple of recon boys who will point y'all in the right direction tomorrow morning, but they won't be going all the way up with you. Once you get up into the mountains, you are 'off the reservation,' so go easy. There are only a couple of passes in and out of the border, and plenty of bad guys use them. You'll also see Lur tribesmen and other small groups of herders up there. Those guys are usually okay, but it's best to avoid contact with anybody if you can. Guess that's about it then. Unload and we'll get you a tent setup. The major has made arrangements for your new wheels tomorrow. Good luck with whatever you're doing up there, boys." With that, they opened the rear doors of the Bradley and stepped out into the strong sunshine of the rolling hills.

While the Marines set up a temporary base camp, the six

guests walked around the area and scanned the mountains and town of Halabja. Knowing the story of the massacre that had occurred there left them all uneasy. There was a sadness in the quiet of the mountain breeze. A silence left by thousands of dead children, who wouldn't run through the streets and laugh and play games. Small monuments stood outside the town where mass graves had been dug to bury the slaughtered townspeople. While it was Iraqis that had done the killing in Halabja, the Iranians they were trying to stop were no better. The six of them walked quietly, crunching over the gravel and small stones of the hills, each lost in their thoughts. They knew why they were there. As they looked at the mountains of Iran, they wondered what the coming days would be like.

At 0600, the six men got up and joined the rest of the Marine base camp that was already in full swing. The three rangers had changed out of their Army-type clothes and, along with Still, Tee and Mackey, had put on black jumpsuits with no markings, uniforms reminiscent of their last mission when Still, Tee and Mackey had been dubbed "The Men in Black," like the Will Smith movie. Changing into their new uniforms changed their moods as well. The three rangers took off their dog tags and gave them to Mackey, who would later give them to the Marine major to bring to Baghdad for safekeeping until they could be reclaimed. They also gave the major all of their IDs, another scary moment. Nothing made a man feel more naked then giving up all proof of U.S. citizenship in a hostile foreign land. They would truly be walking the wire without a net.

The six men cleaned and loaded their weapons, refitted their supplies in their rucksacks, and waited for the major. Duce made them all instant coffee, heated up over a small piece of burning Sterno, which they drank quietly in the cold morning air. They were all looking east into the mountains when the major arrived, followed by an interesting sight. Behind him, several Marines were leading donkeys, one of which was loaded with colorful clothing.

"Good morning, gentlemen. As promised, I have your new wheels. These aren't white chargers, but they are sure-footed and easy to ride in the mountains. You won't have to be expert horsemen to make this work." This was a good thing, since only Mackey and the sergeant major had ever actually been on a horse before. "The clothes should be put on over your jump-suits until you get to wherever you are going. Wear the head-scarves and let them cover your faces a bit, especially my brothers of the darker persuasion, as the locals aren't black. You'll look like local tribesmen and no one will pay any atten-tion to you. You start running around in jumpsuits, every vil-lager within a hundred klicks is going to know the Americans are running around the border. Any questions?"

No one spoke up, and Mackey started pulling the robes and scarves off the lead donkey. The men pulled the clothes on, and Mackey helped them with the headscarves. When they were dressed, they said their good-byes, and the small band of "tribesmen" pulled out their radio. Don, the sergeant major, spoke into the radio. "Wrecking Ball One to base, come in, over."

The radio squawked back. "Wrecking Ball, this is base, you are five by five, go ahead, over."

"Base, six-pack on the way. Be advised we are dressed as locals and traveling by donkey. We should be at your location before nightfall, over and out."

"Roger that, out."

As they shut off the radio, two donkeys rode up at a trot. Two young Marines, recon scouts, smiled as they pulled back on their mounts. "Morning, gentlemen," said one of the men. "Ready for your pony rides?"

"Very funny," said Duce, not too happy about the idea of sitting on a mule through winding mountain passes.

The men loaded the equipment and watched as Mackey pulled himself up on his donkey. They imitated him and tried not to look too horrified at the idea of riding the smelly ani-mals. Once they were all mounted, the recon scouts started guiding them out of the camp. The four new riders were re-lieved to be walking and not galloping as they headed east toward the mountains of the Iran-Iraq border. They rode in single file, one recon scout in front and one in the rear, for almost three hours as they slowly climbed into the rocky mountains of eastern Iraq. Narrow paths, worn into the mountains by thousands of years of primitive travelers, were their guides. When they reached a wider flat area, the lead Marine stopped and dismounted. They all followed his lead, and took a knee in the rocky outcropping.

"Okay, fellas, this is as far as Danny and I are going. This path is going to climb another couple of thousand meters. It'll start getting cold up there, so hydrate now and eat something to give yourselves some calories to burn. When the path splits about a klick ahead, you keep right. When it gets steep—and it does—dismount and lead the donkeys. You may have to smack their asses to keep them moving, but it shouldn't be a problem. They know the way better than I do. Chances of coming across anybody up here are pretty slim, but remember that only the bad guys have mortar tubes and RPGs. The locals use muskets, not AK-47s—so you see anyone that is carrying heavy, you shoot first and ask questions later. The locals only use these paths to move around goats and sheep, and this isn't the time of year for that trek, so most likely, any contact is with bad guys. If you do get in a pickle, you can call in for air support, but it comes from Camp Eagle quite a ways back, and gunships will take a long time to get here, not to mention it will be tough finding you up there. Most likely, you won't see anybody anyway, but that's the skinny. I leave anything out, Danny?"

The other scout cocked his head and thought a second. "You better call your boys and tell them you are at waypoint one. You'll be at the forward observation post in about three or four hours. You don't want any of their snipers taking you for insurgents. Wally up there holds the east Iraq record for farthest kill. That sumbitch can shoot." He smiled with admiration when he said that, his own Marine sniper rifle slung over his back.

"Okay, guess that's it. Eat, drink and be merry, fellas. Keep your eyes open, and good luck."

The recon scouts worked their donkeys around to the back of the pack and started down the same way they had come. Mackey radioed the FOP again, and they each ate an MRE and drank a liter of water. Once remounted, Don took the lead, followed by Mackey, Duce, Still, Tee and Ramon on rear guard. All six of them had M4s across their laps, but under colored poncho-style coverings that hid them from view. The two donkeys with their extra supplies, including the vest full of CX-10, were roped behind Still's donkey in the center of their little caravan.

They rode in silence for almost two hours, the only sound being the clicking and scraping of donkey hooves on hard rock, and the occasional noise of the smelly beasts breaking wind or coughing in protest. Eventually the path did indeed get very steep. They had to stop and dismount, and Don and Duce changed places. Duce slung his M4 over his back and started pulling himself up along the steep rocky trail. They pulled and pushed the donkeys along, all of them huffing and puffing and sweating in the cold mountain air. After another half hour, the trail flattened out again, and they took another break to drink and catch their breath. The radio squawked.

Mackey spoke into it quietly. "Wrecking Ball here, come in, over."

"Base here. We have visual. Sit tight and safety your weapons, out."

Mackey relayed that to the group, who circled up the donkeys and looked around their location. In less than ten minutes a voice called out softly. "Wrecking Ball, I'm coming in. Hold your fire."

A ranger stepped out onto the goat trail not more than twenty yards ahead. He was in a gilly suit and no one had seen or heard him approaching. That got a smile out of Don, who admired good soldiering. When a second ranger stepped out behind him, they all smiled, with Still laughing out loud.

"These guys are some sneaky mutha fuckers," he joked.

The rangers walked to the group and smiled through camouflage-painted faces.

"Welcome aboard. Base is only about half a klick ahead.

Easy walk from here on in. The area is covered in all directions by our snipers. You can relax and enjoy the view; you are safer than sitting in a police station, boys. We own this mountain."

Ramon gave him a *hooaaa* for that, and they all mounted up as they jammed their MRE wrappers into their saddle bags. True to his word, the ranger led them to the FOP within fifteen minutes, and the view *was* spectacular as they came over the ridge and took a look out toward Iran. The sun was low in the sky, getting ready to paint the mountains in orange and pink streaks. When they were at the small camp, several rangers came out to greet them, followed by two men in local clothes— Jerry Woodcrest and Mike Skripak. Woodcrest and Skripak looked relaxed and comfortable, like they were sitting in their livings rooms awaiting company.

When Mackey saw Skripak, he smiled broadly and yelled out to him, "God damn! You're still alive?" He laughed out loud, and Mike grinned and walked over to him quickly. They gave each other the hugs that two brothers would exchange after a few years apart.

"It's good to see you, man. How's it going?" asked Mackey.

"Been better, been worse. It's awfully nice to be out of Iran, to tell you the truth. I have heard more English in the last three days than I have in the last three months, and it sounds *good*. I haven't been this homesick in a long time. I'd like you to debrief me as soon as you can. I really want to know what the hell is going on."

"Fair enough. 'Big doings,' as they say. Let me introduce you to my team. It's a pretty unusual assemblage of personnel, but they're good guys."

The two of them walked back to the others, who were taking their gear off of the smelly donkeys and removing their traveling clothes—all except Ramon, who joked that he looked good in a poncho.

"Fellas, say hello to my friend Mike. We go back a long way and have covered each others' asses on more than one occasion. Mike knows the ins and outs of the Middle East, so listen to him. Mike, this is Don, Tee, Bob, Ramon and Duce. Don, Duce and Ramon are on loan from the Army. They're rangers, so they ought to feel right at home playing in the mountains and eating local bugs. Bob is from the Bureau and has done a couple of large covert ops before; Tee is from the Company and has quite a few years of work under his belt."

Jerry Woodcrest walked over and also said hello at the same time. He and Tee also knew each other from previous jobs and talked quietly, trying to catch up. The group walked into the cave, where they met a few rangers who were between shifts, sleeping, eating or working satellite images off of laptops. The guests were impressed by the sophistication of the operation in a cave in the middle of nowhere. They followed Jerry back deep into the cave, and were amazed how big it was inside. One of the side passageways had lights and power lines wired overhead, and they followed it to a smaller chamber that was flat and clean inside, like a small office. A few very large rock outcroppings served as seats, and the group sat around the "room" in a small circle. A few of the men pulled out canteens or MREs and took their boots off. It was time to talk about why they had traveled halfway around the world, and everyone had his game face on.

CHAPTER 20

Forward Observation Post, Iraq-Iran Border

"Welcome, officially, to Forward Observation Post Iron Mountain, gentlemen," Jerry began as he opened a laptop computer and attached it to a small overhead projector to begin his PowerPoint presentation to the group. "That, I am afraid, is the *last* 'official' thing I will ever say to you. None of us, with the exception of those Army Rangers outside, are officially here. The rangers have been babysitting the goat trails out here for two years. They have dozens of insurgent kills and have gleaned some decent intel from the locals and the dead. Their job is to keep the bad guys out of Iraq so it can get its government in order and our people can get the hell out of Dodge. Things are getting better, but the radicals don't want peace and open society in Iraq—God forbid it could spread all over the Middle East. Iran has been happy to keep a steady supply of insurgents coming over the border, and we can't kill them fast enough." He pressed a button and a picture of Grand Ayatollah Kamala appeared on the screen.

"Other than Mike, any of you know this man?" Tee and Bob were both studying his face carefully.

Bob spoke up first. "Ayatollah somebody, right? Iranian mullah or somebody?"

Jerry smiled and said, "Very good. You get half credit. His name is Grand Ayatollah Kamala, a major imam and religious leader in Tehran. His mosque has attracted more sociopaths and psychotic murderers than San Quentin." He pressed the enter key and the slide showed a picture of a similar man, much younger and without the beard or clerical robes.

"This man here is Bijon Mujaharov." He pressed enter and another slide came up, showing them side by side. "These are the same man, gentlemen. You have just been given a dirty little secret that not even the president of the United States knows. In fact, by telling you, I have more than doubled the amount of people on this planet who know. Anyone inside Iran gets an inkling, Bijon is a dead man, and not the quick way, either.

"Bijon and his family were living quite nicely when the shah was deposed and the clerics took over Iran. They killed his entire family. Long story short, he wants his country back, and has been helping us since before Duce over here was out of diapers. This holy man is one of us, more or less, set up in Iran and sending out intelligence reports every week for decades. His handler is Mike over there, and Mike has sacrificed more than any of us will ever know to keep this thing going over the years. I have been fully briefed by Langley and Skripak, and I know what the plans are. Just so we are all on the same page and everyone has heard it correctly at least once, I will explain fully.

"Bijon, who I will refer to as the imam, has made it a point to attract the hard-liners and terrorists for many years. He is in tight with the president of Iran and his clerics, as well as the important international figures who move money and weapons. The big news is, Iran already has a nuclear bomb—finished. They are a few years ahead of what everyone thought. With the current government in Iran, that is unacceptable to our own government and to the Israelis. The Brits and several other nations feel the same way, but are taking a softer approach.

"Any interference from outside forces merely solidifies the Iranian people, most of whom want change from their current state. We don't want the Israelis bombing Iran, and we can't do it ourselves without risking another all-out war in the Middle East. There are a few generals and politicians in Washington who are pulling a MacArthur and saying why not attack now and get it over with, since we have the troops here anyway, but they are the minority. For the most part, Washington wants a different approach. With Russian and Chinese oil interests in Iran being what they are, the situation gets complicated fast.

"That's where the imam comes in. You have delivered a new top-secret high-explosive halfway around the world for the sole purpose of handing it off to Mike, who will get it to the imam. The imam will invite the president and high-ranking conservatives to his mosque, at which time he will blow them all to hell. According to CIA analysts, probably the same ones who designed the Bay of Pigs, the locals will begin a civil war, the Iranian Army will put down their weapons, and we will achieve a regime change.

"If we are not successful, the Iranians will transport their nuke by ship through the Red Sea and into Israel, where they will simultaneously detonate the nuke while unleashing a widespread chemical attack and pressing the Palestinians, led by Hezbollah and Hamas, into all-out war against Israel. The plan is to kill the entire Jewish population, and then have neighboring Arab nations intercede on behalf of the destroyed Israelis, guaranteeing the end of that country forever. Of course, a nuclear strike inside of Israel would not go unanswered by them or by us, and there begins World War Three, complete with nuclear and chemical weapons. You all with me so far?"

"Holy shit" was all Duce could muster.

"That would be a good assessment, Duce."

"So what is the suggested plan?" asked Mackey.

"That's what we are all here to discuss. The short answer is, get Mike back to Tehran with the CX-10 and let the imam send them all to Allah. The tougher questions are these: Can Mike make it back to Tehran without being stopped? Can we sit back and do nothing with the chance of that nuke being transported?"

Skripak answered right away. "I made it here, I can make it back."

"Well, if anyone can, it's you. Problem is, we can't leave that to chance. I suggest you have some backup for the trip. The other problem is, we don't know where in Iran the nuke is. Washington has repositioned satellites to try and find the damn thing, but the clock is ticking."

Still sat up and glanced around the room. "Look, I know I'm not the expert, but I guess I was sent along for an outsider's view. Here's what I think. The only way we stop the bomb from being moved and used is by taking out the government *now*. After the civil war starts—the one that we don't know will actually occur *at all*—the Grand Ayatollah is going to have to do more than get things reorganized. He is going to have to be *it*. The man in charge. If he can use his sway to recreate a government similar to what they have now, but use his position to slowly change things for the better without a radical overt difference, then the hard-liners will go along with it in the beginning, and he can slowly start replacing people as he gets more control."

Skripak replied, "I understand where you are going with that, and it is logical, but there are some problems. First, I'd have to convince Bijon to try and become their new president. That's risky. If they start really checking his background, he may get caught for what he is. Second, Hamas is already in full swing to get World War Three started over here. Even if the government goes through a coup and the country is in chaos, that may not stop the attack. If the Israelis attack Iran while Iran is in the middle of a civil war, who knows what happens—maybe the Russians back the Iranians and it's World War Three. Maybe the Chinese back the Iranians, and it's World War Three. Maybe the Jordanians and Syrians jump in. It would be a total disaster if the Israelis attack. If we don't stop that bomb, and it gets detonated inside Israel, you can bet your ass they will counterattack."

"Wouldn't you?" asked Duce.

"Damn right, I would—which is exactly my point. The Palestinians have already stepped up their attacks. If they go into full-scale war mode, there is no stopping the dominoes."

Don sighed slowly and then spoke. "We do not have the ability to remove the nuclear material from the bomb to disable it. That means detonating in Iran, or scuttling the ship and sending it to Davy Jones's locker, which is my first choice, by the way."

"Yeah, poppin' a nuke isn't my idea of a good time," said Tee quietly.

"And we haven't addressed the chemical weapons yet, either," said Still. "These fuckers have stashed chemical weapons all over the Israeli border and are prepared to run suicide attacks into civilian areas. The Israelis have a right to know."

"And I'm sure the president will tell them," said Jerry.

"Which means I have to get my ass to Tehran now," said Mike. "I need the Grand Ayatollah to take these people out now. Every day that goes by just decreases our chances."

"Exactly," said Jerry. "That's why you guys were thrown together so quickly. But we still haven't answered any of the operational issues. Who is going with Mike, and how far? And what do we do about the nuke?"

Mike stood up. "Fellas, with all due respect, and appreciation for your concern, I have worked alone for the last thirty years. I speak the languages, I know the country and the people, and I'll move faster alone."

"He has a point," said Tee.

Jerry scowled. "Look, Mike, this is different. Do you have any idea how big of an explosion that CX-10 is going to make? The people in Tehran are going to think *that* was a nuke! And we are going to take out their president and ministers and clerics . . ."

"That's got nothing to do with it. I'm talking about getting it to Tehran as fast as possible."

"Yes, and not letting it fall into the hands of the Iranians," said Jerry.

Duce raised his hand and said in Arabic, *"We will follow you, from a distance."*

Everyone looked at him like he had three heads. Mike answered him in Arabic. *"You speak fluently?"*

"No," he replied, *"but I understand pretty well. What if Don, Ramon and I were to follow you from a half a klick or so, just as backup. If you get stopped or something goes bad, we got your back. A little insurance is all . . ."*

Jerry jumped in, also in Arabic. *"I like that idea. It's a good compromise, Mike."*

Still stood up. "Somebody want to start speakin' English and tell me what the fuck is goin' on?"

Jerry switched back to English. "Don, Duce and Ramon will tail Mike through the mountains. Once he gets back on the main road to Tehran, they can get their asses back over the border."

"And what are we supposed to be doing? Sitting on our asses in this cave?" said Still, feeling a little left out.

"Actually," said Chris, "you and Tee and I can work satellite recon with Langley via remote. We try and find the bomb and the ship. When we figure that out, we call in the Navy and let them sink the damn thing."

"What about the chemical weapons?" asked Tee.

They all looked at each other. "Langley is going to have to figure that one out. They are going to have to alert the Israelis. Maybe bring them on board a little further even."

"How much further?" asked Mike. "The Israelis can't know about Bijon."

"True, but they better know that something big is about to break in Iran, and it is being handled."

"I'd go easy on that. They have their own spies in Iran. I don't want to be tripping over anyone in Tehran. Let's not get into the fourth quarter and blow the game."

"All right, I'll make your point to D.C., but no guarantees on that. In the meantime, I'll have some rangers recon the trails back into Iran. You get your shit together and the three of you leave ASAP. Chris, you and Still and Tee will set up in here with as many laptops as I can put together with satellite images. Langley is poring over them also. We can't really narrow the area down too much, but we'll go by Bijon's clues."

The three Army Rangers walked out of the cavern behind

Mike and headed outside to start assembling gear and supplies. Jerry, Tee, Still and Mackey sat on the floor of the cavern in a small circle.

"I wish I had my damn plane," said Mackey, referring to the spy plane that the CIA had allowed him to fly on more than one occasion, including during the operation that sank the Crescent Comet and saved the White House from a Scud attack.

"You couldn't fly it over Iranian airspace anyway," said Jerry.

"Watch me," he countered.

"Really, Chris. Langley was very specific. We aren't here. None of us. The company is catching enough crap from the European Union already about some of the 'illegal' flyovers and snatch-and-grabs we've been running. If Mike or any of us gets caught, we aren't to be taken alive. I didn't mention that yet to your three rangers. Mike already knows the deal—been living it for years. But that *is* the deal. We are *not* here. The United States cannot be caught spying in Iran, or interfering with its government."

"So while *those* guys go back to Tehran, we are just supposed to look at satellite pics from *our* side of the border and hope the Iranians don't nuke Israel or start World War Three?" Tee said, sounding pissed.

"Pretty much," said Jerry. "We have less than a week to try and figure out how they are moving the bomb. We have a few assets in Iran other than Bijon. Langley will have to shake the trees. I figure they'll move it by train most likely, but that's not a guarantee."

"Let's see if we can overlay a rail map over the satellite intel and see if it means anything," said Still.

"I knew there was a reason they brought you out here," said Jerry.

"Hey, I got it," said Mackey slowly. No one really paid any attention to him at first. "Guys—I got it. I know how we find the bomb!"

That got Bob and Jerry's attention. Jerry looked over at him quizzically. "What have you got?"

"The bomb—we use the mullah. We have him bless the fucking thing."

Bob and Jerry looked at him blankly.

"You don't get it? We have this religious guy tell the rag heads that he wants to bless the bomb before they send it off to Israel. He finds out where it is and then we can grab it."

Bob and Jerry looked at each other. Bob cocked his head. "He has a point. What if they went for it? He could locate it for us."

Jerry sat back and put his hands behind his head. "I'm not sure if that is total genius or total lunacy."

"Why lunacy?" snapped Mackey. "Why wouldn't they go for it? You said before that this guy knows all the big players. Your guy can find it for us."

CHAPTER 21

Langley

Dex and Darren were in the large conference room with their satellite intelligence people. They had been looking at pictures, comparing new images of certain areas to older images of the same places. There were some new rail lines in western Iran in places where it didn't necessarily make sense. They had been looking at an area a few hundred kilometers west of Tehran and comparing photos for almost two hours. Almost forty kilometers of new train tracks led off the beaten path to the middle of nowhere and linked up with nothing. There were no cities, no manufacturing plants, no nothing—just tracks.

One of the younger analysts sat back and exhaled, rubbing his tired eyes. "This has to be it. Why would they run a rail line here? There is nothing out there."

Dex was looking at the same pictures. "It certainly is a possibility. We'll retrain the new satellite with the thermal and deep scan over this area to take a better look. How long will it take to realign the orbit?"

Darren grimaced. "I'll make a phone call. That satellite is being used over the northern frontier of Pakistan looking for bin Laden and his crew. We'll have to work some magic to get it realigned to western Iran. I'll call the director myself and see if I can get it done today. The joint chiefs are going to be pissed when we pull the new toy off their hunting expedition."

The younger analyst sat up, looking a little more excited. Dex and Darren looked over at him and Dex asked, "What is it?"

"I missed it the first five hundred times."

"Missed what?" asked Darren.

"The earth. Look at the texture. We need higher resolution, but look near the end of the tracks. The ground is different. If they were moving earth to tunnel underground, they'd need to get rid of it. They must have been spreading it out over this entire area. That would explain the difference in the color and texture. It's just a hunch. I need higher resolution. We need to get that satellite moved as fast as possible. If we can take some deep scanning pics, I bet we'd find tunnels. I think this is their bomb factory, boss."

Darren stood up and straightened his tie and put his jacket back on. He grabbed some of the pictures from the table and headed out of the room. "I'm on my way to the director's office. I'll call you when I know something."

Dex looked back at the analyst. "Alright, maybe you have something. In the meantime, assume this isn't it and keep looking. I'll get on the horn with our field guys and run this past them. Get me exact coordinates, and the names of the nearest villages." He stood up to go to his office and contact the Wrecking Ball crew, then turned back to the analyst. "And if this does turn out to be the place—then what?" He said that more to himself than the analyst, and then headed out of the room.

Two hours had gone by in a blink, with everyone either in high-level meetings, on phones, or poring over satellite images. They reconvened in the conference room with a few additional people from the Middle East department. Dex and Darren had met for a few minutes before this meeting to catch each other up. It had been a very busy day, but things seemed to be going fairly well. They walked into the conference room together, and the multiple conversations all stopped. Thirteen people were in the room, ranging from young women to old men. Some were tech-geeks, some former field agents who could still manage a few hundred push-ups. Their attention was instantly fixed on Darren Davis, who sat down at the head of the long table. They had all been brought up to speed on various parts of the operation, which was obviously growing based on the size of the staff.

Middle East Desk Chief Davis began. "Thank you everyone for putting this all together so quickly. I know some of you have been here since yesterday, and I promise you a couple of hours of sleep one day soon."

That brought a few semi-macho chuckles, although everyone was indeed exhausted.

"The director has arranged through NASA to have our satellite repositioned. It will be ready in about another hour or so. Fortunately, it doesn't have to be moved much to change its mission from where it was.

"The area we are looking at is in this vicinity," said Darren, pointing to a picture blowup from earlier in the day. "We will re-examine this area with the new satellite and see what we can find. We know that the Iranians have a bomb and a secret facility where they made the damn thing. We need to know exactly what they have and where. Once we have satellite resources, we will know what we're talking about. In the meantime, ground operations continue. We are putting together several contingency plans, but can only do so much until we have more information. Those of you working sat-intel, you are excused for one hour. Find a dark office to crash in, then a pot of coffee or two. The rest of you, stay here."

Most of the staff at the table got up and left the room. They would all grab a quick nap before putting their eyeballs to the test for the rest of the night. The only ones left were Darren, Dex and three agents who had field experience as well as high-level clearances.

Dex was first to speak when the others had left. "I spoke to our people on the ground in Iraq a short time ago. The CX-10 has been delivered to our people, and they are safely at the border. Operation Wrecking Ball is officially on the clock. Our deep cover man in Iran is going to deliver the CX-10 to a high-ranking religious leader that works for us. The short version is this: The mullah will invite the president and his highest ranking clerics and officials to his mosque for a religious service, at which time the CX-10 will be used to 'cut off the head of the serpent.' Our field-ops guys have another twist to this as well. They are going to try and have our mullah friend convince the president to allow him to bless the nuke. If that were to happen, our lives will be much easier. The mullah can take them all out in one shot, but there is a downside. A pretty big one actually. The CX-10 can be used to take out the nuke without detonating the warhead, but it will most likely create a dirty bomb in the center of Tehran. Aside from the fact that it becomes a suicide mission for our man over there, I don't think the president would sign off on that, which leads to scenario two. The bomb will have to be found first, and then the government taken out. That leaves quite a few balls in the air."

Darren stood up and starting pacing around the room. He was thinking out loud. "Let's assume for the sake of argument that the imam is successful in convincing the president to allow him to bless the nuke. One of two things happens: Either the imam goes to the nuke and blesses it there, or they bring it to Tehran. If they bring the nuke to Tehran, and we are correct in our assessment of the location, then we could track the train and potentially hit it before it arrives in Tehran, avoiding contamination of the city. If he goes to the facility, the imam could contact us afterwards and tell us where it is, and we could potentially hit the facility or, at the very least, track the nuke to the port where we could deal with it."

One of the agents sat back and continued the thought. "Okay, so what is more likely? A grandstanding of the nuke in the town square to show off their power, or a secret run to the facility? If it was the Chinese, I think it would be a parade with tanks and troops and a big fat nuke, because they really don't intend on *using* them. At least not for now. But *these* crazy fuckers, I think they'd do it in secret rather than risk the Israelis or us hitting them during the big show."

Dex nodded his head. "Darren, I have to go with that, too. I don't think they'd move the nuke to Tehran. Too dangerous. They'll want to move it *one time*, from the facility to the ship to Israel. The more time it spends aboveground, the more likely someone takes it out. I'll be honest with ya though, I doubt the imam gets near the damn thing."

Darren exhaled slowly. "Yeah, I've been wondering about that myself. How much do they trust him? Although I have to say, I have a lot of confidence in our boy. If he says our guy can get it done, I have to believe that."

Another agent spoke up. "Boss, let's say for argument's sake that the imam gets to the facility. Could he bring some CX-10 with him and detonate it there? He's probably got enough to blow that mosque ten times over. A little dab will do ya."

They all quickly exchanged glances. It wasn't a bad idea. A small piece placed inconspicuously on the bomb while it was being blessed would do the trick. Even better, the facility would be taken out with it, and all in an area that was far away from civilians, if in fact their hunch on the location was correct. For the first time in several days, Darren smiled.

"That is actually the best-case scenario. The CX-10 would more than do the job, and the bomb would contaminate their underground facility, rendering it useless for the next few thousand years . . . I will get a transmission to our field unit and give Wrecking Ball some additional instructions. Good work, everyone. We'll meet up with the satellite crew in a bit and take a better look at the area in question. I'll also update the director."

CHAPTER 22

Operation Wrecking Ball,
FOP Iron Mountain

It was 0500 when the computer beeped that it had un-scrambled a secure message from Langley, Virginia. Every-one was up, drinking coffee and reviewing the terrain maps with the rangers and Skripak. Mike knew Iran like the back of his hand, but the mountain passes along the northwestern border were another story. A right instead of a left at the wrong spot could have you walking for days in the wrong di-rection.

Jerry sipped his coffee and opened the mail. He read qui-etly, destroyed the e-mail, and spun around in his folding di-rector's chair. "Got some news, boys."

The rest of the crew walked over and either took a knee or stood, waiting.

"Langley has been doing some homework. Seems like they may have located a possible site for the nuke facility. We'll check our map and see if it means anything to you, Mike. They also have another idea that may work. If we can get the imam to the facility, he could potentially place a small piece of CX-10 on the bomb *there*. He has more than enough to do the mosque. A small piece would be enough to destroy the bomb and the facility. Another scenario—they move the bomb to Tehran, but Langley thinks that is more unlikely. Too risky to have it above ground where the Israelis or we can destroy it. So, that brings us back to Mike getting his ass back to Tehran ASAP—this morning, with you three guys trailing as sniper support. Chris, Still and Tee will stay with me here and work the maps and satellite intel. If it happens that we can confirm the location of the nuke factory, maybe we pay it a visit ourselves, but that's not plan A."

"This is stupid," said Still. "If we can find the damn nuke, why not just send in a commando team and do the whole thing in one shot?"

Everyone just stared at him. Mackey smiled and asked quietly, "You got ADD? Not paying attention in class? We are trying to avoid World War Three. We are being *sneaky*—shhh. FBI man can't go arrest them in Iran . . ."

Still apologized and Jerry continued. "Mike, the rangers will take you through the mountains as far as the Iranian border, but that's it. After that, Don, Duce and Ramon will cover you through the scrublands until you get to a safer area. From there, you get your ass back to Tehran, hand off to the imam, and we wait and watch. Any questions?"

There being none, everyone except Mike and Jerry got up and headed outside to the waiting donkeys. The sun was just starting to rise over Iran, the pink and orange fingers stretching over the mountains of Iraq like invading armies. Mike sat on the cave floor looking at Jerry.

"If I make it out of this, I'm done, man. The Iranians can rebuild their country, and I am going home." He paused thoughtfully. "Wonder what it looks like."

"Where are you from?" asked Jerry. It was funny. They had known each other, "sort of," for years, but knew absolutely nothing about each other.

"Florida, mostly. We moved around a little bit when I was a kid. Dad had changed jobs every few years. He died when I was a still in high school, and Mom could barely keep a roof over our heads, so college was out of the question. I joined the Marines with a buddy of mine right out of high school and stayed in for eight years before I ended up doing 'other jobs.' It's been so long since I've been home—not even sure what home means anymore. Mom died while I was away, my only sister died in a car accident while I was away. Home is sort of an idea at this point, not really a place."

Jerry cocked his head and looked at his friend like he was meeting him for the first time. "We are in a lonely line of work, my friend. But you . . . Jesus, could it be any worse? You can't even go to the beach and get laid in Iran."

"Coulda been worse! I could still be in Afghanistan!" They both laughed, images of burka-clad women in their heads.

"Really, man, you have been in Iran so long, you are practically Iranian. You ever get laid?"

Skripak laughed. "For a few rials, you can get laid in Iran just like anywhere else. I don't do it too often though. I'm afraid I might cum in English!"

They both laughed at that. And it was true; getting laid was one of the basic necessities of life when doing very long operations. Some places in the world were easier than others, the Middle East not being one of the world's hot spots for picking up chicks. The smiles disappeared. It *was* a lonely life.

"I did take a few weeks off last summer. Met a Navy corpsman in Dubai and had one helluva week. She was amazing looking. Of course, the fact that I hadn't seen a blonde with blue eyes in eight months may have had something to do with it, too. I almost didn't go back to Iran. No shit."

"So why did you?" asked Jerry.

"Why do we *always* go back? I'm not done. I have spent half my life on Iranian soil. I want to leave it a liberated country, or at least better than when I started."

"I hear ya. It's hard to know when to hang it up. I tell ya though, I am surprised Langley left you in so long. Nobody stays on a job for this many years. You've missed your whole life, man."

"Like I said, home is just an idea. There's no one waiting for me in the U.S. And I can do some good out here. Hell, I might help prevent World War Three." He smiled and stood up.

Jerry stood up also, and gave him a quick hug and patted

his back. "Tell ya what, bro. You get this job done, come out in one piece, and I'll buy you the biggest lobster you ever saw in Florida."

"And another beer or two?"

"Deal."

They shook hands, faked smiles and headed outside where the rest of the men were ready to start down the trails.

CHAPTER 23

CIA Headquarters

The satellite had been nudged slightly in its orbit, and within a few hours was able to use the world's greatest technologies to start combing western Iran. Cameras thousands of miles away in space were taking pictures of soil, and, more importantly, *under* the soil. The electromagnetic thermal imaging systems were looking for anomalies underground—anything that might give a clue to the whereabouts of Iran's nuclear bomb. The grid had been shot for a few hours, all data being sent to Langley, Virginia, where a small crew of overworked, overtired men and women tried desperately to find the needle in the haystack.

The young analyst who had first noticed the soil abnormality was looking at the electro thermal imaging pictures under magnification. The pictures didn't provide instant information—you had to really study them. Underground abnormalities could appear for many reasons—underground streams, changes in rock strata, caves—but those were different than man-made structures. Humans liked right angles and boxes, and steel appeared as very straight lines that normally don't appear in natural formations. They were at it for about twenty minutes when the analyst stood up, holding a picture over his head like a trophy.

"Got it!" he announced loudly to the room. "This has to be it."

All activity stopped, and Darren called back to him, "Grid reference?"

The analyst rustled through papers and then announced back to the room a series of numbers and letters, which Davis typed into a computer. An overhead projector changed photos and displayed a piece of Iran ten square kilometers in size. The computer image was a grayish red blur, but there were the unmistakable outlines, right angles, and long, straight lines that told the story of human construction underground. With the image blown up so large, all eyes worked the picture, and several analysts caught the underground rail lines that appeared where the surface line ended.

The group discussed the photo for almost an hour, comparing the underground imagery to the surface pictures. The rail line was the piece of evidence that was the clincher. While the underground construction could have been a dozen different things, the rail line disappearing belowground and continuing into one of the large underground rooms convinced the group of the purpose of such a project. The underground images were from a new technology, and were not particularly easy to read, but combined with the other information they had, and a ticking clock, they were good enough.

Davis and Murphy conferred for several minutes, then thanked the group for the work and excused themselves. They headed to Davis's office and called the director to tell him they were eighty percent sure they had found the bomb factory. Was the bomb still there? That was a whole different problem.

CHAPTER 24

Just East of
FOP Iron Mountain

The small team of rangers from FOP Iron Mountain had led the caravan by donkey through the mountain passes that headed to the Iranian border. As the mountains leveled out to a scrubby plain, the Iranian border appeared. There was no barbed wire or fence along the invisible political line. There were, however, occasional signs that warned of minefields, and huge billboards of Iranian clerics stood in the distance. Ironically, the most menacing face was that of the Grand Ayatollah Kamala. The rangers who had led them through the mountains dismounted as they started to lose their cover in the rocks. Everyone else followed suit. The others moved carefully through the rocks and pulled out powerful binoculars to study the border area.

There were no signs of activity anywhere, just the light warm breeze over the scrubby hard ground. Very little grew in the baked earth and rocky soil other than clumps of scrub grass, and there wasn't much cover in crossing the open border. An Iranian patrol could be anywhere, with their *own* binoculars, looking over the same ground. They sat quietly for a long time before anyone spoke. Finally, a ranger lieutenant scrambled over the rocks back to the small group.

"All right, it looks pretty clear out there for right now, but the sun is already up and there is one small problem. Land mines."

Everyone exchanged nervous glances.

The lieutenant continued, addressing Mike. "When you came in, you crossed near a guarded border. You can't go back the same way with these three following you, even with disguises. Too many smugglers in and out near here. You'd be stopped and questioned. I think you could cross here, though, following Ben."

"Ben who?" asked Mike.

"The donkey. We call him Ben Laden. You make him lead—if he gets blown up, fuck 'im." He smiled.

"Oh, that's just great. And what if he *does* trip a mine? The explosion will bring every guard within five miles," said Mike.

The lieutenant smiled. "Sir, I'll be honest with you, I know the signs say minefield and all, but I really doubt you'll encounter any. We come down here sometimes and watch the border. Smugglers use it almost every day. We have *yet* to see a mine go off. My guess is the signs are supposed to scare you off."

"Yeah, well, it's working," mumbled Mike.

"I'll go first with the donkey," said Duce.

They all turned to him. He repeated himself, then added, "Mike needs to get through with the vest. I'll go first with the donkey, walking in his steps. I'll stay as far back as I can, and hope the mines are small. Mike can follow, with Don and Ramon covering. I'll cover from the other side when I get there. There is a rocky outcropping over there," he said, pointing to a small landmark in the distance, over the invisible line. "I can make it to that point, set up my sniper rifle, and cover you guys coming across."

Don, the sergeant major, put his hand on Duce's shoulder and interrupted him. "It's a good idea, except *I'll* go first. You're a better shot—you set up here and cover my crossing. I'll make it to the rocks, and I can cover you from there. It's a half mile closer and I might actually hit a target from there. Ramon crosses with Mike, and you come last."

The ranger lieutenant interrupted to save the Don and Duce arguing over who pulled point. "With all respect, Don, Duce going first makes more sense. He can set up across the way and pick up an extra half mile. My guys won't miss from here anyway. Duce on the other side sure would add some insurance. He speaks Arabic pretty well—let him escort Mike for a bit with you and Ramon trailing. When they get away from the border, Duce can drop back and rejoin you two."

Mike stood up and looked out over the no-man's-land between the two countries. It was completely vacant and wide open. He turned to the lieutenant and asked, "You said you've been this way before?"

"Yeah, we come down every now and then. Popped off four jokers from Ansar-Al-Islam last month. They were trying to cross over into Iraq with RPGs and AKs. We watched them walk over this area without being stopped on either side, and let them walk up on us in the mountains. When they got close enough, we bagged all of them before they got a shot off. And they didn't hit any mines, by the way."

"Good enough for me," said Duce, standing up. "Let's get this show on the road before the Iranian Army decides to take a drive over here. It's almost oh-six-thirty."

He walked over to his donkey and pulled down a large colorful native shawl that he put over his head and shoulders, and then pulled himself up the mount. He flipped the safety off of his M4 and balanced it in his lap with the shawl over it. He looked down at the rest of the crew and smiled his crooked half smile. "See y'all in Iran."

Everyone else got up and started checking their weapons and gear. One of the rangers that had been out spotting for a ranger sniper came back to the group and approached the lieutenant. They chatted for a few minutes, and then he hustled off again. The lieutenant addressed the group.

"Okay fellas, here's the deal. We have a sniper team about half a klick north. They can see an Iranian outpost on the border, but so far there is no sign of any activity. They will sit on it from their location and will radio back to me if they see movement. Border shootings between the Kurds or Iraqis and the Iranians are more common than you would think, so if we do have to take out anyone across the border, it won't necessarily start World War Three. It will bring other Iranian patrols, though, so we'll hold off unless it gets critical."

Mike was looking over a map, locating the small village he passed through on the way out. It was nearby, and the Lur tribesmen wouldn't hassle him, so he decided he would follow the same route back. Mike saddled up and, like Duce, placed his M4 across his saddle under his poncho. He looked down at the lieutenant and said a quick thanks, then kicked his mount to start him down the hill after Duce.

The rangers moved through the rocks silently, taking up positions in sniper teams in a 180 degree arc. Don and Ramon laid down on their bellies on a large flat rock and watched their friends head out. Ramon assembled his sniper rifle and Don set up a small tripod for his extremely powerful binoculars. When Duce reached the end of the hills where the rocks turned into crusty earth and scrub, he dismounted. He took out thirty feet of rope and attached it to the donkey's tail, and then smacked the beast and told him to git, like a regular cowboy. The donkey started walking across the open plain into the no-man's-land, with Duce walking as far back as he could and still hold the rope. Anytime the donkey stopped, Duce would snap the rope, sending a wave through the rope that popped the donkey in the rear and got him going again.

The walk was slow and excruciating, as Duce waited for the donkey to explode into a million pieces and shower his face with the familiar heat of shrapnel. He controlled his breathing and heart rate as best as he could, fighting off the panic attack in his stomach. The crunchy, scraping noises of hooves and boots over the hard earth was deafening to Duce. It took fifteen minutes to reach the rocks on the other side of the border, at which time Duce jogged up behind the donkey and pulled it into cover in the rock outcropping. He knelt down and assembled his sniper rifle, then used binoculars to scout around. When he was satisfied that he was alone, he radioed back to

Mike. Mike had watched his progress from the Iraqi side of the border and was mounted and ready to go. He followed the faint trail left by Duce, but it was pretty useless, since his mount didn't step into the exact footprints anyway. He was just as likely to hit a mine following this trail as any other, but luckily, he made it across without incident.

When Mike was across, he hopped off his donkey and pulled it into the rocks with Duce's. They called back to the rangers, who reported all quiet on the eastern front. Mike and Duce waited for five more minutes, and then, satisfied that no one was around, started heading east toward the Iranian foothills. Don and Ramon scrambled off the rocks and hopped on their donkeys, pulling ponchos of the Lur tribesmen over their heads and shoulders. Ramon still had his sniper rifle assembled, and it stuck up behind him a little, but he didn't bother to take it apart. Don and Ramon hustled down to the trail left by the others, and moved quickly in single file across the plain. When they arrived at the rocks, Mike and Duce were already gone.

Don took out his binoculars and watched Mike and Duce heading quickly into the foothills. He was sweeping the binoculars in all directions, not seeing anything, when his radio squawked. It was the lieutenant.

"The border guards at the outpost just stepped outside. They are starting to scan the border. Sit tight."

Don hopped back down into the rocks and signaled to Ramon, who moved around in a better position to see the guards who were almost a kilometer away in a small outpost. Don crawled over to Ramon. "The LT says to sit tight, but if we don't move now, we could be stuck here all day. What do you think?"

Ramon cursed under his breath and looked through his scope, his rifle on the bipod. He watched a guard come around the corner, followed by a second one. One of them unzipped and started urinating. Ramon chuckled quietly.

"What is it?" asked Don.

"I could shoot his dick off," he whispered back.

Don took out his spotter's eyepiece and took a look. Sure enough, the guard was peeing off the small porch of the wooden cabin—not more than a shack, really. Don called back on the radio to the lieutenant.

"LT, we need to get out of here *now*. How many guards are in the shack?"

"We make it three, but can't confirm. There may be more inside," he answered.

"We have a shot on two of them, can you get the third?" asked Don.

The lieutenant made him hold for a few seconds, then confirmed that his snipers had shots on all three of them. Don and Ramon looked at each other. Killing a man from almost a mile away required skill, but it wasn't glamorous. It was more like murder than combat, but they had a mission, and it was "them or us."

"I can hit the targets from here, Don," said Ramon quietly.

Don radioed back and said, "LT, I am requesting your snipers assist us in taking out the guard house. We need to get on the trail and can't wait here. This is an authorized request."

The lieutenant again asked them to stand down for a minute, at which time he contacted Jerry Woodcrest at Iron Mountain for additional authorization, which was given quickly. The lieutenant radioed back after instructing his snipers, who all changed to the same channel. The lieutenant spoke slowly to all of the snipers who were zeroed on the house.

"Acquire target closest to your position. Prepare to fire . . . three, two, one, fire-fire-fire."

Don watched through his spotter's scope as Ramon gently squeezed off a 7.62-mm round at precisely the same time as three other snipers across the border. Ramon's round, being slightly closer, hit the guard who was zipping his pants up a split second before the second sniper across the border almost decapitated him. The guard next to him flipped over the railing in a mist of red blood and dropped to the ground. A third guard, around the corner and out of their sight, also dropped like a stone. The lieutenant called back on the radio, confirming three kills.

Ramon immediately broke down his weapon while Don grabbed the two donkeys and hopped up on his. He used his binoculars to find Duce and Mike in the distance. They had stopped and were looking back toward the border. Duce had binoculars out and they were trying to assess the gunshots. When they saw Don and Ramon on their donkeys heading out of the rocks toward them, they double-timed it. The two pairs of men continued east, at their interval of almost a kilometer, as they headed into the rocky hills of western Iran.

CHAPTER 25

Tehran

Morning prayers echoed throughout Tehran. State-run radio broadcast sermons from mosques around the country, but most listeners were tuned into the Grand Ayatollah Kamala's mosque. He was being particularly interesting today, his speech going beyond the usual rhetoric that echoed the president's stance on Israel and America. This morning, he was more impassioned than ever, citing verses from the Koran and then spinning them with his own brand of hatred, but with some mystery entwined. He made poetic references to the "dead tree in the desert that was Israel being burned to the ground by the winds from the East," but stopped short of any nuclear reference. By the time prayers were over, over one hundred thousand Iranians had taken to the streets of Tehran, cheering and chanting for their favorite cleric.

The Grand Ayatollah stood out on a small balcony above the crowds, using the large speakers on the outside of the mosque to praise the holy and faithful who heard his voice and understood. The more he praised them, the more they cheered, unified in their allegiance to him. He would be counting on this allegiance in the days ahead, although the crowds of the faithful didn't understand that part of the plan just yet.

When he was finished with his speeches, he left the balcony and walked inside, surprised to find several of the president's aids as well as Muhammad Ali Basri and Kumani Mustafa Awadi waiting for him. He bowed slightly, as if honored by their visit, crossing his arms over his chest respectfully.

Muhammad Ali Basri spoke first. "You were brilliant this morning, Ayatollah. The president has been listening to you every day. He is taken with your strong support and wishes to invite you back to the presidential palace for a feast three nights from now. I believe he will have some news for all of us." He smiled.

Grand Ayatollah Kamala smiled back, again bowing slightly, and said, "I would be honored to join our great president again. He is about to change history and the balance of power in the Middle East for centuries. As you can see, our people are eager to fight for our leader."

"Not all of them, I am afraid," said Muhammad. "At the universities, the liberal students are tempted by the West. They sneak satellite dishes into our country and view scandalous television and listen to music that would make Satan blush. It is poisoning our youth. The president has had some of them arrested, but there are hundreds, perhaps thousands of these students protesting against Iran having nuclear weapons. Their minds have been corrupted by the Americans who believe only *they* should be allowed to make atomic weapons."

Kumani Mustafa Awadi interjected, "Perhaps the Grand Ayatollah could speak to the students directly to remind them of their loyalties to our president and to the Koran. When we attack Israel, the UN and the Americans will make ridiculous threats and demands. We cannot have distractions in our own country. These students must be dealt with before that happens."

The Grand Ayatollah nodded thoughtfully. "I understand," he said. "Perhaps I can find the words to remind them of their duties. God willing, they will stop their protests and give our president the support he deserves."

Kumani and Muhammad smiled and bowed, having made their point to the imam.

"We shall call you in a few days to remind you of the dinner party. The president will be most pleased to hear you address this little problem."

The small entourage left and the ayatollah told his assistants he was not to be disturbed. He would be praying quietly in his room and studying, as he prepared his words to correct the behavior of the university students. He walked the stone steps to his chambers and locked the ancient door behind him. Sitting on his soft bed, he rubbed his eyes and exhaled slowly. He had been preparing his whole life to do something for his country. The day was approaching when he would be called upon to act, and he did pray—not for wisdom to squash the rebellion of the students, but for strength to prevent the murder of millions of Israelis and perhaps Iranians. Every war ever started in the history of mankind was expected to be much shorter than they ever actually were. Was the president crazy enough to believe that Israel would be destroyed in a week, and there would be no repercussions to Iran? He pushed the bed a few inches and picked up the carpet. Pulling up a few boards, he took out the burst transmitter and typed a message directly to CIA headquarters, something he had only done a few times before. Almost all of his information went through Skripak, but Mike hadn't answered his messages the past few weeks. He was trying not to panic, but he typed quickly:

Dinner party with president in 3 nights—awaiting possible announcement. No word from my friend. I believe situation is getting critical. Do you have instructions?

He hit send and took the dish apart carefully, putting it back into the hole in the floor. Once the bed was pushed back, he lay down and closed his eyes, trying to compose a few speeches, each greatly different from the other, for the coming days.

CHAPTER 26

Tehran

The imam had just finished his evening radio broadcast, more radical and violent than he had ever been in the past. The president was present at the studio for the sermon, along with several of his highest ranking officials, and he was very pleased. The Grand Ayatollah was treated like royalty by the radio sound engineers. They all complimented him on his fine speech and his call to the students to "stop protesting and follow the path of Mohammed which the president had shown them," and which the Grand Ayatollah supported. The Grand Ayatollah was clear in his speech that the president spoke directly for the Koran in his calls for the destruction of Israel and the West.

The imam walked out of the sound studio to the observation room where the president and his entourage waited. The president smiled and bowed slightly, a gesture that was returned by the imam.

"You were very inspirational, as always, Ayatollah. Your commentary on the student protests was masterful. Tomorrow, the police will arrest all those students still causing problems. They have now been very clearly warned and will have only themselves to blame. Our nation will stand united in the coming days."

The imam smiled and thanked him, but in his head he repeated those words, "in the coming days." Time was running out. Where the hell was Skripak? He decided to push his luck.

"As always, your wisdom builds a stronger Iran. How long before the storm cleanses the desert?" the imam asked quietly.

"God's plans are a mystery to humble men like myself, Imam. I leave it in the hands of our prophet, Mohammed, blessed be his name." He smiled.

The imam bowed and didn't push further—perhaps the president truly didn't know. In any case, he wasn't going to share any information about the timeline with the Grand Ayatollah.

"Well, Mr. President, I shall look forward to the coming days myself, helping you build a new Iran—one that will become a superpower to overshadow the crumbling West."

The president smiled and turned to leave with his men. "I shall see you in two days for dinner, Ayatollah Kamala. We shall celebrate the future together."

With that, the president and the Grand Ayatollah, along with their entourage and bodyguards, left the building and headed out to their waiting limousines. The imam was dropped off at his mosque, which was quickly becoming the center of all religious activity in Iran. The fact that the president was now appearing alongside the Grand Ayatollah on a regular basis cemented the ayatollah's importance in the eyes of the Iranian people. And of course, the fact that the imam supported the president gave religious justification to any actions the president would take on any issue at any time.

The following morning would begin the "cleansing of Iran" by the president, which the Grand Ayatollah had not been told about. There was no way for the imam to know that his words would be used as the excuse of the president for the subsequent arrest, incarceration and execution of tens of thousands of young Iranians who did not share the president's view of totalitarian religious rule of their beloved country. There would be no trials, just the rounding up of the troublemakers, most of whom would simply disappear. Families and friends who asked too many questions would share the same fate. The president wanted one people, fiercely loyal to only him, who shared his vision without question. The last ruler to govern with such draconian measures had lived only across the border in Iraq—but this president was determined not to share the fate of Saddam Hussein.

CHAPTER 27

Western Iran

Don and Ramon had dismounted and were watching from a rocky hillside as Duce and Mike walked toward the small village. At a little over a half kilometer, Ramon could help take out any hostiles. Don was using his spotter's scope and quietly relaying wind speed and direction to Ramon, who was prone on a rock with his rifle up on the bipod. They had observed radio silence the entire trip, for fear that Iranians might triangulate and discover them. In an area where very few people used any electronic devices, their radios might be compromised.

It was getting close to dusk, and Ramon didn't like the lighting conditions. It was too bright for his night vision scope, but getting a little dark from this distance. The hills and mountains made funny shadows, and Ramon was stressed. They watched Mike and Duce walk their donkeys into the village. They were approached by a couple of villagers, probably the village elders or local chief. Ramon could see their gray beards through his scope. Mike was doing the talking, and Duce was tending to his donkey to keep busy and stay out of it.

Within a few minutes the four of them were smiling, and

Mike made a peace sign behind his back that Ramon could see. Ramon spoke quietly to Don. "Did you catch that?"

"Affirmative. Looks like he's fine. Just stay on him as long as you can. What's he up to? Looks like Duce is moving stuff from Mike's saddle to his."

They watched as Mike followed the two older men down the dirt path. All of a sudden there was commotion from the village, with people coming from many directions.

"Heads up, Ramon. You watching this?" asked Don.

"Yeah. What the hell are they doing down there? Duce looks calm, though."

"Yeah, I see that, too. He just made a peace sign behind the donkey. What the hell are they doing down there?"

The villagers assembled by the older men, then jogged off together. Don and Ramon watched them disappear down the path, while Mike started fishing around in a bag in his robes. He was counting out rials to the older man.

"He's giving him money," said Ramon quietly.

"Roger. Maybe they are paying them off to keep quiet?" asked Don.

"Wait!" said Ramon. "Check this shit out."

The crowd of villagers had reappeared, pushing what looked to be the filthiest car they had ever seen. The car was small, and obviously old and beaten, but the villagers were excited and pushed it back to where Mike stood with the village elders. The elders shooed them away, perhaps so they wouldn't see the amount of money they were about to make, lest they had to share any. Evidently, they drove a hard bargain, because Mike gave him another stack of bills, and Duce handed him the reigns of the donkey he had stripped of its cargo.

Mike walked over to Duce and the two of them spoke for a moment. They watched Mike look in their general direction and give a big dramatic smile to them as he stripped the other donkey with Duce. The filthy car was pushed closer to them, and the locals used small gasoline cans to fill the tank. Mike hopped into the driver's seat and turned the key in the ignition, and by some miracle, the car actually started, spitting black smoke out the tail pipe to the cheering of the locals.

He got out and helped Duce quickly throw their gear, all wrapped in Lur blankets, into the backseat, or what was left of it. After some formal cheek kissing and bowing good-byes to the local chiefs, Mike and Duce peeled out of the village.

"Where the fuck is he going with Duce?" asked Ramon. "Isn't he coming back with us?"

Don frowned. "I thought that was the plan. Just keep watching them."

As the car left the village, the crowd of villagers broke up after the excitement, and returned to their activities. The car continued down a dirt road out of sight of the village, but still within binocular view of Ramon and Don. It eventually stopped, and they could see the passenger door open and Duce hop out with his Lur poncho over his weapons. Duce was double-timing it away from the road, toward Don and Ramon, and then Mike gunned the engine and sped off toward Tehran and the fate of the Middle East.

"Got him," said Ramon quietly as he watched Duce circling back toward them, away from the village. Don used his spotter's scope to keep an eye of the village, while Ramon watched Duce bobbing and weaving through rocks and open ground, trying to avoid detection as he worked his way back toward his rendezvous point.

It was almost twenty-five minutes of stress as Don watched the villagers moving about less than a kilometer away, until Duce made it back to them. When he was a few hundred yards away, Ramon signaled him to their rocky hiding spot. He scrambled over to them and hopped into the small area. Breathless, he sat back as Ramon handed him some water.

"No problems?" asked Don.

Duce caught his breath and answered, "No problems. Mike spoke with the chief and traded him the two donkeys and some rials for the car. Funny thing was, it was the same car Mike had sold them last week. In one week, they totally beat the shit out of that thing, man. It was so filthy, Mike didn't recognize it at first. They pulled out the backseats for the chief's house—it's his new couch—and also pulled apart the dash. I have no idea if they'll ever actually use that radio again, but it's gone. Anyway, Mike got off okay, and says he can be in Tehran by tomorrow if all goes smoothly."

"Like anything ever goes smoothly in this part of the world," mumbled Ramon.

"Roger that," replied Duce.

"Alright, well, take five so you catch your breath, and then we need to start getting back to the border," said Don.

"Want to wait until it gets darker, Sergeant Major?" asked Ramon.

"Ramon, there is no way in hell I am staying on Iranian soil one second longer than I have to. Let's get the fuck outta here. Our mission is finished—it is time to go home. Besides, by the time we get to the border, it'll be dark"

"I'm good to go, Sergeant Major," said Duce. "But we'd better take it low and slow. Those border guards we popped might have brought a whole division down by now."

"Yeah, I thought about that, too," said Don. "But from what the LT said, border shootings happen all the time. I think they'll be looking west at the Iraq border, not at us. I hate the idea of being here in Iran without any backup. Let's just start moving west and keep our eyes peeled."

With that, they checked their weapons and started moving quietly through the rocks toward "home."

CHAPTER 28

Tehran

Skripak had driven straight through the night, stopping only once on the side of the road for gas, which he filled himself from the cans in his trunk purchased along with the car in the old village. He was tired and hungry, and for the first time in many years, actually scared. The vest he wore under his tunic was explosive enough to disintegrate the mosque and everyone in it. And then there was the other possibility, too, if Bijon could get close to the bomb. While he had been assured the nuclear bomb would not detonate a nuclear explosion, the idea of blowing up a nuke was downright terrifying. Unlike so many of the people around him in the Middle East, Mike did not seek martyrdom.

As Mike approached Tehran, the sun was coming up, and there were military vehicles rumbling everywhere. When he passed a tank at a large intersection, his heart sank.

"Oh, God," he mumbled, "am I too late?" Several divisions of Iranian soldiers marched with a great show of force through the main avenue toward the mosque where Bijon would be waiting for him, also scared out of his mind, no doubt. Mike slowed down and searched everywhere with his eyes . . . What was going on? Why the Army?

As he made a left turn down a back street that would take him to the mosque, he saw a platoon of soldiers with their AK-47s pointed at what appeared to be a very young crowd, hands in the air, and faces looking scared. Mike slowed down, and then stopped, afraid to get closer. A loud bang on his car door made him jump.

"What are you doing here? What do you want?" screamed a soldier.

Mike stammered, then took a deep breath. "I am trying to get to the mosque. Can I get around this?"

The soldier turned away from the car and screamed at the platoon of soldiers, who pushed the group toward the wall of the small alleyway so the car could pass. He turned back to Mike and grunted something, and Mike drove around the group without looking back. His heart was racing, but he drove slowly and deliberately out of the alley onto the main street again, only to have a column of trucks loaded with young men and women seated at gunpoint pass in front of him.

Mike was trying to catch up in his mind. He had been gone a few days and no one had mentioned any trouble in Tehran at the forward observation post. Something had happened that the CIA was unaware of, and he was hoping it wasn't the beginning of the attack on Israel. The staccato sound of several AK-47s being fired from the alley behind him made him jump in his seat.

"Jesus Christ," he exclaimed, and drove on down the avenue toward the mosque. He was praying that Bijon would be there waiting for him, and all would be normal when he got there. He picked up speed and passed several intersections that had police and military checkpoints, but no one stopped him. It appeared to be mostly a show of force for something, yet he couldn't help but assume the worst about the gunfire back in the alley.

When Mike got within sight of the mosque, he pulled over and parked his filthy car. It was, without question, the dirtiest car on the street. When he got out, he said a quiet thank-you to the piece of crap vehicle that had somehow managed to get him all the way back to Tehran in record time. He walked quickly toward the mosque, ignoring the crowds of people on the street who appeared to be in a quandary as to what was going on all over Tehran. He heard more than one old man comment about the police arresting the troublemakers or students, but never slowed down to learn more.

Mike used the rear door to the mosque, took off his shoes, and went upstairs to the Grand Ayatollah's chambers. A large bodyguard stood outside, but recognized Mike. He greeted him by one of his aliases, and allowed him in. Mike was in the outer room where one of the imam's aides sat at a large gold-gilt table scribing from the Koran. He also greeted Mike by the same alias, and asked if he was expected, to which Mike answered "yes." He was allowed to knock at the Grand Ayatollah's door himself, one of very few people who had that privilege, only because the imam had told them that Mike was his cousin and should be allowed in at any time.

The door opened slightly, and the Grand Ayatollah Kamala, Bijon Mujaharov, closed his eyes and said, "thank God" quietly. He allowed Mike in, and closed the door behind them and locked it. They walked quickly to the study and sat down. Bijon was frantic and trying to talk slowly and calmly.

"For God's sake, where have you been? I thought you were dead! Do you have *any* idea what is going on around here? Where the hell did you go?" he whispered quickly.

Mike put his finger over his lip to signal him to be quiet. "Look Bijon, it's getting dangerous as hell for us to be together. The shit is about to hit the proverbial fan, and you are in the middle of it. I have a lot to tell you and very little time. The day you have been waiting for has come. It may not be our time of choosing, but be that as it may, your country is about to embark on a new beginning—and you are going to lead your people out of the Dark Ages."

"What are you talking about? Did you see the trucks outside? It's *my* fault! The president had me make a fire-and-brimstone speech yesterday to warn the students to get back on the path of righteousness, and today they are being rounded up and arrested. I think they are being shot, Mike! I have heard machine guns all day, and there are trucks filled with kids everywhere. It is insanity out there, and it's *my* fault. What have I done? He is massacring *children*!"

Mike grabbed him by the shoulders. "Get your shit together, Bijon. Whatever that psycho is doing, he was going to do with or without you. At least you gave them a warning. Maybe some of them went home. In any case, we have a plan. We have no extra time to debate any of this—I just need you to trust me totally. We only have one shot. If we blow it, we're both dead, World War Three starts, Israel is wiped off the map, and God knows how many people are going to die, including most of Iran. Langley has given me something special for this operation. It's called CX-10 and it's an explosive strong enough to take down this entire mosque—every brick. You are going to invite the president here with all of his highest-level people—every conservative in the government. We are going to get this place packed with every extremist we can find, and you are going to slip out the back and watch them all go to hell."

"Blow the mosque? How will you get all of the explosives to Tehran? Or are the Americans bringing it?"

"I have it here right now," he said, and lifted his shirt to show the heavy vest underneath. "This vest will take down this entire building and everything it in."

"This is insanity, there will be hundreds of people in here. I can't kill innocent people coming here to pray."

"We will exclude everyone but the most important government and military people. It will be a special sermon and blessing specifically for them. You will announce it today, calling for it tomorrow morning. Get your people on the phone to the president and convince him he has to be here with every VIP you can think of."

"And what if he doesn't come? I can't make him come here, you know."

"You have to, Bijon. No pressure, but the fate of the world

is depending on you getting him here with his cabinet and generals, and us blowing them all to hell before they start World War Three."

Bijon leaned forward and rubbed his temples. "This is impossible. There isn't enough time to plan for this . . ." He was visibly shaken and Mike cut him off.

"Get it together, man! We don't have a choice. You *must* get them here tomorrow. I'll set the explosives myself."

"How will you get close enough?"

"You don't understand, Bijon. This vest is going to take down the whole building—every brick. I don't have to get close."

Bijon squinted at him and asked again, "That vest is enough to flatten this building and kill everyone inside?"

"Every brick. It is the most powerful conventional explosive on the planet. It will make a hole where the mosque used to be. Everyone will be dead except for you—saved by Allah, himself. And you will immediately get back on the radio calling for peace and order. You will set the course for the new Iran, Bijon. It is time for you to step out from behind the president and become the new leader of this country."

Bijon shook his head. "It's impossible, Mike. I can't do this. Even if I can get them here and blow this place, I'm no president . . ."

"You will learn to be. Right now you're simply a spiritual leader who will call for elections and pull this country back together."

"There isn't enough time, Mike. I can't get all of these VIPs here tomorrow. I'll need a few days. Wait—I'm having dinner at the palace tomorrow night. What if we do it there?"

"No good. You'd never get out. Damn. Tomorrow night? For sure?"

"Yes. It's a big event. I have been asked to say a special blessing there already—they won't come here."

"Bijon, they have to come here! You aren't listening to me. We don't have a bunch of options here. We had two simple plans—one is to have you locate the bomb and blow it in place, the other is to take out the whole regime. There is no way to get the bomb now. We don't have time. Judging from what I saw on the way back to Tehran, and your dinner plans tomorrow night, the attack is most likely within two or three days. I'll need to contact our people ASAP. I'll do that while you arrange for the big sermon here tomorrow, Bijon. I don't care how you do it—but get those people here tomorrow afternoon."

Mike got up to head out toward his flat, where he would send the news to Iron Mountain and Jerry Woodcrest.

"You are leaving? Right now? You just disappear for a week and then pop in and tell me we are wiping out the heads of state and I am supposed to just make them appear here by magic tomorrow?"

"That is pretty much it, yeah. You've been waiting for half your life for this, Bijon. Did you think it was going to be planned for three months with tons of agents helping us? It's me and you, Bijon. That's it. And we're going to get it done. Now take a deep fucking breath and make your phone calls. I'll be back later tonight. And remember to act normal—don't say shit about the students. We need the president to think you support everything he does. Now is no time to criticize him."

"Easy for you to say. Your speech didn't sign the death warrants for a few thousand people."

"Remember the mission, Bijon. We have one chance, and that's it. We blow it, and millions die—remember that. I'll be back as soon as I can. Keep your head on straight."

Mike stood up, then stopped. "Shit. I better leave the explosives with you in case I get stopped outside. It's chaos out there. Look, I am going to give you a quick lesson in CX-10. If anything happens to me, your mission doesn't change, you understand? Your entire country—fuck it—the *world*, is counting on you."

Mike spent the next ten minutes explaining how the CX-10 worked, and how to set the charges. Bijon would set the explosives before the guests arrived, and find the right time to sneak out the back and get the hell out before the entire building came down. The fact that the explosives were so strong meant that close was good enough, and the only thing that needed concentration was setting the proper amount of time to get out and being far enough away when the explosion occurred without raising suspicion.

Mike went over it one last time with Bijon, who was still in shock, then left him to brief Jerry about the current state of affairs in Tehran. The sense of urgency was in the air all over the city, even if the average citizen had no idea about the atomic and chemical attacks being planned for the next day or two.

Mike went out the same door he used to enter and walked very quickly to his apartment. He stopped several times, once at a fruit stand and once to buy a coffee, to make sure he wasn't being followed. Military and police vehicles were everywhere, and large transport trucks filled with civilians roared by regularly. From what he could gather from casual chatting with people on the street, several thousand students had protested Iran's nuclear armament program despite the Grand Ayatollah's speech yesterday. The military and police had swarmed the large gathering, arresting thousands of students. There were rumors of violence, but no one would say too much about that.

When Mike had finished his circuitous route and double-checked against being followed, he headed to his apartment. The tiny slip of paper he had inserted into the doorframe was still there when he opened the door, so most likely no one had been in his apartment. He turned on the lights and walked around the apartment several times, checking a few gadgets he had to make sure he was safe from eavesdroppers or secret police. He washed his face and drank a gallon of water before using the bathroom. He was dying to shower, but needed to get the intelligence report out immediately. He went to his room and opened his closet, where he removed the false Sheetrock ceiling and fished out a heavy wire that hung behind the wall. At the other end of the wire was his burst transmitter kit in a small black plastic box.

He took it into his room and sat on the floor, away from the closed windows. He took a deep breath and began typing to Jerry:

> Situation changing every minute—police and military arresting thousands of protesters. Bijon feels responsible for students arrests, may be close to panicking. We are out of time. No way to get to traveling package. Attempting to host big party at Bijon's tomorrow. Repeat, tomorrow. Hoping we are not too late. You will have to find another way to find westbound package. This may be last transmission until after party is over. Will hope to see you for another cold one soon. God help us all.

Mike hit send and the encrypted message was gone. He relocked the computer, which automatically wiped his entire drive of all correspondence. He dropped the box back down into the wall and resealed the ceiling, then took a shower until the hot water ran out. When he had showered and brushed his teeth, he set his alarm for three hours and lay down on his bed. It would be a long couple of days and he would need his wits about him. He was fast asleep in ten minutes.

T he Grand Ayatollah Kamala sat on his floor, cross-legged, in quiet meditation. He had, over the years, gotten into the habit of meditating for several reasons. First, it truly helped him to relax and keep his sanity under the great stress of leading a fictional life for so many years. Second, it helped him concentrate when he needed to write speeches or sermons. And third, it made him appear more scholarly to his assistants. When he opened his eyes, his assistant was sitting quietly across the room waiting for him. It was the perfect opportunity—it would require pushing the envelope like never before.

"Bopal!" the Grand Ayatollah yelled.

The young man ran to his imam and fell to his knees, "Yes, Grand Ayatollah? Are you all right?"

"I have had a vision! Mohammed's voice rings in my ears, blessed be his name!"

The young man's hair stood up on his arms—he had never seen this great man look like this before. The imam looked visibly shaken and wild eyed. He reached out and took his hand. "Holy one! What does the voice say?"

"We must contact the president at once! I have heard a sermon from the Prophet himself that I will repeat tomorrow morning. The president and all of our great leaders must be there! It is a miracle of Allah, blessed be his name. I need to begin writing it down immediately! I am not to be disturbed by anyone, unless it is the president himself. You must gather all of Iran's greatest patriots for tomorrow. Get the word out immediately—I have had a vision. Our great president must appear with me tomorrow with all of the great imams from all over Tehran. The Majlis and the ministers must all attend—but only the purest, only those that support our great leader."

"Was the vision about the president, great one?" asked the young man.

"Yes, he was in the vision, along with many of our leaders. But I cannot say more until tomorrow, when I will share it with all of Iran. Get all of our assistants gathered and tell them the news. I have had a vision for the first time in my life directly from Allah, blessed be his name, and we will all meet here tomorrow morning! Go now!"

The assistant stood up, stumbling toward the door, in his excitement not even saying good-bye. He was running and yelling inside the mosque, something that was never done, and the crowd followed him downstairs as he repeated something about a great vision from the Grand Ayatollah Kamala.

The imam stood up and closed the door behind his very excited assistant. He walked to his closet where, hidden inside one of his robes, there was enough CX-10 to vaporize the building in which he had spent so many years. He stood there, feeling the material on the robe, his most ornate, and contemplated his fate. He walked to his small balcony and watched military vehicles rumbling through the city and listened to the occasional sounds of machine-gun fire. The streets were

growing empty of civilian vehicles as most people headed
home and stayed there. Bijon felt heartsick. He had been used
by the president again, but this time he could see the actual
death his words had brought.

"Enough," he said quietly. "Tomorrow I will end this once
and for all."

And with that, he really did pray to God for help in saving
his country.

CHAPTER 29

Iran-Iraq Border

Duce, Don and Ramon had moved quickly and quietly through the scrub countryside toward the Iraqi border without seeing so much as a goat until they were within sight of the border. It was past midnight and the countryside was pitch black. If not for their night vision, they wouldn't be able to move at all through the rocky terrain. When they were within sight of the border, everything changed. Military trucks were rumbling toward the border, filled with soldiers. Duce was looking through binoculars at the passing vehicles for quite a while before giving them to Don. Ramon sat looking in the other direction, searching behind them for any movement.

"Apparently, they didn't like our little border shooting," said Don quietly. "They must be reenforcing the border with an entire company."

"So now what?" asked Duce quietly. "It's almost oh-one-hundred hours. We don't get across in the next four hours or so, the sun is going to start coming up and then we're stuck here for God knows how long."

"I think we should just keep heading west and snake

through the patrols as best we can. We maintain absolute silence and get to an isolated border area, and then we'll have to take our chances with the minefield."

Duce replied, "Mike had said something about crossing through some mountain passes just north of the patrolled official border gate. What about heading north by northwest and seeing if we can get around these guys?"

"No good. First of all, we'd have to go straight through these fuckers, and second of all, I was talking to some of the rangers about these mountain passes. You get lost in there and you are seriously fucked. We better head due west—straight line to the border, and hightail it across the border ASAP. Once we get into Iraq, we break radio silence and get a dustoff from the nearest outfit we can find."

Duce nodded his head. "Okay, boss. That's fine with me. You tell Ramon and I'll take point about fifty yards out. It's dark as shit out here—I won't go farther ahead of you than that. We get separated, we just keep heading west to the border."

"Roger that. But don't get separated. We all go home together. Take it slow. We have four hours to make a three-hour hump. There's no rush."

Duce nodded. "Good, because I can't see shit out here." They gave each other a quick pound on the fist, and Duce headed out, low and quiet, toward the border and a few thousand Iranian soldiers.

Don briefed Ramon, and they followed Duce from about fifty yards back. In the dark, moonless night, without lights from any city nearby, Duce glowed green in the distance. Don prayed quietly that the Iranians didn't have decent night vision out here. They weren't that close to the patrols yet, but when they got to the border, they'd be sitting ducks.

CHAPTER 30

FOB Iron Mountain

Jerry read the message from Mike and sat back rubbing his eyes. They were out of time. He had the sinking feeling in his stomach that they were too late. He rarely felt defeated, but he was starting to feel that way now. Any chance at locating the nuke at the facility was shot—there simply wasn't enough time. Bijon was going to try for tomorrow morning, less than twelve hours away. That was a long shot, at best.

Jerry fired off a long message to Dex back in Langley and then found Still, Tee and Mackey, who were sitting in another chamber of the cave looking at satellite images, road maps, rail lines, shipping schedules and piles of other papers.

Jerry walked to the group and announced, "Looks like the clock just pushed ahead a little bit, boys. I think, as they say in the field on days like this, we are fucked."

Tee asked, "What happened?"

"I just got a message from Mike. Apparently, Tehran is under marshal law. Student protesters, the same ones we've been rallying to start support for the upcoming regime change, are being arrested. Maybe worse than just arrested. I have a message to Langley with a long list of questions, but frankly, if we don't have answers, I doubt that they will either."

"What do you mean, 'the ones we've been rallying'?" asked Still.

"We have contacts inside Iran besides Mike and Bijon. We actually have many students in the universities who are forward-thinking young people envisioning a different future than what they see in Afghanistan. They aren't agents, per se, but they give us information, and are receptive to our help. We had suggested that they start organizing in the universities and protesting publicly against the nuclear program. It helped our position in the UN and drew attention to it here in the Middle East. We hadn't counted on them being rounded up and slaughtered."

He sat down next to Mackey and sighed. "Mike has instructed Bijon to hit the targets tomorrow."

"Tomorrow?" all three of them exclaimed in unison. Mackey continued over the other two, "We were supposed to have at least two or three more days! What about getting Bijon to the nuclear facility? What happened?"

Jerry looked around the room. These were good men, even if they were slightly out of their element. "Look guys, I'm not going to bullshit you. Mike walked into a shit-storm in Tehran. Bijon was slightly panicked, feeling guilty about a speech he made warning the students to stop what amounted to sacrilege. I guess he feels like he has legitimized the president's actions—put his stamp of approval on this roundup of the students. Anyway, Mike made a judgment call. He was afraid that this dinner thing they have might be a post-bomb celebration, instead of a pre-attack get-together. Anyway—it's done. The wheels are in motion. Bijon is trying to get all the bad guys in one place at one time tomorrow morning, and they are going to blow the mosque. After that, who knows what happens. Hopefully, the Grand Ayatollah calls for order in the face of national disaster and is well received."

"Jesus, what happened to finding the nuke? And where the Hell *is* the thing, anyway? If the attack starts the same day the Iranian government goes down, the Iranians will blame the

Israelis and World War Three starts anyway. I thought that's what we were here to avoid," said Tee.

"Yeah, this whole thing is fucked if we don't stop the bomb. This is a mess," said Still.

Jerry cringed. "You are all correct in everything you said. Which brings me to the next possibility, and it makes my ass pucker just thinking it out loud . . ."

The silence was deafening as they all stared at Jerry.

"We have all this intel sitting right here on the floor. We could go after it ourselves. It's a crazy idea, given that we have no time for planning how to get in or out, and don't even know where to begin looking. That said, I'm not sure we can sit back and do nothing."

There was total silence as each man in the room pondered the possibilities.

Jerry looked around at the glum faces. "Look, guys, you are a weird assortment of commandos, no doubt. I've got one pilot with some spy-craft training, one street cop, and one special operations guy. Quite frankly, we really should have two or three SEAL teams for something like this. I'm not sure how we would possibly even go about this with the time frame being what it is. Like I said, I'm just thinking out loud."

Still grinned. "So we'd sneak into Iran and somehow travel a few hundred miles to a secret nuclear facility and break in without being detected by probably a few hundred soldiers and then steal or destroy an atomic bomb. I don't see what the big deal is," he said sarcastically.

"Right. No biggie," mumbled Tee.

"Like I said, guys, I'm just thinking out loud. Anybody has any other ideas, I'm all ears, but I don't think we can just sit and wait for tomorrow and do nothing." Jerry stood up and stretched his back. "We're fucked," he mumbled to no one in particular. "If we take out the Iranian government but don't stop the attack, we still failed. The president should be advised. This may require an overt military strike. I don't think we have a choice."

"An overt military action may be the only choice, but that still muddies the mission," said Mackey. "The whole point of the mission was to facilitate regime change from the inside to avoid solidifying the Iranian people with their leadership. We take out their leaders *and* our Air Force takes out a nuclear site, who do you think gets automatically blamed for blowing the mosque?"

"What a mess," mumbled Still. "I should have stayed in D.C. and arrested drug smugglers. This is FUBARed."

Tee stood up. "Look guys, the Iranians still have to *move* the fuckin' thing. They don't have a missile; they are moving it by boat, right? We have the *Kitty Hawk* and a good-sized float in the Persian Gulf. Why not have them run interdiction or throw a blockade? It would be out of the eyesight of the media. No one would know shit."

Jerry cocked his head. "That's actually a great idea. I'm so friggin' tired I'm not thinking clearly. Let me call Langley direct. I'll do it as a conference call with you guys present. We'll get Dex and Murphy on the other end with the joint chiefs. Maybe there's enough time to throw a net across the Persian Gulf before they get out to the Indian Ocean. Damn, I wish we had more time. This is nuts . . ."

Jerry started walking out of the small roomlike cavern. He turned back toward the group. "Guys, keep looking over that stuff. Check rail lines from the facility to the nearest ports. See if you can narrow this down for the fleet. There's a few thousand square miles of water out there."

"God, this is like déjà vu . . . and not a good one either. It wasn't that long ago we were flying around looking for that fucking Scud. This is too weird, man," said Mackey.

"Yeah, and look how that worked out," said Still. "We saved the fucking universe."

"Great—and it was all quiet and peaceful in the world for, what? About five minutes?" Mackey smiled.

Jerry walked out, yelling back to the group, "Get on it boys—meet me in fifteen minutes."

The three men grabbed the maps and charts and picked up where they had left off. They had the rail lines already marked, along with the ports. It was what they had been working on before Jerry walked in. They began circling the ports in grease pencil and writing them down.

"I still think Abadan," said Tee. "The rail lines follow the oil pipelines from the north, and it links here to where the tracks end at the facility," he said pointing to the map. "Abadan is a deepwater port for tankers—it would make sense to load it on a large tanker or freighter there. They'd go through the Persian Gulf, hook around the Indian Ocean and right through the Red Sea, through the canal to Israel. It makes more sense than moving it east overland to get farther out of the gulf. They'd feel safer when it was aboard ship and out to sea."

Mackey and Still agreed. "Okay, look, we can't rule out other possibilities, but if they do go via Abadan, it gives our ships more time to throw up a net up at the Strait of Hormuz. It's a narrow piece of water—twenty-one miles across—and it only has two channels about a mile wide each that a large ship can pass through. It's our best chance," said Mackey.

"Assuming they haven't already offloaded the fucking thing in Israel by now," said Still.

"Yeah," said Mackey, "assuming that."

CHAPTER 31

Iran-Iraq Border

It was daylight, and Duce, Don and Ramon were hiding in what amounted to a large pile of boulders not far from an Iranian military column. They had gotten somewhat disoriented in the dark, and even following their compass headings, had managed to get lost while dodging Iranian patrols. They had moved all night alternating between west and northwest, trying to get around the increasing numbers of Iranian patrols, but every time they tried to get closer to the border, they came perilously close to detection.

At night, they had traveled fairly quickly considering some of the area was wide open, arid scrubland. Now, with the sun up, there were very few places to hide, and there were trucks and soldiers everywhere.

"How many you make, Sergeant Major?" asked Duce.

"Too fuckin many," he said quietly. There were a few hundred soldiers setting up what appeared to be a small camp or firebase. "They must be reenforcing the border in case we send anybody in after they start the attack."

"A lot of good it would do. We'd roll through them without slowing down if we wanted to."

"Yeah, well, if we had a couple of Abrams, maybe. It's probably just a scout patrol. There will be more coming soon, with armor, no doubt. If we don't get out of here soon, you'd better start thinking about your next career as a goat herder in Iran."

"Fuck that, man. But we do have a situation. There is no cover around here, and we've been wandering around in circles. I think we're farther from the border now than we were last night," said Duce quietly.

"Roger that," said Don, who was then interrupted by Ramon scrambling over on his belly.

"We've got company coming up behind us. I don't think they've spotted us, but there is a vehicle making dust big time coming this way," whispered Ramon.

Don used his binoculars and watched the dust coming at them. "Son of a bitch," he mumbled. "There is nothing out here except this pile of rocks, and those rag heads are headed right for us."

"Think they've made us?" asked Duce, getting a little nervous. "We squeeze off any rounds from here and we are totally fucked. Shots will bring that entire firebase over here in two minutes."

Don moved in tighter into the rocks for cover. "Everybody just sit tight and get as covered up as possible. If they fire at us, we'll take them out and go for the truck. If they just stop here for some other reason, we'll play it by ear. They get out and wander around, we kill 'em quiet and take the truck if we get a chance to go in close, but only if we can do it with no shooting. Everybody understand?"

"Roger that," said Ramon and Duce, and they took out their Ka-Bar knives as they crouched deeper into their little hiding spot—a pile of rocks in an otherwise flat wasteland. There were clearly not a lot of options, and they were too far inside Iran to call for an evac chopper. With no help coming, they maintained radio silence with Iron Mountain and waited.

The vehicle continued to close in on their position. Duce used his sniper scope to watch the vehicle as it approached. "I only see two people in that truck. Looks like somebody important, too. The passenger looks like a fucking general or something with all the gold shit all over his uniform. Driver is just a grunt, looks like. They are heading right for us, man—beeline."

"Okay, sit tight. Let's see if they stop," said Don.

The next few minutes took forever. Even if it hadn't been so damn hot, their mouths would have been as dry just from nerves. The truck stopped at the base of their rocky location, and the doors opened up as the driver killed the engine. The officer was yelling on a phone at someone, looking downright pissed off. The driver just stood there, looking at him. The officer was getting louder, and Duce could almost make out some of what he was saying—something about not having enough men. Apparently, the officer was going to climb the rocks to take a better look at the border area and the troop movements in the area.

The driver followed the officer up the narrow path through the rocks, climbing the steep grade by pulling themselves along the rocks. The officer was bitching and moaning the whole time, the driver silent as he tried to keep up.

Don signaled a finger across his throat and a finger over his lips, and they crouched silently. They let the officer walk right by them first, heading up to the top of the rock pile. As soon as the driver passed Duce, Duce jumped up behind him, one hand over his mouth as his plunged the Ka-Bar into the man's throat, releasing a fountain of blood. He used the momentum of the lunge to take him right across the trail, making room for Ramon to rush the officer from behind, bringing down his Ka-Bar as hard as he could into the man's spinal cord, dropping him like a stone. He knifed him two more times to be sure, and wiped the blade off on the officer's dressy uniform. Apparently, they had just killed a very important person.

Don was already working his way down the rocks to the vehicle, scanning all directions as he moved to make sure they were still alone. Duce and Ramon hustled after him to the heavy jeep. Don hopped in and smiled to find the keys in it, which he cranked to start the engine. Duce hopped into the other side, with Ramon hopping into the back and kneeling to face the rear, his sniper rifle across the rear bench seat.

Don spoke calmly, but his words were serious. "Fellas, we have one chance to get out of here in one piece. I am heading away from that firebase as fast as this piece of shit will move and running across the border the first fence I see. Duce, you get that radio up and ready, but maintain silence until we either get to the border or get spotted. I'm not stopping for anything under any conditions, so hang on tight. That hotshot upstairs looked like a fucking general, and I don't think his disappearance will go unnoticed for too long."

Don floored the jeep and headed out from behind the rocks, keeping the rock pile between them and the firebase for as long as possible. Ramon stayed down so there appeared to be only two occupants, like before. They were flying over the hard ground at full throttle, leaving the firebase and a few hundred Iranian soldiers behind them.

Duce was hanging on to a bar on the dashboard. He started screaming as he spotted the back of one of the huge billboards with Grand Ayatollah Kamala's face on it, facing west toward Iraq. He pointed and shouted to Don, who saw it at the same time.

"There it is, baby! That's the border! Stand on that fucking pedal and get us the hell out of here."

Their truck bounced and jostled over the rocky ground, with Don struggling to keep the throttle maxed yet keep control of their vehicle. Don headed straight for the billboard in the distance. The base of the pole was blurry in the heat of the desert, but as they grew closer, they could see what looked like two vehicles.

"Shit," said Duce. "We've got company straight ahead. Slow down so I can take a look at what's up there."

Don backed off the accelerator and Duce used his sniper's scope, trying to hold it against the side of the windshield to steady it and focus on what was ahead. Ramon used the moment of smoother driving to check behind them. He pulled out his scope and balanced it on the rear of the jeep, but it was difficult to use the high-powered scopes with such vibration and jostling.

"Sergeant Major!" yelled Ramon from the back of the jeep. "You'd better put your foot back down. We've got something coming up behind us. I can't see what, but there is definitely dust heading this way, maybe two miles back."

"Yeah, well I've got two vehicles dead ahead. I count six men standing around. So far I don't see any of them using binoculars on us."

Don slowly started picking up speed again. "Duce, scan out as far as you can between them and the border. We are going to have to go through them to cross. After we get past them, I just want to know if we're clean and green. Ramon, just keep your eyes behind us."

They continued in silence, but Ramon and Duce both snapped their scopes onto their sniper rifles and loaded their weapons. Duce checked Don's magazine and slapped it back into his M4, which he chambered and slid across Don's lap. Duce pulled out two fragmentation grenades and hung them on his breast pockets.

He shouted to Don over the engine. "I'm thinking we go straight through them and I chuck a couple of grenades. You don't slow down, and Ramon and me cover our rear while you drive fast as hell to Iraq."

Don looked over and saw Duce's grenades. "How many you got?"

"That's it, just two. What about you, Ramon?"

Ramon yelled back over the noise. "None, man! I'm a fuckin' sniper!"

Don gripped the wheel tighter and stood on the accelerator. "Okay, boys—hang on tight and we are going straight through these fuckers. When we get in close, one of you use my M4 and spray and pray."

"Okay, man, just don't slow down, 'cause I think we've got the whole Iranian Army behind us!"

Duce craned his neck and looked back. Sure enough, there was a huge cloud of dust in the desert behind them. There was no way to count the number of vehicles, but there was definitely more than two traveling at high speed. Duce cursed, and Don screamed to him, "Okay, looks like things are gonna get loud real soon—fuck radio silence. Get on the horn and tell Iron Mountain we are trying to get home, and we have the whole Iranian Army behind us. Give them whatever landmarks you can. Tell them we would sure appreciate a little help from their side of the border if they can!"

The two Iranian vehicles ahead were now less than a mile away, and the soldiers there were walking out toward them with their AK-47s, looking fairly casual. Apparently, there was no radio broadcast yet about a stolen jeep or a dead general, and the fact that Don, Duce and Ramon were in an Iranian vehicle helped confuse whoever might be looking at them.

Just then, one of the men sitting in one the vehicles ahead of them hopped out of his truck, running and screaming at the others, who immediately leveled their weapons at them. Apparently, the word was out from the column behind them.

Don yelled to Duce, "Get on that fuckin' radio! Prepare for assault! We've been made!"

Ramon repositioned himself, leaning outside of Duce trying to use his sniper scope to get a look at the group ahead of them from their bouncing jeep. It was impossible, and his rifle barrel was swinging around wildly. The men in front of them were close enough now to realize the vehicle approaching them wasn't going to be slowing down, and they ran behind their own trucks to take cover and get into a better firing position.

Duce was talking quickly into the radio. "Wrecking Ball to Iron Mountain! Come in Iron Mountain!" He repeated it over and over and finally started screaming, "U.S. Army patrol to any listening ears! We are under attack inside Iranian border and need immediate assistance! Come in *anyone*!"

Jerry Woodcrest's voice at the other end of the radio was a welcome sound.

"Wrecking Ball, this is Iron Mountain, sit-rep and twenty, over."

"We are traveling to the border in a stolen truck with a large force behind us in pursuit and a small force ahead of us near the wire! I do not have exact coordinates, but estimate within three kilometers of where we entered. We need help, over!"

"Wrecking Ball, we cannot enter Iranian airspace, but will send air cover and notify all troops in your area. Wait one, over."

The sound of AK-47 rifle bursts broke over the sound of their radio.

"I'm not slowing down! Try to get some fire on that position!" yelled Don. The rocky roadway they were on funneled between natural rock formations, and there was no way to go around the enemy to get to the border. The only way home was straight ahead, through the opposing force.

Duce looked through his sniper rifle and put it back down. "Impossible," he said, and grabbed Don's M4. He picked it up and started firing at the trucks, watching them disappear momentarily in a cloud of dust as his rounds sprayed all over the area. Enemy fire was everywhere, but so far only one or two rounds had pinged off of their truck's hood. A huge explosion echoed behind them—the column following them had armor, maybe a TOW or some type of rocket. It wasn't even close, but it was incentive enough to keep going forward. All six of the guards ahead were now firing at them. Ramon fired his sniper rifle, but it was impossible to use the scope with the bouncing—he merely pointed and fired, the noise deafening Duce in front of him, who cursed out loud.

When they were within two hundred yards, the incoming rounds started hitting the jeep regularly. Don was swerving all over the road to keep the enemy from getting clear shots, but it was futile. The windshield popped and the glass spiderwebbed in the upper right corner near Duce's head. He called out that he was okay, and then returned fire until he was out of ammo, and switched magazines. Ramon was firing and reloading as fast as he could, but he was pretty sure he wasn't hitting a damn thing.

"Hey!" yelled Ramon. "What if you stop this thing for twenty seconds, let me and Duce get a couple of shots off, then we run 'em? Maybe we can improve the odds!"

Duce yelled to Don, "Not a bad idea, Don—give us two shots each!"

Don slowed down and yelled back over the incoming rounds pelting their truck, "Okay—you got ten or fifteen seconds *tops*! I am gonna lock 'em up—you guys make 'em count! Hang on!"

Don slammed his foot against the brake and cut the wheel, making them spin so that Duce and Ramon were facing their enemy. They balanced their rifles on the top of the door and squeezed off a round each within the first three seconds of stopping. Ramon hit his target in the neck, sending him flying. Duce hit the officer in the chest, and he dropped in a heap. One of his men tried to run to him, but Ramon squeezed off a second round and dropped him. Duce aimed at another target, this soldier smart enough to hit the ground when he saw his comrades falling. Duce knocked his helmet off, but was unsure whether he hit him or not. As he started to chamber another round, Don yelled, "That's it!" and floored the jeep again, sending Duce and Ramon falling back against their seats. Another incoming artillery round exploded, this one closer than the last one, and the shrapnel showered the back of the truck, blowing out the rear windshield.

Ramon screamed in pain from the back seat. "I'm hit!" he cried, holding his neck, blood squirting out between his fingers.

"Hang on!" yelled Don, and he kept the jeep headed straight at the trucks. With their officer and two others dead, the three remaining soldiers stayed on the ground, firing their weapons without aiming. Even at twenty yards, they were only occasionally hitting the jeep, and Duce pulled the two pins off his grenades. Don drove like a maniac, straight at the two trucks, then weaved through the small space between the two bumpers, sideswiping the truck on his side. Duce flipped the two grenades out of the truck, and then grabbed Don's M4 and started firing behind them as they broke through the roadblock. Ramon was laid out in the back seat, squeezing his bleeding neck, while Don struggled to keep control of the wheel as the two grenades exploded behind them with ear-ringing violence.

The radio in the jeep squawked and a new voice came over. "Wrecking Ball, this is border patrol leader. We have visual of artillery and smoke. Three gunships inbound, but we are not cleared to fire into Iranian airspace, over."

Duce leaned out of the truck and looked up in both directions. In the distance, he could see three Apache helicopters flying low to the mountainsides. He craned his neck back toward the two trucks, one of which was burning from his grenade. There was no fire coming from them anymore. Duce climbed over his seat into the back to where Ramon was grimacing and tried to control his bleeding. Duce pulled a pressure bandage out of his side pocket and moved Ramon's hand away, which released a torrent of blood.

"God damn it! Get us a medivac!" he yelled to Don. Don kept his foot to the floor, and as they crashed through a light barbed-wire gate that was the Iranian border, he grabbed the radio.

"Border patrol, this is Wrecking Ball—request immediate medivac for one wounded, over."

"I read you, Wrecking Ball, request will take some time. You are out of the normal AO. Keep heading straight, there is a ground unit due west eyeballing you, over."

"How's he doing back there?" asked Don, driving as fast as the jeep would move.

"I'm cool, Sergeant Major," said Ramon, slurring slightly.

Duce was holding the bandage against Ramon's neck, and yelled back to Don to just keep driving as fast as he could. An incoming shell exploded less than fifty yards from the rear.

"God damn it!" yelled Duce. "Those fuckers are following us over the border!"

It was true, in the no-man's-land between Iran and Iraq, the column of soldiers from the firebase was still behind them, firing wild shots with their fighting vehicles. Fortunately, they were older Soviet vehicles that lacked radar guidance systems, and they weren't very accurate firing at moving targets while they themselves were moving. The three choppers broke right off the mountainside and wheeled around, hovering. The radio squawked and the same voice returned.

"Be advised, Wrecking Ball, targets have crossed the Iranian border and we are cleared to fire."

A second later, the *whoosh* of rocket pods from the three helicopters roared overhead. The smoke trails raced overhead from the choppers to the advancing column, which disappeared in a maelstrom of fire and smoke. A second and third wave of rockets followed.

"Wrecking Ball, targets destroyed. Be advised, medivac is inbound to our location, fifteen minutes out."

"You hear that?" yelled Don to Ramon. "You hang in there, man. Help is on the way."

Ramon tried to force a smile, but instead closed his eyes and fainted. Duce yelled back to Don, "They better hurry, man—he's losing a lot of blood."

Don started to slow down as they neared the Iraqi border, nothing more than a barbed wire fence that was down in more places than it was up.

"Hey man, don't slow down!" yelled Duce, but the truck came almost to a stop.

"I think you have to drive," said Don quietly as he rested his head against the seat.

"What are you doing, man?" yelled Duce, trying to control Ramon's bleeding as best he could. Don didn't answer, and their truck stopped. Duce grabbed Don's shoulder and gave him a shake, but he was out cold. Duce leaned into the front seat and saw some foamy blood coming out of Don's mouth, a sure sign of a lung wound. Duce leaned back toward Ramon and tied off the pressure bandage on his neck, careful not to strangle him, then hopped into the front seat and tore open Don's shirt. He had a Kevlar vest on, but the bullet had entered under his left arm. There was bloody foam coming out of the small hole there as well.

Duce pulled out another first-aid pack and ripped open a plastic adhesive sheet that he slapped over the sucking chest wound. He pulled Don's shirt and Kevlar vest off, cutting off part of it with his Ka-Bar knife and putting on another pressure bandage. It took every ounce of Duce's strength to pull Don out of the driver's seat into the passenger seat, and Duce ran around to the driver's side. He hopped in and gunned the engine, blowing through the small wire gate on the Iraqi side that was totally unguarded. He grabbed the radio as he drove, aware of the total silence inside the jeep now—no incoming gunfire, no artillery shells, and not a word from his friends. Duce was operating without thinking now, his many years of training kicking in to fight back the fear in his gut. He grabbed the radio in Don's lap.

"Border patrol, this is Wrecking Ball. Where is my medivac? I have two wounded, both seriously."

"I have visual on you and the inbound chopper, Wrecking Ball. Continue west on your present heading—medivac will be here in two minutes, and we have your back door covered."

Duce drove, but continually checked his two silent passengers. Ramon was mumbling, so at least he was alive. Don was white and out cold, and Duce was starting to get panicked. He pulled over and ran around to Don's side of the truck and opened his door. He dragged him out of the seat and laid him on the dirt road, cocking his neck back and clearing the blood out of his mouth. He started mouth-to-mouth, but Don remained unconscious. He continued mouth-to-mouth for what seemed like forever, until the thumping of rotor blades washed hot air over him, and two medics ran to him with a stretcher.

They were screaming to each other over the rotors—and one of the medics pulled out a metal instrument that he punched into Don's chest, releasing blood and allowing his lung to re-inflate. While they worked on Don, Duce ran back to the jeep and pulled Ramon out of the back seat. Ramon opened his eyes and looked up at Duce.

"Hey, bro, we home?" asked Ramon.

"Yeah, man, we're almost there. We're out of Iran and you'll be in the hospital in a few minutes. Sit back and enjoy the ride."

The medics had loaded Don into the chopper and ran back to help with Ramon. They loaded Ramon into the chopper as Duce retrieved the two sniper rifles and Don's M4, along with their three packs. He waddled back toward the chopper under the heavy load. The medics screamed at Duce to hurry up and get on board with them. He dropped one of the packs, and said "screw it," leaving it there, and half fell into the open door of the chopper, pushing the gear ahead of him. He was only halfway in when the chopper lifted off the ground and headed to the nearest field hospital on the other side of the mountains. Duce watched glumly as the two medics on board worked on Don and Ramon. The Iranian border and the smoldering column slowly faded in the distance, and Duce finally became aware of just how exhausted he was.

CHAPTER 32

Tehran

The Grand Ayatollah sat alone in his study. He had avoided all of the many phone calls, except for the president's. Whether the president really believed him that he had a vision or not was unimportant; the fact was it *was* to the president's advantage to have his chief cleric and sponsor receiving direct messages from God that would support the president's position. To that end, the president had insisted, with some prodding by the Grand Ayatollah, that all of his senior staff and conservative ministers accompany him to the noontime special service. It took some major schedule shuffling to free up over two hundred of Iran's most important political and religious figures, but when the president insisted, that *was* the final word.

The president seized the opportunity to make a big show of his arrival at the mosque. The streets were lined with Iranian soldiers, and the Iranian news radio and television crews had been talking about the Grand Ayatollah's vision all morning. By eleven o'clock, the streets were jammed with tens of thousands of Iranians, ranging from the fanatically religious to the curious. Skripak, dressed in traditional robes, blended into the large crowd outside behind the mosque. He stayed near a rear door, where the Grand Ayatollah himself would emerge if all went according to plan.

The night before, while most of Iran was asleep, Bijon and Skripak had placed two wads of CX-10 in the center of the mosque, against two large support columns, setting the fuses to go off at a little past noon. Bijon had been up the entire night, contemplating the results of his upcoming actions. He thought about his family, and the thousands of other families that had been tortured and murdered. He thought about the thousands of young Iranians who had been arrested yesterday, and wondered how many of them had also been tortured or murdered. He thought of an atomic explosion in Israel, followed by an all-out war that would ultimately leave the entire Middle East in ruins.

He tried to meditate, but it was no use. In a few hours, the mosque that had become the center of Iranian fundamentalism because of his hate-filled words would be vaporized, along with everyone in it. What would happen afterward was anyone's guess. Would he have an opportunity to lead his people down a new road, or would he be discovered as the assassin and publicly executed or tortured to death? He was exhausted and nauseated from nerves.

The sound of knocking on his door snapped him out of his troubled thoughts. It was Bopal, his young assistant. "Imam, his Excellency the President is arriving outside. It is almost noon and you aren't downstairs yet. Is everything all right? You should be dressed, holy one. Let me help you."

The Grand Ayatollah Kamala suddenly realized that he had been half thinking, half dozing, since the wee hours of the morning, and in fact was not dressed in his finest robes yet. He stood, feeling a bit unsteady on his feet.

"You don't look well, your eminence. Is everything all right?"

The Grand Ayatollah smiled and took a deep breath. "It is the visions—they have returned. Help me dress, we don't have much time."

His assistant was honored to help the imam dress in his finest robes as they prepared for the imam's revelations.

Downstairs, at the front of the mosque, soldiers lined the steps as hundreds of dignitaries began entering the mosque, leaving shoes in huge piles by the front doors. The leadership council, the heads of the Ministries of the Martyr Foundation, the Housing Foundation, the Literacy Movement, the Supreme Council of Cultural Revolution, the Islamic Propaganda Organization, the Land Allocation Committee and several smaller government agencies were all arriving. Onlookers in the street tried to spot the VIPs as they arrived by limousine, the way stargazers in Hollywood would look for the latest movie star.

The president's limousine door opened and his bodyguards stepped out to lead him to the large doors of the mosque. At the sight of the president, the people in the street began to applaud, as much out of fear as true admiration. The president climbed the steps of the mosque and stopped to turn to the crowd. He waved to the increasing applause, and then turned and went inside.

Inside the mosque, the worshippers took their positions on the floor of the giant domed chamber. The president was taken to the front, where the Grand Ayatollah Kamala was waiting for him, now dressed in his finest robes. They exchanged formal greetings, and the president whispered that he was anxious to hear about the imam's great vision.

"Your excellency, I promise you that you will never forget this day," said the Grand Ayatollah. "I will return in a moment and explain what I have seen to all of Iran."

One of the last to arrive was Grand Ayatollah Seyed Ali Mustafa Bin Azed, the number-two man in Iran after the president. Ayatollah Azed was smart enough not to criticize Ayatollah Kamala in front of the president, but was jealous of the ayatollah's rising stardom and favor. He allowed the other dignitaries in the mosque to come to him, where he offered somewhat cold salutations, and was sure to offer body language that showed his derision for the Grand Ayatollah Kamala. He commented to a few VIPs that his mosque, the Ali Hamshi Mosque of the Martyrs, was still the most important mosque in Iran, and perhaps would have made a more appropriate place for some great revelation.

Those he spoke to avoided comment either way, lest they fall out of favor with either of the powerful and somewhat radical and violent men. The president might one day be replaced by election, coup or some other means, but the ayatollahs tended to stay for life. Neither of these men would make a good enemy.

When Ayatollah Azed made his way toward the front of the mosque, the president saw him and gave him a warm, respectful greeting. Bijon took a deep breath and approached the imam, bowing respectfully as well.

"Welcome to my humble mosque, Imam Azed. You honor me by coming today," said Ayatollah Kamala. "I have reserved a special place for you and the president—Bopal!" he called. Bopal, his young assistant, came at once, bowing to the two most powerful men in Iran, then bowed and walked backward, his arm extended as he invited them to follow him. The president and Grand Ayatollah Azed followed Bopal to prayer mats next to the thick carved columns of the mosque, where a brick of CX-10 lay hidden beneath tapestries, its timer counting down the seconds.

The Grand Ayatollah Kamala sneaked a glance at his wristwatch, which was hidden by his long robes. It was noon. Seeing the hands of his watch on top of each other brought another wave of nausea to his stomach. He looked up at his mosque, which was packed with every conservative political and religious leader in Iran, and felt the sweat run down his back beneath his robes.

CHAPTER 33

FOP Iron Mountain

Jerry was sitting on a crate inside a small part of the cavern. Several battery-operated lamps made the cave feel bright and comfortable, all things considered. Large generators outside with wires running into the cave provided power for their laptops and satellite uplinks. Jerry had been up for most of the night, worrying about his team in Iran. He had gotten an update on Don and Ramon and had called Tee, Still and Mackey into the chamber of the cavern where he was working.

As the three of them walked in, the weight of worry filled the room.

"Take a seat, guys," said Jerry. He had just gotten off the phone with the field hospital, where Don and Ramon had been treated before being sent by helicopter to a hospital ship in the Persian Gulf. The three of them sat down on the ammo crates that were the fine furnishings of the cave.

"Ramon and Don have been stabilized and are en route to a hospital ship. Ramon took two units of blood, and they'll operate on board ship to remove the shrapnel in his neck. It was very close to his carotid artery and he almost bled to death. He is stable now and should have a complete recovery. Don is in worse shape. He's an ox, and I wouldn't bet against him, but one lung was collapsed, and the other was partially perforated. He was in surgery for three hours just to get him in good enough shape to fly him out to the ship. The surgeons at the field hospital say his condition is guarded, whatever the hell that means. If you guys know anybody upstairs, put in a good word. Duce is catching a chopper back here from the hospital, but most likely won't arrive until tomorrow. By then, who knows *what* is going to be happening in the world."

Jerry stood and stretched his back, then walked over to a tin of coffee he had warming up over some Sterno. He offered it to the others, who turned it down and waited for him to continue after a sip that burned his lip.

"I am waiting for word from CENTCOM regarding the fleet. Last night I was on the horn with Dex and Murph back in Langley, and they met with the joint chiefs. The president authorized moving the *Kitty Hawk* and her battle group to the Strait of Hormuz, and they changed heading last night.

"There are over a hundred and fifty commercial ships in the Persian Gulf area. If we eliminate all U.S. ships, we're down to eighty-seven. If we start with Iranian registries only, that narrows it to eighteen as of last night. There *is* a big question about jurisdiction here. Technically, U.S. Navy warships do not have authority to stop and search foreign vessels in the Persian Gulf or the Arabian Sea. Of course, if that ship *is* out of the Gulf already and into the Arabian Sea, I think we've lost it."

Tee was the first to interrupt him. "Jerry, let's assume for a second that it's one of the eighteen Iranian ships still in the Gulf—what can the Navy do?"

"That's the call I'm waiting for. The president is in a cabinet meeting along with the joint chiefs. With the current hostile relationship between the Iranian government and our own, boarding or seizing the vessels may be an act of war. At the very least, they'll be kicking and screaming at the UN General Assembly. Then there is the other question—do we only stop Iranian vessels? The Saudis, Iraqis, United Arab Emirates and a few other countries have ships in and out of there as well.

While they probably won't bitch too much about a stop-and-search, what about Chinese or Russian vessels? You see the problem? We don't have time for a bunch of lawyers to argue this shit out in world court. In any case, it won't be the Navy doing the boarding and inspecting."

"If not the Navy, then who?" Tee asked.

"Coast Guard," said Jerry.

Still smiled. "Sneaky lawyers." He chuckled. "Coast Guard ships routinely stop and inspect vessels for a million different reasons. It will skirt the legal issues a little easier than the Navy throwing a blockade."

"Roger," said Jerry. "The Coast Guard has a station in Bahrain, Patrol Forces Southwest Asia, with four one-hundred-and-ten-foot patrol boats. They've been doing maritime intercepts for three years already without significant bitching from any of the countries whose ships have been inspected. Dex said the joint chiefs suggested using the Navy's resources to locate the ships and stop them, then have the Coast Guard do the actual inspections with Navy support in case things get hairy. The Coast Guard ships have tactical law enforcement teams on board who can handle enemy crewmen if it comes to that."

"So what's the hitch?" asked Tee. "What are they waiting for?"

"I'm not sure, maybe for the president to sign off on it or something. Also, that Navy taskforce is running support ops for U.S. personnel in Iraq. We move the fleet; it changes the air support operations for ground forces. In any case, we'll know soon enough."

Still sat back, crossed his arms, and made a *harrumph* sound.

"Yes?" asked Jerry dryly.

"Let's just suppose we get lucky and find the damn thing. What the hell we gonna *do* with it?"

They all looked at each other.

"No, seriously, man," said Still. "They board the ship, kill or arrest the crew, and then what? We take their nuke? I don't *think* so. And we sure as hell don't detonate it, and we can't just sink the boat and leave it there for some other crazy son of a bitch to recover. So what do we do with it?"

"*That* decision," said Jerry with a smile, "I am happy to say, is above my pay grade. Maybe that's what the boys in D.C. are trying to figure out now."

Jerry stood up. "Okay, fellas, I suggest you grab a few winks until I hear back from D.C. In a very few hours, the shit is going to hit the fan around here, and I don't expect anyone to be sleeping much the next couple of days. Everyone is dismissed—except Mack. Can I have a word with you for a sec?"

Tee and Still left to grab some chow and a nap, and Mackey sat down closer to Jerry. "What's up, chief?" he asked.

"Still was right-on about the nuke. That *is* the decision they are working on right now. If we were to seize the nuke and then Iran was to make claim to it, denying, of course, any wrongdoing, what then? Iran will say it was transporting it to another point inside Iran, and they want it back. It belongs to them. So what happens? The president is not going to allow that debate to occur. That leaves two options: sinking the ship after disarming the warhead, or sinking it and detonating it underwater in the Gulf, which would not be a very smart move. The U.S. Army *does* have a NEST team in Iraq, in the event we ever found any of Saddam's hidden nukes."

"NEST team?" asked Jerry.

"Nuclear Emergency Search Team. They aren't military, they're nuclear physicists and shit. These guys are trained to disarm and handle nukes. There's a team in Kuwait on standby. We find this thing and those guys will be brought to the ship to remove the nuclear material. After the nuclear material is removed, it will be transported to a safe location until its fate is determined. The rest of the bomb and ship get deep-sixed, compliments of the U.S. Navy."

"The NEST team will take the warhead back to Kuwait?" asked Mackey.

"Negative. It will be moved to a Navy ship for transfer back to the U.S. or to another location where it can be disassembled.

You may get the call to fly it back, which is why I asked you to stay. It's all pretty sketchy right now, but I just wanted you to be aware that you may be asked to transport the bomb out of the Gulf region by plane. For now, forget about it. If anything changes, you'll be the first to know."

Mackey sighed. "Super. Be sure to drop me a memo if you want me to fly an atomic bomb halfway around the world."

CHAPTER 34

Tehran

Bopal returned from getting the president and Grand Ayatollah Azed situated. He looked as nervous as Ayatollah Kamala, but for very different reasons. The great imam looked at Bopal and felt great hesitation. Bopal was one of the few people in the country that Bijon actually liked. While the young man was extremely radical in his world views, it was mostly because of his great reverence for his imam. The Grand Ayatollah looked at him thoughtfully, trying to figure out a way to spare the man's life in the next few moments.

"We are ready, Imam," said Bopal, smiling. He leaned closer and whispered, "I will be watching Ayatollah Azed's face when you speak of your visions. He is so jealous he looks ill."

The Grand Ayatollah's mind was racing. How could he get Bopal out of the mosque with him without risking everything?

The imam whispered back to him. "Bopal, you are a good man—one of the finest men I know. Do you trust me?" He gripped the young man's arm so tight it made Bopal wince in pain. "Do you trust me with your *life*?"

Bopal tried to smile, but it came out a crooked grin. "Of

course, Imam! You speak for Mohammad the Prophet, blessed be his name. I would do whatever you ask."

"Then follow me quickly," whispered the Grand Ayatollah, and turned and walked quickly toward the back of the mosque. The crowd inside didn't pay much attention, either not noticing at all, or simply assuming that the two of them were still preparing for the sermon.

The imam moved quickly through the mosque, looking so hurried and serious that no one dared question him. Bopal followed him, trying his best to keep up, but not understanding what was happening. When he could take it no longer, he finally whispered to the imam as he grabbed his robe. "Holy one, where are you going? There is nothing this way except the rear exit—everyone is waiting for you!"

The imam ignored him and moved at almost a run down some ancient steps that led to a small hallway and rear door. There was an ancient wooden door there, which the imam moved to open. Bopal grabbed his arm and said slightly louder than a whisper, "Imam! What are you doing? You cannot leave! Whatever you need, tell me and I will get it! The president and Ayatollah Azed are inside with the most important people in the country! This is no time to be leaving—they are all waiting for you and it is after noon already!"

Imam Kamala turned and grabbed Bopal by the front of his robes. He sneered, only an inch away from Bopal's face, speaking through his clenched teeth. "Listen to me, Bopal! Do not say another word until I speak to you. You said you trusted me with your life—now *silence*!"

The imam pushed the door open and bright, hot light filled the cool stone corridor. The back of the mosque, which would normally be teeming with people, was quiet. The president's security detail had sealed the back alley to the general public. Only those people who lived on that street were allowed into the small alleyway. Two men in dark suits stood outside with automatic weapons. They were shocked when they recognized the Grand Ayatollah, who looked equally shocked to see them. Bijon had not counted on anyone being in the back alley other than Skripak.

For a brief second, the two guards and the Grand Ayatollah just stared at each other without speaking. Bopal stood staring back and forth at the men, not understanding what was happening at all. A man stepped from the shadows of the alleyway as if appearing from thin air. His robed arm came up, the sun glinting off something in his hand. There were muffled popping noises as a silenced pistol spit death at the two dumbfounded bodyguards, who crumpled to the floor. The arm came up again, this time aimed at Bopal, but the Grand Ayatollah stepped in front of the young man.

"No!" cried Bijon. "He is with me!"

Skripak stepped in closer. "What are you doing? Just you!" he said, and prepared to fire at Bopal.

The imam grabbed Skripak by his robes and said, "No—he comes with me!" The imam grabbed Bopal by his wrist and pushed Skripak, who began cursing under his breath.

"You're gonna get us killed," he muttered, then grabbed the imam's arm, and the three of them began moving down the alley. Skripak stepped to the right, into shadows, and pushed open the rear door of an empty house. He pulled out a plain black robe for the imam and told him to hurry. Bijon pulled off his fancy embroidered robe and turban, and pulled on the black hooded robe.

"You, too," said Skripak to Bopal, who was in shock.

"Imam! What is happening? What are you doing? We have to go back! He killed those men—they were the president's bodyguards!" It was when he said that out loud that Bopal realized something was terribly wrong. He looked back at Bijon, who was pulling on his plain black robes.

"No! What have you done?" he screamed, much too loudly for Skripak. Mike fired three silenced shots into Bopal's chest and grabbed Bijon by his arm.

"You listen to me, Bijon—get a fucking grip on yourself. I have no idea what you were doing bringing him along, but if it was because you didn't want to feel guilty about killing him, you can live guilt-free now. We have about three minutes to get the fuck out of here before this whole block disappears, so stay on my ass!" He punched Bijon in the chest to snap him out of the shock of seeing Bopal's blood running onto the floor, and started running through the front of the house.

Bijon said a quick blessing for Bopal as he ran after Mike. They stumbled through a three-room house that opened to a hallway on the other side. The two of them were now running at full speed down the hall and out the front door of the building onto a quiet residential street. Mike's filthy car was at the curb, and he pulled his door open and started the engine. It spit black smoke and died as Bijon hopped into his seat. Mike cursed and turned the starter, and it slowly began whining without catching.

Bijon said a prayer to God out loud, and God must have been listening, because the car started, spitting black smoke. Mike screamed, "I knew you had a direct line, Imam!" as he floored the accelerator and pulled out onto the street. They roared down the quiet, empty street until they got to the end where it opened to a major road. The traffic was heavy there, and Mike cut off some honking drivers and hung a hard right into traffic, weaving and accelerating through cars. They hadn't gone more than a few hundred yards when a shockwave made Mike swerve across the road, almost hitting another car.

The explosion was deafening, louder than any B-52 strike Mike had ever heard, and that was saying something. Windows exploded in apartment buildings a half kilometer away, and a small mushroom cloud rolled out of the city block where the mosque used to stand. For almost a full minute, glass, stone, wood and shrapnel rained all over the area, as Mike continued driving as fast as his car would take him out of Tehran. Bijon let his head fall back on the seat and covered his face with his hands, crying at the destruction he had just caused. The dead would number in the thousands, no doubt.

The sound of the explosion was followed by the screaming of sirens from all over the city as police, fire and emergency vehicles raced toward the black smoke billowing from the wasted city block. Mike craned his neck and thought of the Twin Towers burning in New York. That was the last time he had seen such destruction in a civilian area. They continued moving through traffic, many of the cars having pulled over to stop and see the fire and smoke. Mike used the opening in the traffic to move faster, wishing like hell the damn Lur tribesmen hadn't stolen his cheap radio.

When Bijon had finally gotten hold of himself, he turned to Mike.

"Where are we going?" he asked, his eyes full of tears.

"A safe house I have set up outside of Tehran. We'll wait a day and see what's happening. Local news will catch us up and we'll have to time your reemergence carefully. We want you running this country, not hanging from the town square."

"I feel sick," said Bijon. "I've wanted revenge for my family for most of my life, and now that I have it, I feel sick." The words were heavy, his tongue thick. He could smell the explosion in the air.

"That's because you are a decent human being, Bijon. We didn't bring you in because you are a killer; we brought you in because you are a good man who is going to help your country rebuild itself as a modern nation. I'm sorry about your buddy back there, but he would have gotten us both killed."

"His death is on my soul," said Bijon quietly. "Everything he believed, he believed because of me. I made him grow up to hate. I was going to teach him a new path." Tears ran down Bijon's cheek, and he buried his face in his hands.

CHAPTER 35

FOP Iron Mountain

Word traveled fast. Jerry's satellite phone was beeping like a New Year's Eve noisemaker. It was Murphy himself calling from Langley, Virginia, where several Middle East desk chiefs were trying very hard to contain their excitement. They had just sacked the quarterback and taken him out of the game, but not before the pass was thrown. It was now up to the secondary to make sure the ball never got there, but still, the linebackers felt great satisfaction over their huge hit on the QB.

Jerry grabbed the phone and opened the secure transmission. "You've got Iron Mountain, this is Silver Fox, go ahead." His call sign was a reference to his head of gray, almost white hair. The tinny sound of a secure encrypted phone signal bouncing all over outer space to Jerry's handset made Dexter Murphy's voice sound strange.

"Silver Fox, this is Wrecking Ball Workshop. We have confirmed through many independent sources that a very large explosion destroyed your friend's mosque in Tehran. The president, Grand Ayatollah Azed, Grand Ayatollah Kamala and many of the highest-ranking conservative government officials and mullahs are all reported dead or missing. Most officials cannot be confirmed dead, only assumed dead. The explosion was unprecedented by conventional weapons. The mosque was completely destroyed, down to the last brick."

Jerry was trying to keep up mentally. "Did you say Kamala was reported dead?"

"No, not dead—missing. Most of the hundreds of people inside the mosque were quite literally vaporized. Estimates are approximately twelve hundred dead inside and outside the mosque. The explosion took down two buildings besides the mosque, one of which may have been a weapons storage facility, based on reports of secondary explosions. The president had over a thousand soldiers lining the streets in front of the mosque, at least half of which are missing and presumed dead. There is a hole twenty-feet deep in the ground where the mosque stood."

Jerry quietly mouthed "holy shit" as he listened.

"You reading me, Silver Fox?"

"Loud and clear, sir. Any speculation about who is responsible?"

"So far, no word on that, but things are happening fast in Tehran now. Al Jazeera is already reporting rioting in the streets near the two universities that had reported the largest number of students arrested and/or missing. Understand that this is not yet confirmed, but Iranian police units have been *reported* to have *fired* on each other, as they have received conflicting orders. Looks like the pressure cooker is about to lose its lid."

"Any word from our friends in Tehran?" asked Jerry hopefully.

"Not yet, but we are manning the phones, as they say. The explosion only occurred about an hour ago. Al Jazeera initially hinted at an Israeli rocket attack, but later said a possible coup attempt was being made. Israel made a public statement that they extended their sympathies to the innocent civilians who were killed, denied any and all involvement, and expressed their hope that new leadership would be willing to open dialogue with Jerusalem."

"Wow," said Jerry quietly, as he tried to take it all in. "So what do we do now?"

"We wait and watch, and try like hell to find the package before it gets to Israel. Given the situation, the boss has not yet told the recipients about the package yet. If we can't find it in the next twelve hours, he will be forced to call them and warn them."

"Jesus, they don't know yet?" asked Jerry.

"Negative. The boss wanted to see how this will play out first. If Iran blames Israel for the attack and successfully launches *their* attack, they'll justify it and say it was a counterattack to Israeli aggression. If, on the other hand, we can keep the pot stirred in Tehran and push for a new regime, we can keep Israel out of the picture—but only if we can find that package."

"So where are we on that hunt for the package?" asked Jerry.

"The *Kitty Hawk* has been reassigned to the Strait of Hormuz and all four Coast Guard ships left Bahrain last night for the same area. They have already searched one Iranian vessel, but it was clean. The Navy is tracking several other Iranian vessels and we are hoping to get lucky fast . . . Hold on."

Jerry sat on his ammo box chair and waited for a minute while Dex spoke with someone else. Dex came back on. "Sorry about that, Silver Fox, I have more information out of Iran. It would appear that both Muhammad Ali Basri and Kumani Mustafa Awadi were with the president in the mosque when it blew. That's the good news. The bad news is that Ali bin-Oman, who we had been trying to track down as the third person involved in the package delivery, is trying to get some face time in Iran. He was just on Al Jazeera calling for all Moslems to take up arms against Israel in response to this attack from the Jews. He said, 'All the world will see the might of Allah within one week, and Israel would be wiped off the face of the Earth once and for all.' That's a quote."

"Hey—that's not bad news at all," said Jerry. "In fact, it's *great* news. If Ali bin-Oman says the world will see within a week, it means the ship is still where we can grab it. If he had said tomorrow, we'd know we were too late. You think

Ali bin-Oman is trying to become a player now with the president and his buddies all gone?"

"Could be. We had very little on him other than his constant connections with Basri, Awadi, and Hamas. With the power vacuum we just created, he is definitely someone to keep an eye on."

"Is he in Tehran?" asked Jerry.

"Yeah, the interview was in front of the Ali Hamshi Mosque of the Martyrs, Ayatollah Azed's old mosque. Azed's followers are starting to fill the streets outside his mosque to protest his death, along with the president's. They are hardliners. It will be risky, but I think it's time for Ayatollah Kamala to reappear. If he doesn't get ahold of this thing soon, someone else will."

"You think Mike could get close enough to bin-Oman to take him out?"

"Interesting idea. I'll bounce it off of DD," he said, referring to Darren Davis. "Look, you guys sit tight and gear up. As of right now, we are waiting and watching the news while we search for the package. Our people in Kuwait are en route to the carrier group," he said, referring to the NEST team. "At some point, we may need you to pick up our friend at the border and bring him home, or we'll need to get you out to the strait and figure out what to do with that package if we get lucky enough to find it."

"Roger that, Workshop. I'll be sitting by the phone." They signed off as Mackey, Still and Tee walked in. Jerry brought them back up to speed on everything he had just spoken to Murphy about.

Still was the first to respond. "I just want to know how your ayatollah is going to reappear out of nowhere without a scratch and not get lynched."

Jerry made a sour face. "That, my friend, is the million dollar question."

CHAPTER 36

Tehran

Mike and Bijon had sped to a quiet part of the city where Mike kept a very small apartment. He rarely used it, but kept it stocked with nonperishable supplies, a television, a radio, forged documents and, most importantly, an encrypted satellite phone. Mike hustled Bijon inside the small one-bedroom apartment and locked the door. He immediately flipped on the television, where state-run news was reporting the tragedy at Grand Ayatollah Kamala's mosque. The reporter was going down a very long list of names—the missing and presumed dead, all of which were national figures of great importance.

Bijon sat on the small bed, expressionless. When the story moved from his mosque to Ali Hamshi Mosque of the Martyrs, Bijon sat up. A man was being interviewed, Ali bin-Oman, and was demanding the destruction of Israel. Bijon was concentrating so hard on the man on television that he was oblivious to Mike assembling the satellite phone, which he had uncovered from its hiding places around the apartment walls and floor.

Bijon finally snapped out of his trance when he heard Mike speaking.

"This is Ivan," he said into the phone. "Looking for DD or Dex for a nine-one-one." He sat and waited, hardly breathing, until the phone crackled back. Bijon walked over and sat next to him to try and hear. They heard the voice of Darren Davis himself.

"Glad to hear your voice, Ivan. Is your friend with you in one piece?"

"Roger that. Rumors of our deaths have been greatly exaggerated." He smiled.

"Excellent news. We are watching the news—what are you seeing?"

"Right now, the same news as you, most likely. We are in a safe location, but out of visual contact with the action."

"Can you put Bijon on the phone?" asked Darren, using his real name on purpose, signaling that this was it.

Bijon took the phone slowly, as if it weighed a hundred pounds. He spoke to Darren Davis directly, something he had only done twice before. He tried to use his best American accent.

"Hello, Mr. Davis. This is Bijon."

"Bijon, you have waited your entire adult life for this moment. I can only guess what you must be feeling right now, but I believe, as do my colleagues, that the time for you to act is now. Within a very short time, clerics, radicals and revolutionaries will start to emerge and fight for a chance to rule your country. You have paid your dues, Bijon. It is time for you to set the course for your nation. You will face great danger when you reappear, and, quite frankly, I have no idea how you are going to pull this off."

Bijon gave a tired, thoughtful smile. "How will I pull it off, as you say? The same way I have been doing it for the past thirty years—I will lie."

"We wish you luck, Bijon. Some months from now, Iran will rejoin the world community as an equal trading partner and a modern nation. When we get to that point—and we will—you and I will meet, face to face."

"I shall look forward to the day, Mr. Davis," said Bijon. He handed the phone back to Mike, who announced himself again.

"Ivan, we have one last job for you, if you can do it. If you can't, we understand. This is not to be a suicide mission, you understand me?"

"I've made it this far, DD, and I have no intention of getting killed. What is it?"

"We have a target. Ali bin-Oman. He is trying to rally Ayatollah Azed's followers. He may pose a danger to Grand Ayatollah Kamala when he reappears. It may be impossible to get close to him in the current conditions, but if he was to disappear, it might be safer for Bijon."

"I understand. I'll see what I can do, but right now, my primary task is protecting Bijon. The next couple of days will be interesting, to say the least."

"Understood, Ivan. Good luck to both of you."

"Hey, any news on the package?"

"Not yet, but we're working on it."

They finished their call, and Mike quickly disassembled the phone, stashing the pieces all over the house. It took him over ten minutes to finish hiding the pieces, and when he returned to the bedroom where they had sat for their phone call, Bijon was sitting in the center of the floor, cross-legged, with his back straight. Mike watched him for a moment, and realized he was meditating. He sat in a wicker chair in the corner and watched Bijon, wishing he could clear his own mind. Instead of clearing it, he made a to-do list in his head, and started thinking about a few other contacts he had inside Iran that might be able to help him keep Bijon alive after he returned from the dead.

CHAPTER 37

Strait of Hormuz

The *Kitty Hawk* and her strike group arrived at 0300 on a calm, moonless night. Even on the water, the weather was hot and sticky. The flight deck was fairly quiet, with only a few helicopters flying in and out, along with two E-2C Hawkeye radar planes that had been taking shifts since the first news of the atomic bomb had reached the fleet. The four Coast Guard interceptors had rendezvoused an hour before and followed the fleet into the strait. With a fleet of almost thirty ships, the U.S. Navy and Coast Guard made a wall across the water. The *Kitty Hawk* battle group was the largest in the U.S. Navy.

The smaller Coast Guard vessels were able to get out of the actual strait and into shallower waters, while the larger Navy vessels stayed in the deeper shipping lanes. On the bridge, the captain of the *Kitty Hawk* was speaking with his executive officer about the latest satellite, AWAC, and Hawkeye intelligence. They were plotting the Iranian vessels in the Gulf in grease pencil on a large glass map of the area. Fifteen Iranian ships were under direct observation, while several dozen more from other countries were being monitored on the map. Captain Bennett chomped on his unlit cigar and examined the information in front of him. He was jabbing his stubby finger at two of the ships nearest to their location and snarling at his XO.

"We'll start with these two," he spat out through his tobacco-stained front teeth. "Both of them are freighters, not tankers. Makes sense the rag heads would stick the damn thing in a container if they are going to offload it by truck. Did that NEST team arrive yet?"

The XO, Lieutenant Commander Sawyer, was quick to answer. "Not yet, sir, but they are in the air. We expect them on the flight deck any minute."

"Very well. I want to be notified the second they arrive. We will transfer them to the Coast Guard Cutter *Aurora* after I have briefed them personally. The *Aurora* will stop and search these vessels with Navy support. Inform the Coast Guard that we have three hundred Marines aboard the *Philip R. Reynolds* for backup, but we have been instructed not to fire on these ships if at all avoidable. We are to safely recover the bomb, not sink it with the ship. That said, I also don't want to give these pieces of shit time to detonate it while tied to Coast Guard or Navy vessels. I want our people aboard these ships while it's still dark, so we need to hustle. Tell the flight deck supervisor to get the Seahawks flight-ready and loaded with Marine combat assault teams. Colonel Jacobs is in the ready room with his officers and NCOs, so give him a call and tell him to be aboard the choppers in twenty minutes. We also have two SEAL teams aboard the *Shiloh* and I want them operational immediately, understood?"

"Aye, aye, Skipper. I will notify the flight deck supervisor and Marine Colonel Jacobs immediately." The XO snapped a salute and rushed off to use the phone.

Captain Bennett crossed his burly arms, almost covering the rows of ribbons that decorated his barrel chest. He looked more like a blacksmith than a Navy captain as he made angry faces at the grease pencil marks in front of him. He was still standing there when his master chief walked in. Master Chief Grant Parker was a lifer, and a poster boy for the U.S. Navy. Even at close to fifty years old, he was hard as a rock, and although he was only five-foot-eight, there wasn't a sailor on the ship who would get in his way. Captain Bennett loved the man for the way he ran his crew and kept his boat shipshape at all times. Master Chief Parker snapped a salute.

"Evening, Captain," he said. "The NEST team has just landed and will be in the wardroom in ten. I saw the XO, and he had me call over to the SEAL teams. They are itching to try out their new toys, and I think they may have a good idea, sir."

"Spit it out, Master Chief," said the captain.

"The *Pigeon* has a small submersible. Our SEALs can approach in the dark, in total silence. They can sneak aboard and do the whole deal before anybody has a clue they're there. If these guys do have a nuke, why risk them getting jumpy and detonating it in the middle of the fleet?"

"I share the same concern. The only wrench in the works is Washington. They are concerned that we may board the wrong vessel and shoot up an innocent Iranian crew."

"Is there such a thing?" the master chief deadpanned.

"We are supposed to be preventing World War Three, not provoking it, Master Chief."

"Aye, aye, Captain. But the SEALs are sneaky bastards. I still think they can do the job."

"As do I, Master Chief. But we have one small problem. There are a hundred damn boats out there, and we don't know which one is carrying the bomb, if any."

"Like I said, Captain, the NEST team has arrived. They have radiological detection equipment that we don't. We get them close enough to light up their machine and bingo—we send in the SEALs."

The captain unfolded his arms and slowly reached into his pocket, pulling out one of his fat cigars, which he presented to his master chief.

"Lead on," he smiled, and followed Master Chief Parker to the wardroom where he would meet the NEST team.

Captain Bennett and Master Chief Parker walked into the wardroom to a controlled chaos. The NEST team, with the help of a dozen sailors, was unpacking numerous crates of equipment and piling gear all over the tables in the small space. As they walked in, the master chief barked out, "Attention on deck!"

The NEST team stood at attention, not used to military formalities in their line of work. They all wore dark blue jumpsuits with identifying patches that had some kind of isotope on them and the word NEST; none of them showed a rank insignia. Captain Bennett stood with his hands on his hips, chewing his wet, nasty cigar, and spoke through his teeth. "Who is in charge of this outfit?"

A pretty young woman with blond hair gave a lousy salute and said, "That would be me, sir. I'm Dr. Diane Peters with the Nuclear Emergency Search Team. This is my team, Dr. William . . ."

The captain cut her off. "With all due respect, Doc, we don't have time for formal introductions. We have less than three hours till sunup. I need to know if you have radiation detection equipment with you, and if so, what its range is. How close do you have to be to a ship to be able to tell me if it's the right one?"

"Well, sir," she said, feeling slightly nervous as the two burly sailors glared at her and her team, "that would depend on whether or not the bomb has been shielded, and how far belowdeck it is. Radiation will most likely be leaking from the device in large enough quantities to be detectable from approximately one half mile, in the current weather conditions."

The captain smiled, appreciating her *Reader's Digest* version of Nuclear Physics 101. He spoke more calmly to her. "If I get you up in a helicopter, can you use your gizmo on the ships? How much time does it take to register?"

"If we were to approach the vessels from the downwind direction, the equipment would have the greatest range. It takes very little to register on our machinery, if we set up at the highest sensitivity levels. Once we were within range— that half mile, we would know almost instantly. Unless, of course, like I said, they have shielded the device to prevent all leakage."

The captain switched the wet cigar to the side of his mouth. "If they have this thing in a metal container, in the middle of a bunch of other metal containers, maybe even belowdeck, what then? Would that shield the radiation?"

"No, sir. Not from our equipment. We wouldn't be able to tell you *which* container the device was in from a half mile out, but we would be able to tell you if the ship was hot."

"How many of these gizmos do you have?"

"We had three, sir. But I believe one is out of service. Low bidder, sir."

"Tell me about it," he grumbled, and looked at his master chief. "Master Chief Parker, get two teams in the air. Use the Stalkers." He looked back at the NEST team. "That is classified, ladies and gentlemen. The Stalker is a helicopter we are testing on this float. It is almost completely silent and has excellent nighttime capabilities. We can get you very close without being heard, and at night, without being seen. You will be flying below radar, not that these jokers would have any anyway. Dr. Peters, how much time do you need?"

"Give us three minutes to assemble the units, and we are good to go, sir."

"Go find me a bomb, lady." He smacked the master chief on the shoulder. "I'll be on the bridge. See them off and get on the horn to the SEAL team. Stand down the Marines. We'll find the bomb nice and quiet, and the SEALs will take the ship from the water using the submersible."

"Excellent idea, sir," said the master chief.

"Thought you would like it." He smiled, and walked briskly out of the room.

"Well, you heard the captain, people—let's move."

The NEST team quickly pulled boxes apart and assembled their equipment in total silence, pleasantly surprising the master chief. They had obviously drilled a thousand times before for nuclear emergencies, and worked as a team, handing each other pieces and tools as they went from a dozen boxes of stuff to two very complicated radiological detecting devices.

The spacesuit-like hazardous material suits were thrown to the side. The suits would not shield them from a nuclear blast. The second the two machines were finished, Diane announced that they were good to go, and they hustled after the master chief through a series of doors and elevators back to the flight deck, where two of the world's most secret helicopters sat waiting for them.

A Marine major stood in his flight suit by the two choppers, awaiting the NEST team. He trotted over to the team as they approached, carrying what looked like two very small aerial antennaes attached to laptop computers. The master chief introduced the major to Diane, who introduced three members of her team.

"We can take two of you in each Stalker. Mission orders say to bring you in low and quiet from the downwind side of the target vessels. We have two waypoints already, and if we don't score with them, we will receive new coordinates while we're in the air. We can go two hours, depending on how far out we go—but two hours should cover a lot of water out here. We can make a hundred seventy knots. It'll be a little tight in the rear seat, and you need to put floatation vests on."

"That's reassuring," said Diane.

"Just a precaution, ma'am. Not much of a glide pattern in these things, but we've never had a problem, so don't worry." He knocked on his helmet for luck after he said that.

"Good luck," said the master chief. "Go find us a bomb and we'll take care of the rest. Remember: get in and out undetected. We don't want some nervous A-Rab blowing up the nuke."

Diane picked three other members of her team to board the choppers, and they hustled after the major and climbed aboard the two sleek black helicopters. The Stalker looked somewhat like a black bullet, with the rear rotors completely encased and out of view. Even the top rotors had a winglike apparatus over them to absorb the typical rotor sound. In the dark, the Stalker would be silent and invisible. The flight crews closed the doors, gave thumbs-up to the master chief and silently lifted off the deck. Most activity stopped as sailors watched the strange birds lift off without the normal sounds of helicopters. The black choppers moved out over the water, each in a different direction, and then veered off silently to try and prevent World War Three.

CHAPTER 38

FOP Iron Mountain

Jerry, Mackey, Tee and Still stood in an open area near their base camp. It was the only flat area within half a kilometer, and it was where the Army Blackhawk helicopter would be landing. They crouched in the rocks and watched as the helicopter barely touched the ground. The side door slid open, and lo and behold, Duce hopped out of the chopper. He was now in his camouflaged battle dress uniform—BDU—his black jumpsuit having been soaked with the blood of his friends, who were both now en route to the army hospital in Germany.

Duce had two field packs on his back, along with his team's weapons. He wasn't one to lose stuff. He crouched below the rotor blades as the chopper lifted off and headed back to Camp Eagle. His friends trotted out to meet him, grabbing his gear to give him a hand. Still gave him a smack and welcomed him back over the *whump* of the rotor blades. Duce gave his crooked half-smile, and trotted after the big man.

Once the chopper was gone, Jerry put his arm around Duce. "Hey, man, good to see you in one piece. I hear it was pretty damn close out there."

"Yeah," said Duce quietly. "Don and Ramon almost didn't make it out. I hear they're on the way to Germany now. They should both be okay, but damn, Don was close."

"So I heard. Listen, you did a good job out there, Duce. So far the mission has been pretty successful."

"The mosque?" asked Duce.

"Poof," said Still.

"Big fuckin' hole," added Tee.

Mackey shot them a look. "Yeah, they got the CX-10 into place, invited the president and top clerics, all the local bad guys—got 'em all in there and took it out. Left a hole twenty feet deep where the mosque was, and knocked down two other buildings, one of which may have been a weapons facility. Secondary explosions and a huge fire. You may have helped take out a thousand terrorists in one shot."

"Damn," said Duce quietly.

"Yeah—damn. That was you, Don and Ramon who helped get that in there. Remember that. Those guys are going to be fine. And you have all helped changed history, my friend."

"What about the nuke?" asked Duce.

"Working on it," said Mackey, grim faced. "There is a NEST team on location on the Strait of Hormuz. No word yet, but they're looking."

"Been a busy couple of days, huh?" said Duce, looking pretty beat himself.

"No doubt," answered Jerry. "Let's get back to the forward observation post and see if we can catch up on the latest news. We're not out of the woods yet."

"Any word from Mike or Bijon?" asked Duce.

"Not since they checked in with Langley. They both made it out. That's all I got so far."

"Well, it's a good start, anyway," said Duce.

"Yeah, well now the *real* shit-storm starts," said Jerry. They started the walk back to the FOP, up the weaving goat trails that led to Iron Mountain.

CHAPTER 39

Outside Tehran

It was late afternoon. Calls to prayer could be heard outside, and Bijon knelt on his prayer mat, joining the millions of others around the country. He also added prayers for strength, courage and Allah's blessings to his usual prayers. He begged forgiveness for having killed so many Iranian countrymen, but explained himself as best he could to the Almighty. The president and his cronies had twisted the Koran and made the Prophet Mohammed out to be a murderer. It was not the way it should be. Bijon begged Allah for guidance and wisdom, and words to help bring his country out of despair.

Skripak sat in a chair watching quietly, lost in his own thoughts. To think that what had just happened might have been the easy part was unnerving. There were now several million Iranians that would stone them to death—at the very least—if they knew what they had done. Skripak waited until Bijon was finished, and then spoke.

"My friend, we need to go. It is time we made a few visits to some friends I have around the city. We need people to know that you are still alive, that you will lead the people of

Iran to a new age. And we need to do it before Grand Aya-tollah Azed's followers take the reins of this country with Ali bin-Oman as their leader."

Bijon stood. "I will put my robes back on and emerge from the dead. Perhaps it is time for you to finally go home, my friend. It will be very dangerous now. You have done more than your part."

"Look, Bijon, with all due respect, I have lived in this shit-hole . . ." He caught himself and apologized, then restarted, "I have lived in this *country*, very far from home, for *way* too long. I am not going to leave at the final hour and watch you fuck up my life's work." He smiled, and Bijon hugged him for the first time in his life.

Bijon spoke with watery eyes. "My friend." He took a deep breath and gathered himself. "You have sacrificed so much of your life to a country and people to whom you owe nothing. You have never ceased to amaze me, or to be a source of in-spiration in the darkest of times. I know none of this would have been possible without your help."

Mike cut him off. "Don't thank me yet. I still might get you killed. We need to contact supporters and build up an army of your people around you. If you go stickin' your head up now in the wrong place, somebody is gonna blow it off. Grand Ayatollah Azed's people will not be pleased to see you, my friend. And Ali bin-Oman will definitely put your lights out. No way are they going to believe you miraculously survived that explosion."

Bijon scowled. "I have been wondering what to do about them myself. I thought perhaps with enough supporters we could overcome their opposition. They would be linked to the old ways of the president, while I will be calling for change, and a new Iran."

"That's all well and good, Bijon, but Ali bin-Oman will take you out before you get a chance to do anything that re-sembles gathering support. I will contact my people at the universities, whoever is left after the president's roundup and massacre, and tell them you are alive and prepared to take Iran in a new direction. You leave the other two to me."

"You will never get close to Ali bin-Oman now, Mike. He'll be surrounded by an army."

Mike smiled. He reached into his pocket and pulled his hand back out. He opened his palm and showed Bijon the small round ball of CX-10 he had pinched off the vest before blowing the mosque. "I saved a little for a rainy day, Bijon. I don't have to get *that* close."

Mike got up and walked to the window. It was late afternoon, and the sun was getting low. The streets were filled with people, and cars clogged the narrow road. The city was buzzing with the chaos of an attack of unknown origin. Sirens could still be heard far in the distance, as the buildings around the mosque still burned. Mike turned back to Bijon.

"Look, buddy. I need to get out and see what's going on around the city. I need to do that alone. You need to sit tight. Do *not* leave this apartment until I get back. If I am not back by tomorrow night, I'm not coming back, and you'll have to try something on your own. For now, just stay here. Don't go near the windows or answer the door. There's a pistol under my mattress if you need it—let's hope it doesn't come to that. No one should bother you here. My neighbors are used to me being away. Promise me you won't move till I get back?"

Bijon smiled and said, " I promise. And you promise me that you are *coming* back."

Mike smiled. "I promise. Let's finish this thing so I can go find a beach, a decent bottle of wine and a beautiful blonde."

Mike slipped a Beretta under his robes in his waistband and slipped out the door into the bustling streets below.

CHAPTER 40

Strait of Hormuz

The two helicopters made beelines for their respective targets. The *Kitty Hawk*'s captain had chosen the two ships carefully. They were both Iranian freighters, not tankers. They were also the two closest ships heading their way. The Strait of Hormuz was a bottleneck, and fairly easily patrolled. The *Kitty Hawk* and the rest of her fleet could wait and allow the ships to come to them, assuming the bomb-laden ship hadn't already passed them.

It was dark, and the two choppers were silent as they skimmed thirty feet over the water. The NEST team had divided into two groups of two members each. One of the team members was holding the wand in the direction of the target boat, while the other watched a tiny screen on what amounted to a small laptop computer. They flew in the dark and in silence—only the faint glow of the heads-up display in the cockpit and the screen of the computer gave off any light at all. In the soft green glow, the chopper sounded windy but not helicopter-like, as it rode through the air at 160 miles per hour.

The copilot of the first chopper spoke quietly to his pilot, but all members of the team on board could hear the conversation.

"Radar picks up target at current heading, ten miles out. Time to target, less than four minutes. She is heading straight for us at twenty knots."

"Roger that. Maintaining heading."

Dr. Diane Peters was in the backseat next to Dr. David Tompkins. She nudged him. "Three minutes and we should be lighting up if we've got the right boat." She spoke to the pilot. "Major, remember to approach downwind if possible. It will extend our reach."

"Aye, aye, Doc," he said quietly.

As they approached their target, warning lights began flashing all over the control panel and heads-up display. The copilot was trying his best to sort through the continuous stream of computer alerts he was getting. The pilot asked three times if he should abort the mission, and three times the copilot told him to hang in there, he was working on it. The NEST team tried their best to ignore them and concentrate on their monitor.

The copilot finally came back on the headset. "Chief, I am getting fuel alerts, but I know we are full. I checked manually before we left. I say ignore the damn thing. The problem is in the computer, not the fuel tank."

"You willing to bet our ass on it?" asked the chief warrant officer, holding his course.

"Roger that, sir. Hold our course."

"Increasing to max speed, and advise me of any changes in our warning system," said the pilot. "If we do go down, maybe we can at least get a reading off that damn boat first. I am advising fleet."

The pilot changed channels and called back to the *Kitty Hawk* to advise the captain of their onboard computer system warnings, and that they were continuing their mission. They were given clearance to proceed on their own judgment, and were advised that a search and rescue helicopter would be dispatched on their same heading, but far enough away to avoid detection by the freighters.

The pilot changed his frequency back to the chopper and told the copilot and passengers that a search and rescue chopper was en route, but that they would continue toward their target.

Meanwhile, aboard the submarine tender *Pigeon*, a twelve-man SEAL team prepared their SCUBA equipment and weapons for a night dive and ship assault.

CHAPTER 41

Tehran

Mike entered the apartment in the dark. It was three o'clock in the morning, and the area was fairly quiet. Bijon had passed out on the sagging bed, the pistol lying next to him. It had been an emotionally draining few days, and the stress had literally knocked him out. He didn't stir when Mike walked into the room. Even when Mike turned on a small lamp, Bijon didn't wake up. Mike had spent hours running from contact to contact, organizing a crowd of centrist Iranians who had not been fans of the radical Ayatollah Kamala, but who *would* be fans of the new and improved version. They were not told anything about Kamala's interesting life story—only that he was alive, and now with the threat of the president removed, was prepared to bring Iran into the world community with a more open, liberal government. It was met with some skepticism, but they trusted Mike, and knew he was in constant contact with the Americans. They did not know that he himself was in fact an American CIA agent.

When it was explained that the Americans would agree to sit down with the new leadership of Grand Ayatollah Kamala, which would lead to actual democratic elections, the contacts

he had immediately begun working through their various
channels to put together masses of followers to counteract the
extremism of Grand Ayatollah Azed's followers, who were
gathering around Ali bin-Oman.

As predicted, Grand Ayatollah Azed's mosque was already
putting up one of their own clerics as the ruler of Iran until a
new president could be "elected." The name Ali bin-Oman had
already been mentioned as a possible successor the late president, and Grand Ayatollah Azed's clerics warned the Iranian
people that strong leadership was required in these troubled
times, in the face of Israeli aggression. The big lie had already
started. No doubt it would be only a few days before the Iranians were broadcasting proof that Israel was directly responsible for the mosque attack. Rumors were already circulating
about Iran trying to get Syria and Lebanon to join them in
claiming Israeli responsibility.

Mike made a pot of strong coffee and sat in the kitchen.
He was trying to stay focused, regardless of how exhausted he
was. He needed to keep Bijon alive, organize enough supporters to give him a national spotlight and show of strength, and
take out Ali bin-Oman. There would no doubt be more violence as the many local clerics jockeyed for positions of power
in the large vacuum created by the block of CX-10. To say the
morning would be interesting would be the understatement of
the century. As he sat drinking his coffee, lost in his thoughts,
Bijon woke up abruptly and looked to the light in the kitchen.
He walked sleepily into the kitchen, feeling like he had been
run over by a truck.

"How long have you been here?" he asked quietly.

"Not long. Just making coffee. You want some?"

Bijon walked to the small metal table and sat down, ac-
cepting the small demitasse of strong coffee. He sat down,
stirring in sugar and feeling like crap.

"Where did you go? What happens next?"

"I was running down old contacts. In four hours, you and I
are going to meet a large group of supporters. You have a few
hours to think of the speech you will give them and march
your ass down to the center of town where your mosque used

to be. We have made plans to stage a rally. Al Jazeera will be there, along with state-run radio and TV . . . We have it leaked out that you are alive."

Bijon rubbed his eyes and drank the coffee. "I have my speech as prepared as it will be. I am ready, Michael. No matter what happens when the sun comes up, I am ready."

Mike sat back and sipped his coffee, looking at the tired man in front of him, a man he had "invented." Bijon saw him smiling and asked what was so entertaining at a little past three in the morning.

"You know, you and I have been fictional characters for so long, I'm not sure if either one of us knows who we are anymore. Or did we actually become the people we portray? I think my Iranian accent will stick with me forever now."

Bijon laughed. "It's a wonder you were never arrested. Your Farsi is terrible."

"Bullshit!" laughed Mike. "Besides, in another week, I can forget every word of it. In fact, that's my new mission. I am going to get drunk, get laid, shave off this ridiculous beard that I can't stand and forget every word of Farsi I know. From now on, when you and I communicate, you will speak to me in English!"

Bijon whispered back, "Not for another few weeks, I think, my friend."

Mike drank back the last few dregs of coffee and stood up. "Yeah, we better wait a bit before we start celebrating. I'm afraid we're done sleeping for the day. You need to get showered and back into your formal robes. We need to be out of here in another hour to meet our people. You need to talk to these people yourself, one on one, before we can put together an army of followers. Your regular customers may be looking at you funny when you reemerge. You will need a strong support base that can out-scream Azed's people and those who question how you survived."

Bijon stood up, and they gave each other a serious handshake. Bijon whispered, "The sun will rise over a new Iran, God willing."

CHAPTER 42

D-Day

Jerry was finishing his call with Langley when Duce, Tee and Still walked into the small corner of the cavern that was his communications room. They sat and waited for him to finish.

"Okay, boys, here's the deal. Mike is going to try to hit Ali bin-Oman today. Grand Ayatollah Kamala is going to return from the dead. There will probably be a small civil war starting today, and the Navy is going to try to locate a nuke and steal it without getting blown to kingdom come. Oh, and we will probably have to help extricate Mike from Iran in the next forty-eight hours. Just another day at the office. Any questions?"

Duce, Tee and Still exchanged glances. Still spoke up. "So nothing new?"

"Nothing yet. Where's Mackey?"

"He's catching z's," said Duce.

"Good. He may need them. You three gear up. As soon as you are ready, take a squad of the rangers and head out to the border. They will take you to the extraction location. Once you are there, you will hunker down and wait for word that

Mike is coming out. Bring supplies for five days. If we have to, we can get more out to you."

"Is Mackey coming with us?" asked Tee.

"Negative. That's all for now. See me before you take off."

On board the submarine tender USS *Pigeon*, twelve of the most well trained, dangerous close-combat warriors of the United States Navy donned black wet suits and zipped up their watertight equipment bags. They were getting ready to climb over the side of the ship and enter a tiny submarine that could hold the twelve men and their equipment. The small sub bobbed in the water of the Strait of Hormuz, tied to the *Pigeon* like a baby attached to its mother by the umbilical cord. The SEALs climbed down the rope ladder and entered the top hatch of their vehicle. They would be exiting out of the bottom, where a larger hatch would open and allow them to swim out into the black ocean. It was only a couple of hours until daylight, and everyone was anxious to get under way.

The SEALs were commanded by Chief Petty Officer Chris Cascaes, another lifer who began his career as a rescue swimmer and ended up as one of the baddest of the bad-asses, as the operators of SEAL Team Six would attest to. The eleven men on his small combat team would follow any order he gave, or die trying. They had followed him into harm's way on too many missions to count, and he had never lost a man under his command. He was competent, respected and fearless, and his men loved him.

For this mission, they had been equipped with MP5 "room brooms" for close-quarters combat, specially fitted with noise and flash suppressors. They had also loaded their sub with three thousand-pound magnetic bombs that could be attached to the hull of the ship when it was time to deep-six it. They loaded the sub and sat inside in the extremely cramped quarters. CPO Cascaes would be steering the sub himself, with his squad's second in command, Chief Petty Officer Montoya, assisting.

The sub, the USS *Intruder*, was a very special design. It

could serve as a disabled sub rescue vehicle (DSRV), a deep-water submersible for exploration or intelligence gathering, or most often, as in this case, it could be used to sneak up on other ships or into harbors where the team could unload underwater and enter areas undetected. The sub was only thirty feet long, with the steering and command console located forward. The passengers all sat behind the commander, with the large bottom hatch opening at their feet. Two long benches faced each other, holding eight men each at maximum capacity. When ready to go, they would simply open the large hatch between them, the air pressure keeping out the water, and drop out the bottom in their SCUBA gear.

The three heavy mines had been attached magnetically to the belly of their own sub, where they would remain until they were transferred to their target, assuming the NEST team could find it. Their plan was simple enough. Find the ship, board it and kill everything that moved, and call in the NEST team to disarm the nuclear weapon and remove it. After that, they would attach the three mines and sink the ship after they had reboarded the sub and disappeared into the rising sun. Of course, it was pretty rare that anything actually went according to plan.

Standing atop the bobbing sub, CPO Cascaes handed each member of his SEAL team a potassium iodide tablet to be swallowed before they entered the sub. In the event of radiation leakage, the potassium iodide might save their lives from radiation sickness. Each man threw it back and gulped a swallow of water from the CPO's canteen. When the last SEAL was aboard, Cascaes took his own tablet and dropped into the hatch, sealing it behind him. As he powered up the USS *Intruder*, the sailors aboard the *Pigeon* cast off the tender lines and watched as the small black submersible cut through the ink-black water.

Dr. Diane Peters was watching the screen closely, trying her best to ignore the warning alarms that kept going off in the helicopter. The copilot still insisted that the diagnostics equipment was wrong, and they weren't having a mechanical failure, but that didn't keep the lights and alarms from unnerving the two NEST team passengers in the back seat. The pilot was about to say they were within range when Diane's screen lit up with a radiation detection light.

"We're hot!" she said loudly into her headset. "I say again, I have radiation confirmation, getting stronger."

The pilot remained calm and stayed on course for the moment. "Do I need to get any closer, or do you have enough to confirm presence of the atomic warhead?"

"If you can stay on course for another minute, the radiation levels should be large enough to confirm a warhead. Right now, it is minimal, but I can confirm radiation."

The lights inside the cockpit went on again, screaming warnings and alerts about multiple system failures. This time, a red light in the cockpit control panel began flashing, dancing to the alarms. It was the Master Alarm switch, indicating critical failure.

"God damn it, Major! I have to abort," yelled the pilot over the alarms.

The major was typing away at a systems analysis computer to no avail. "Sir, just hold us steady for another thirty seconds and let the doc get her reading. I still think we're fine. It's the damn computer! We are flying straight and steady and I know we have fuel."

The pilot was reading gauges and holding his course amid the chaos of the lights and alarms. "Doctor! You have twenty seconds and I am turning this bird around. Your ship is dead ahead."

"Roger that, sir. Our radiation readings are increasing. I'm at fifteen rads and climbing."

"Fifteen rads? What does that mean to me, Doctor? You find the bomb or not?"

"Affirmative, sir. Unless they are transporting other fissile material or nuclear waste, we can confirm the package is on board."

The pilot spoke to his copilot. "You heard the lady, Major—I am turning this bird around. Changing frequency to the flagship." The pilot flipped a switch and spoke directly to the *Kitty Hawk* bridge. "Stalker One to flag, come in, over."

"This is flag, go ahead Stalker One," came the voice of Captain Bennett himself.

"Flag, we confirm package aboard target two. I say again, positive reading for package aboard target two. We are returning to the deck with Master Alarms and multiple system failure readings."

"I understand you to say positive reading for package aboard target two. Are you holding steady, Stalker One? We have a rescue chopper inbound."

"We are flying one-hundred percent. It may be a computer error rather than mechanical, sir, but I have changed course and we are heading home. Advise rescue that we are inbound. I pick him up on radar three miles out. Time to the deck, fifteen minutes at present speed, assuming we are still flying."

"Stay on this channel, Stalker One, and keep us advised of your situation. I am advising pick-up team of the target. Over and out."

Captain Bennett switched channels and radioed the sub, which was still at periscope depth and able to receive radio transmissions. The captain confirmed the proper target and again personally authorized the use of lethal force to remove all hostiles from the ship as quickly as possible. He wished them luck and signed off, then went back to monitoring his multimillion-dollar secret prototype helicopter that was threatening to drop into the ocean with its crew of four.

The sub would be arriving at the ship in less than forty minutes, and the chopper would be landing on the deck in a little over ten, if it landed at all. Captain Bennett chomped nervously on his unlit cigar and called his XO to man the bridge—he was going out to the deck personally and to wait for the damn chopper. Master Chief Parker was right behind him.

Bijon and Mike drove through the quiet neighborhood back toward central Tehran. It was still completely dark. The sun wouldn't be up for another few hours, and there was still a power outage in much of the central city following the explosion. There was an apartment complex on the way back toward where the mosque had stood the day before that would serve as a rallying point for Grand Ayatollah Kamala and his supporters.

They pulled Mike's decrepit car to the curb and the two men got out, walking down the dark street into a large apartment complex and through the back into a courtyard. There, almost one hundred men stood around talking in hushed but excited tones. Some were arguing, some debating, some making speeches. When the Grand Ayatollah Kamala entered, he was immediately recognized, and silence spread through the crowd. The small sea of people opened, ironically like Moses entering the Red Sea not far from there.

The Grand Ayatollah lifted his hands and waved the crowd closer to him. They slowly approached, many of them seeing him in person for the first time, although they had seen his face on billboards and TV for many years. For these Iranians, he represented the oppressive conservative hard-liners, and they regarded him with great caution. He turned around inside the crowd slowly, making eye contact with as many of them as he could, then slowly began, in a steady strong voice that carried over the dimly lit courtyard.

"Grand Ayatollah Kamala is not dead, but rather reborn," he began, to the perplexed faces around him. "I had a vision and called upon the president and Grand Ayatollah Azed to hear the message from Allah and his Prophet Mohammed, blessed be his name. I had been summoned by the great one himself to deliver a message that would change the course of action in our beloved country. It was a message that flies in the face of everything you have ever been taught about the outside world. It contradicts teachings from myself, from imams all over Iran and all over the world. It will shock most of our great nation. But hear me now—it is the *truth*."

The crowd shuffled in closer, captivated by his intriguing speech. "We live in a violent world. We live in a world where we feel oppressed and threatened by the West, by the Jews, by the Christians, by our Sunni brothers—yes, *brothers*. The

Sunnis are our brothers. But here is the real shocking truth—
so are the Jews and the Christians."

He paused and looked at the shocked faces around him.
There was not a sound uttered from anyone. Some mouths
actually hung wide open at his words.

"For how many years have we fought the Jews, the Christians, each other? A hundred years? A thousand? Two thousand? We will kill each other for another ten thousand if
someone does not end the madness. At what point did it become acceptable to strap explosives onto our children and turn
them into walking bombs? The Israeli Prime Minister Golda
Meir once said 'there will never be peace until the Arabs love
their children more than they hate us.' " He screamed, "She
was *right*! When is this going to stop? How much more blood
do we need to see before the world changes and we open our
eyes?" He paused and looked about him. The crowd was incredulous. They could not believe it was actually Grand Ayatollah Kamala—it must be an impostor!

"My eyes are open!" he screamed, and began to walk
through the crowd. He grabbed an old man by the arm and
screamed at him, "Open your eyes! In a single flash of light
that removed evil from our midst, I can now see! Open your
eyes! All of you! Do you care if the Jews live in Jerusalem? It
is not our Holy City! It is not Mecca! It is not even mentioned
in the Koran—so why do we fight so hard for it? Because we
want to kill every last Jew? For *what*? What has any Jew ever
done to *any* of us? Can any of you name one Jew you have
known in your personal life that has wronged you? No! Of
course not. You don't even know any Jews. But we live in
poverty and oppression by our own government and they need
to blame someone for their own lack of leadership and inability to govern a nation."

He was walking through the crowd now, touching each person as he slowly moved among them. Those he touched followed him without even realizing it, thunderstruck by such
outrageous comments coming from the most vocal Jew-hater
in their country.

"Our president, Mowad Asmunjaniwal, is dead. Ayatollah

Azed is dead. Every hate-filled member of our government is dead. *It is time to rebuild our country*. It is time to take back Iran from those who would oppress you and blame others! Who will help me rebuild our nation? Who among you is brave enough to stand beside me when I address our nation and tell the world that Iran is not the evil empire! Iran is a nation of good people and wants to be part of the modern world! We will build industries; we will build schools—*real* schools with *real* teachers who will show our children the future! A future of knowledge and learning and science! We will never turn our backs on our religion, but we will stop using the Koran as an excuse to kill those who don't have the understanding of the Koran. We will show them that the Persians and Arabs can be as successful as the Jews, as the Christians, as any people anywhere, but not until we teach our children a different understanding of the world. We will build a new Iran!"

The crowd began cheering, slowly at first, but it continued to build. Kamala continued to work his way through the crowd, asking individuals if they were with him. Some kissed his hands, some merely said yes as they touched his robes. It was going better than could have been anticipated until one older man grabbed his arm and spoke angrily through his clenched teeth, "Who are you? Ayatollah Kamala is dead! Who are you?"

"You know who I am," he said quietly to the man. "I have preached to you wrongly for my entire life. The time for change has come, before the world is immersed in so much blood we all drown." Kamala held the man's arm and turned back to the crowd, shouting.

"I am Grand Ayatollah Kamala, and I was *wrong*! Do you understand? Everything I have been taught—everything I have taught the people of Iran—it was *wrong*! We can change the course of our destiny! We can build a better Iran for our children!"

The crowd began cheering again, this time louder, and lights in the surrounding apartments began coming on. The crowd began chanting his name and the Grand Ayatollah spoke to as many of them as he could, urging them to get their families and friends and gather with him in front of his ruined mosque, where he would address his nation and the world.

"God is great!" the Ayatollah shouted, "and he will show us the way to build a new nation!"

The crowd cheered with him. "God is great! Kamala! Kamala!"

With the Grand Ayatollah leading the way, the people began to exit the courtyard out into the street, where others came out of the buildings to see what was happening. The word spread quickly, and by the time the Grand Ayatollah marched onto the scene of his ruined mosque and shattered buildings, there were thousands of followers in the streets behind him, carrying banners and Iranian flags, cheering and singing national songs.

As the sun began to rise in central Tehran, the scene was dramatic. Emergency vehicles and soldiers still had the area sealed off, and were still pulling dead mangled bodies and body parts from the still-smoking wreckage. As Grand Ayatollah Kamala walked down the street with thousands of supporters marching behind him, the soldiers and rescue workers stopped dead in their tracks. Hundreds of people on the scene stood, incredulous, as the man who was supposedly buried beneath the stone wreckage of the smoldering mosque appeared before them. Word spread throughout the crowd quickly—the Grand Ayatollah was alive!

By the time the Grand Ayatollah stood on top of a pile of rubble that was across the street from what had been his mosque, there were over five thousand people around him, and more filled the streets with each passing moment. Television cameras and reporters that had been filming the scene of the disaster were now moving their cameras and setting up across the street, where the Grand Ayatollah had reappeared from the dead.

Kamala spoke quietly with supporters, a few at a time, shaking hands, being hugged and kissed by loyal hard-liners who were sure he was killed. Some of them cried and knelt before him, unsure if he was real or an angel returned from

Paradise. Soldiers who had been guarding the area removed their weapons and hats and knelt before him, causing a ripple effect of thousands of people who knelt and quieted, until the Grand Ayatollah stood on his little pile of rocks, high above the thousands of Iranians who waited for his words in this time of great crisis. . . .

Jerry Woodcrest walked out of the cavern to where Tee, Still and Duce were assembling their gear with a platoon of rangers. They would hike on foot down to the border crossing, where hopefully Mike Skripak would show up in a few days. Mackey was obviously missing, still sleeping as he prepared for a flight out to the Strait of Hormuz where he would be landing on the USS *Kitty Hawk*. Jerry pulled his three men aside and spoke quietly, out of earshot of the rangers.

"Okay fellas, I just got off the horn with Langley. Things are going surprisingly well so far, but of course we are only one trigger finger away from taking out an entire carrier group. Special Ops is en route to hopefully take down the ship carrying the nuke. Turns out it was on a cargo ship, and the NEST team got lucky and found it before it slipped past the fleet. Assuming our boys secure the nuke, it will have to be made safe, and then transported to the *Kitty Hawk*, where Mackey has the fun job of flying it out of here. I don't know to where, and frankly, I don't care. Just let him get that thing out of the Middle East. In the meantime, you guys sit on the border and watch for Skripak. I don't know if it will be easier or harder for him to get out now in all this chaos, but let's just make sure we get him out in one piece. With the turmoil in Iran, you may have Hezbollah and a hundred other groups moving in and out across the borders. Stay together and keep your shit wired tight. You will have air support if you need it once you get in position, but be careful in the mountains. Once you are off Iron Mountain, you are in Injun country. Any questions?"

There weren't any, so they said a quick good-bye and hustled off to the rangers to begin the very long walk down out of the mountains. As they walked away, Jerry stood and looked out to the east, over the mountains toward Iran, where the first orangey-pink wisps of sunrise snuck through the azure sky.

Gonna be a helluva day, he thought to himself.

By the time Stalker One approached the *Kitty Hawk*, all of its on-board warning systems were screaming and lighting up louder and brighter than a local fire department. The co-pilot had been correct, there were no mechanical failures, just computer foul-ups in the diagnostics equipment. That was the good news. The bad news was the fear that, at some point, the safety overrides would automatically shut down all systems and drop them out of the sky like a rock. The copilot continuously battled the computer, which by now he had nicknamed HAL after the monster in *2001: A Space Odyssey*, and tried everything he could to turn off the alarms as they kept coming back on. He had eventually changed channels and been patched through to an engineer in Florida, routed through Washington, D.C. And so, there they were, thousands of miles apart, while the chopper flew at 130 knots about a hundred feet above the ocean, speaking to each other about how to override the damn computer without shutting down the engine. In the meantime, the pilot ignored everything except his route to the carrier, where he would hopefully be landing within the next five minutes. About fifty feet off of his port side flew a rescue helicopter with two rescue swimmers ready to jump at any second.

On the bench seat, Diane Peters leaned back and decided she really didn't like flying in helicopters very much. On her right, Dr. Tompkins was making his final mental arrangements for exiting the helicopter while upside down under water. Both of them clutched their equipment tightly, even though it was turned off with their readings safely recorded in the memory file. The pilot speaking to them over the screaming alarms made everyone jump, then smile.

"I have visual on the *Kitty Hawk*. Time to dry feet is two minutes."

Dry feet, thought Diane, *please God, let us keep our feet dry.*

The Grand Ayatollah waited patiently for the cameras to set up. He had used his time wisely, speaking one on one to as many people as he could. He had found the highest-ranking officer he could in uniform, and asked for his protection lest something go wrong. The colonel was honored to be chosen for the task and wasted no time in gathering a show of force nearby. When he asked the Grand Ayatollah how he had survived the blast, the cleric just responded that everything would be explained shortly, but to have faith in Allah and place his trust in the Grand Ayatollah, who would open the eyes of the Iranian people on this day.

As the sun rose in a brilliant pink fireball, it illuminated the streets of Tehran, which was now filled with tens of thousands of curious citizens. The news had been carrying stories of the Grand Ayatollah surviving the blast, but he wouldn't speak to reporters yet. Instead, he had just directed them to set up a podium, where he would address all of Iran at the same time. This news had also made it to the Ayatollah Azed's mosque, where Ali bin-Oman tried his best to convert Azed's followers into his own. He had already spoken to one of Azed's surviving clerics and told him he would be the next Grand Ayatollah, under the leadership of the new President Ali bin-Oman, and was not pleased to see news that announced Kamala's return from the ashes.

Skripak had slipped away from Bijon, once again the Grand Ayatollah Kamala, and headed across town to the Ali Hamshi Mosque of the Martyrs. A small crowd was beginning to assemble there as well, although nowhere near the size of the one around Ayatollah Kamala. This only added to Ali bin-Oman's anger. Ali bin-Oman stood on the outside steps of the mosque, looking down on a crowd of Azed's supporters and trying his best to fire up the crowd. Unfortunately for him, he was excellent at killing people—particularly unarmed civilians—but a very poor public speaker. For all of his rage and impassioned rhetoric, the faces of the crowd remained fairly uninterested. There were still many clerics claiming to be Azed's successor, and the man that Ali bin-Oman had chosen was not the most popular—his first mistake.

Ali bin-Oman's second mistake was standing outside. Skripak stood across the street, holding an Iranian flag. Inside the flagpole was the small piece of CX-10 he had saved for this special occasion. It was small compared to the brick that had taken down the mosque, but slightly larger than the piece the team had trained on in Virginia, which had vaporized a small house. Skripak waited until a group of supporters showed up carrying banners and chanting Azed's name, and handed the flag to the most obnoxious of the group, whispering to him that the TV cameras would arrive soon, and Ali bin-Oman should have a national banner behind him for the picture. The man wasted no time in forcing his way through the crowd to get as close to Ali bin-Oman as he could. Oman was actually smiling when he saw the man approach, waving the flag and screaming, "Ali bin-Oman for president." That was what he heard when he saw the flash of white light. He never heard the noise the followed it.

Skripak had crouched down behind a car across the street and watched the flag move through the crowd. He looked at his wristwatch, and right before the explosion, rolled under the car and covered his ears. Even the small piece of CX-10 was enough to completely obliterate the crowd and the front doors of the mosque. The front of the mosque was completely covered in human remains, to the point that it looked like it was dripping with red paint. Whatever was left of Ali bin-Oman and his followers was running down the front wall.

Skripak joined the other survivors in running away from the explosion. He didn't stop when he got out of the smoke, however, and continued all the way back to the huge crowd gathered to hear the Grand Ayatollah Kamala. By the time he got close to where Kamala's mosque had been, there was no way to push through the huge crowds. The sun was up, and it was so loud in the streets that the explosion had been only a dull thump in this part of the city. Mike pushed and weaved as

best as he could to get closer, but could see early on that it
would be impossible to get all the way to Bijon. He pushed
back out of the crowd the same way he had come in and
walked several blocks out of his way to get to his jalopy of a
car. He stood there for a moment and looked at it, pondering
what to do. He had sanitized his safe house and destroyed all
of his equipment after sending one last burst transmission to
tell Langley that he was still alive and today was D-Day. If all
went well, he would be heading to the border. If all turned to
shit, well . . . he just had to pray that everything went well.

He had spoken to Bijon in the morning for quite a while,
but hadn't really said good-bye. As he sat on the hood of his
partially demolished car, he realized he probably wouldn't
have a chance to say good-bye to Bijon at all now. The lion
was out of the cage, and it was time for the handler to disappear. In the midst of the total chaos that was Tehran, Mike felt
quiet and calm. A mission that had become his life's work was
ending. Whatever would happen now would have to happen
on its own. He was no longer running the show. It was sad, the
finality of it all. Of course, the thought of getting back to the
United States was what kept him going most days, but now
that it was almost here, it seemed bittersweet. He realized that
his part of the mission was over, but that the work in Iran was
really just beginning. He finally came to the conclusion that
he had passed the torch, and Bijon was eminently more qualified to change the course of Iran than he was. As he made
peace with leaving in the midst of total chaos, the missing
bomb popped back into his head. If the bomb went off in Israel, then everything he had accomplished was for nothing
anyway.

He opened the door of his car with a creaking whine, and
by yet another miracle, it started. He pulled away from the
curb and his cheek actually felt wet. As much as he hated living in Iran, it had become his life. There were people here he
cared about, and the markets and countryside could be beautiful at times. He hated to admit it, but he might actually miss
some of it. His car coughed and belched black soot, bringing
him back to the situation at hand. He had a lot of driving to

do, a mountain range to cross and a border crossing ahead of him.

"Good-bye, my friend," he said softly over the whining motor. "And good luck to you, Bijon . . ."

The SEAL team made almost forty knots in sixty feet of water. They approached the large container ship from the side and turned into the bow, slowing their speed to match that of their target. When they were in position, they slowly dropped their speed and allowed the ship to start passing them. CPO Cascaes waited until they dropped directly behind the ship, and then held his position. He had one of his men use the robot arm of their sub to hold twenty feet of ship's anchor chain they had brought just for this purpose. Even under water, the huge chain was heavy and cut their speed. Cascaes spoke to his man via headset, and the ensign used a camera located on the robot arm to see under the stern of the ship. There, beneath the stern, they could see the single huge screw of the ship. Using the robot arm, the ensign carefully brought up the end of the anchor chain until the whirring propeller ripped it out of the grasp of the mechanical arm and wound it into the prop. With an audible sound of metal on metal, the screw stopped spinning, and somewhere in the engine room of the old container ship, dials and gauges began signaling the crew that they had a major mechanical problem.

"That's it, Skipper!" said the ensign. "She is dead in the water."

"Roger that. Excellent work. Pull in the arm, out." CPO Cascaes killed his own engine, and began slowing down at about the same rate as the huge ship above them. "We are go! Prepare to assault!" he said to his crew, who immediately sprang to action.

Within seconds, the bottom hatch door locks were spinning and pulled open. The SEALs buddied up, and the two-man team that had oxygen tanks checked their air hoses, and then dropped out of the bottom of the ship. Cascaes turned command of the sub over to his second, and dropped out the bottom with his men. With one man on board, the other nine swam up the side of their own sub, holding small rungs that acted as a ladder to the surface. The two with SCUBA tanks had a different task. They would be transferring the explosives from their sub to the center of the ship's hull.

Once on top of their submarine, the nine SEALs attached a cable with an electromagnetic end to the ship to keep the ships tethered together. Using hand-held magnetic cups, the nine men climbed up the side of the old tub. It was a large, rusty vessel, and the climb was almost a hundred feet straight up. With weapons and night-vision gear on, the climb was difficult, but these were SEALs. In less than three minutes, they were topside. A few crewmen were standing outside of the bridge, screaming down to another group of men on the deck. They were yelling in Farsi, and were obviously furious that they had stopped moving. Something about transporting a nuclear weapon illegally aboard a ship that refused to move always made people nervous.

All of the SEALs were equipped with close-quarters automatic weapons, except for their one sniper. Still attached to the outside of the ship via magnetic suction cups, he assembled his weapon and scope and took aim at the top deck and the screaming man who appeared to be in charge. The SEAL sniper waited until his companions had silently stepped onto the deck of the ship and moved into cover. Four of them moved aft and four of them moved forward, including Cascaes. The sniper stayed where he was, using the ship's metal wall for cover. They were all equipped with throat mics, earphones and night-vision goggles or scopes. As soon as Cascaes whispered, "Take them down," all hell broke loose.

The sniper fired four shots in as many seconds, and dropped all four men on the bridge. He stayed where he was, scanning right and left for new targets. The four SEALs in the aft of the ship were running between huge stacks of multicolored containers, piled ten high and eight across. A spray of AK-47 machine-gun fire pinged all over the deck, ricocheting off the containers and sending the SEALs diving for cover. One of the SEALs called over to the sniper, advising him that they were under fire from the crane above the containers. A few seconds later, the sniper fired and the window of the crane exploded. A Hezbollah guerilla who had volunteered for the suicide mission fell a hundred feet to the metal deck below, dead long before he splattered on the deck.

The SEALs continued moving through the containers, stopping every few meters to check around corners. They were trained in urban warfare, and this wasn't much different than working a building. Two of them had small Geiger counters that they used to test each container as they passed by, but so far they only had background readings. The mother lode was still hidden in the mass of containers.

In the forward section of the ship, CPO Cascaes led his team quickly through the doorway to the bridge. They flipped up their night-vision equipment in the dim light of the entryway and moved quietly up metal stairs until they could hear screaming in Farsi, then stopped in firing positions. The sound of voices was followed by boots clanging on metal steps. The SEALs held their position until the Hezbollah fighters appeared above them running down the steps. In short, controlled bursts, the SEALs dropped four of them before they could get off a shot. The SEAL team sprinted up the steps until they got to the bridge. They stopped outside the door, and two of the SEALs threw in grenades. After the explosion, they jumped in and sprayed the room. Three men were dead inside, one of them apparently the ship's captain.

Cascaes spoke into his throat mic to the entire team. "Teams one and two are heading to the bow. Bridge is secure and ship is dead in the water. One and two will work from the bow to midship. Team three and four, keeping working to the stern. Any radiation readings yet?"

"Negative, Skipper. We have not located the package yet. Team three is belowdeck working aft. We are still working through the containers, over."

"Roger that, team four. We will work our way toward you and secure the container area. Once we have the package, we will call for dust-off and drop this tub, over and out."

Rifle fire continued outside as their sniper found more

targets. In the rear of the ship, the Hezbollah suicide bombers who were there to guard the bomb ran up from their quarters. There were ten of them, all armed with AK-47s. Team three was pinned down by the sheer volume of bullets being blindly sprayed at them in the dark, and they called for help. Team four was halfway up the stack of containers when the call came in, climbing through the containers with their Geiger counters to find the package.

The two SEALs of team four, both petty officers second class—the equivalent of sergeants—were experienced fighters. They never split their team in combat, but now they had a problem. They had to find the package, and they had to reinforce team three. PO2 Hernandez called over to PO2 Wilson, "You stay and find the bomb, man. I'll go back up team four. Sparky, you on channel?"

The sniper, nicknamed Sparky by his shipmates, who joked that he could light a match from a mile out, answered back. "Roger, three. I am holding current position amidships."

"We need you back here, man. Team three is pinned and I am going to assist. Top deck is clear. Hustle back here, man!" With that Hernandez started climbing down the sides of the containers as fast as he could. He jumped the last eight feet and ran back toward the continuous spray of AK-47 gunfire.

Sparky climbed over the rail and sprinted toward the stern of the ship. Two decks below him, Cascaes and his three men worked back toward the stern as well. When they got to the engine room, they found half a dozen terrified crewmen being guarded by one fanatic, whom they dispatched quickly and without incident. They left the crewmen on their own to find a lifeboat or go swimming, and continued aft.

PO2 Hernandez worked his way back toward the rear entryway. The two SEALs of team four were back-to-back between two containers and were outflanked by a group of Arabs who were screaming and firing magazine after magazine at them. Hernandez worked his way quietly around the outside rail until he could see four of them, hidden behind some steel drums, taking turns shooting at the SEALs. Hernandez pulled the pin of a grenade, waited two seconds and rolled it across the deck toward them. With the noise of gunfire, it wasn't heard rolling across the deck, and when it exploded, it sent the four men and the drums flying. The two trapped SEALs used the explosion to cover their movement and ran from their location to a better position behind a ventilation housing.

AK-47 fire again opened up, this time from the other side of the aft deck. The two SEALs crawled toward it, while Hernandez again worked to flank around behind them. Sparky had climbed the containers to the ladder of the overhead crane, and worked his way up the huge ladder to the small platform. He crawled out and looked down on the aft deck, where he could see two men trying to work behind Hernandez. He called to Hernandez on his mic as he fired the first shot, dropping one of the men. The second one opened fire and hit Hernandez in both legs, dropping him screaming to the deck. Sparky got off a second shot but missed, and the target disappeared behind another container.

The two SEALs in team three heard Hernandez scream and worked toward him as fast as they could. They arrived at his location at the same time as the man who had shot him the first time. The Hezbollah terrorist stood up to finish the job when both SEALs of team three fired bursts into him, exploding his chest. They ran forward to Hernandez and one slapped pressure bandages on his legs while the other covered them.

From above, Sparky spoke to team three. "You still have movement behind you and I have no shot yet."

He was interrupted by lights coming on all over the ship. Temporarily blinded, the SEALs ripped off their night-vision goggles and hugged the deck. Steady gunfire rained over the three SEALs, with ricochets bouncing all over the deck and containers. The SEAL who had put the pressure bandages on Hernandez flopped on top of him and used his body to shield his fallen friend. Sparky put his eye back in the scope and scanned the deck as fast as he could, locating the source of the gunfire from a small shedlike building where the Iranians had taken shelter after flipping on the light switch.

Sparky fired and hit the first target, sending the second one prone inside the building. He called back down to team three. "Three! One target down, one inside the shed. I will keep him down in there, but you need to take him out!"

Seaman White grabbed his teammate, Seaman Jones, and screamed in his face for him to stay with Hernandez. White scrambled across the deck, between containers and steel drums, working his way toward the shed. Every time the man inside the shed tried to move, Sparky fired a round of suppressing fire at the shed door or window. White timed the shots with his own movements, crawling and scrambling closer with each shot. He moved into position to get a clear shot at the shed, when the man inside rushed out directly at him, screaming *"Allah Akbar!"* and firing his AK-47 wildly all over the deck. One bullet caught White directly on his own weapon, rendering it useless. White dropped and rolled, throwing off his weapon and pulling his Ka-Bar knife out of its shoulder holster. The Hezbollah terrorist continued spraying in his direction until he clicked empty, and White used that split second to rush him. He tackled him like a linebacker and brought the knife up into the Iranian's kidney as hard as he could, then pulled the knife up the man's back with as much force as he could muster. He pulled the knife out and thrust it into him three more times on sheer adrenaline until he realized the man was very dead.

White rolled off of him and crawled into the shed, but the one man left in there was dead from Sparky's earlier bullet. White's headset came on at the sound of Sparky's voice. "Hey, three, you okay down there?"

White spoke back quietly, feeling somewhat naked with only a bloody knife. "I'm okay, target down. Jones, you copy?"

Jones voice came back, sounding quiet and shaky. "I'm here, Hernandez didn't make it . . ." His voice trailed off.

"Sit tight, I am on my way. Cover me, Sparky." White sprinted across the deck, grabbing the AK-47 and two magazines the dead man had in his waistband, then hustled back to Jones and Hernandez. When he got there, Jones was cradling Hernandez in his arms, sitting in a pool of his blood.

"I couldn't stop all the bleeding, man. I'm sorry." He was crying.

White knelt beside them and took Hernandez away from Jones and laid him on the deck. "We'll come back for him, man. Keep your shit together. There may be more rag heads on this tub, and we still have to find the bomb."

White put down the AK-47 and took Hernandez's weapon and ammo. "Come on, man, we gotta bounce." He grabbed Jones and pulled him to his feet, baby-slapped his face, and jogged off through the containers back toward the other half of team four, Ensign Taylor.

"Taylor, you copy?" asked White.

"Roger," came the reply.

"What's your twenty?"

"Third row of containers, on the top. I am definitely getting warmer. I have readings starting to show up. Look for the bright orange containers in the center of the row. I'm on top of them working forward."

Sparky's voice chimed in. "Four, I have visual. I am over your head, watching your back."

White and Jones quickly worked their way through the containers, the sunrise just starting over the Iranian coastline in the distance. Cascaes's voice popped into their headsets. "Team one and two are topside aft, working our way through your mess. Looks like you had company—everybody okay?"

White grimaced at having to say it out loud, "Negative, Skipper. Hernandez is KIA. I am with Jones, working back to Taylor. Sparky is in the crow's nest."

Cascaes voice was slow and steady. "Copy that, we are moving up your six. Keep your eyes peeled. There is no movement right now, but I am not sure if the ship is clear. There are a few crewmen belowdeck that may head up for lifeboats. If they are unarmed, don't fire on them."

"Roger that, Skipper. We are climbing up the containers."

By the time Jones and White were on top of the containers with Taylor, Taylor was sure he had found the right container. It was padlocked like the rest of them, but each team had a set of bolt cutters between them just for that purpose.

"This is it," Taylor said. "This is the hottest spot on the ship, and it's on top of the stack to be taken off first. Do we open it?"

Cascaes voice came back, "Negative! Secure the area and wait for us. I am contacting fleet." He grabbed his radio and called the *Kitty Hawk*. The bridge transferred his radio call to the deck, where Captain Bennett was watching the beleaguered Stalker land. A sailor ran to the captain with a radio as he stood on the flight deck.

"Sorry, sir, but the bridge says it is urgent," said the sailor as he handed the captain the radio.

"Captain Bennett here, come in," he barked.

"Captain, Cascaes here. We have the package, but it is inside a container. Should we open it?"

"Wait one, over," said the captain as he watched the Stalker unloading its four passengers. He jogged over to Diane Peters, who looked fairly shaken up from the interesting chopper ride.

"Hey, Doc! Our SEALs have the bomb in a container. Now what? Do we pull it as is, or open the container and take a look-see? What if they have the damn thing booby trapped?"

Dr. Peters scowled. "Sir, obviously we have never done this before outside of practice drills, but I don't think they would booby trap the doors. And even if they did, it wouldn't set off an atomic explosion. That can only be done with the main trigger device. Jesus . . ."

"What is it?"

"What if opening the door is how they start the sequence for the main device? We don't know what these lunatics have done. Oh, Christ."

"Well that's just great, Doc. There is no way in hell I am bringing that thing aboard one of my ships until we know it is secure."

"I need to go back," she said.

"What?" asked the captain. "Go back for what?"

"Your men need to open the door when I get there and see what we have. If the device can be made safe, I'll do it aboard the ship, and then you can transport it off of there by heavy helicopter."

Master Chief Parker was standing next to the captain. "Captain, we can take a Sea Dragon back to the ship and let it circle until we get the nuke turned off, then lift it back here. I'll go back with her."

Captain Bennett's radio squawked again. "*Kitty Hawk*, this is team one leader, do you copy?" It was Cascaes again, sounding a little antsy.

"Yeah, I copy. We are sending back a NEST team with the master chief to take a look. Sit tight and do not do anything until we get there." The sound of AK-47 gunfire in the background was loud over the radio.

"We are still taking fire, this is a hot LZ! Do you copy?"

"We copy. Sit tight and secure that area! Team is en route!"

Bennett turned to his master chief, red-faced with anger, "Master Chief, there are still rag heads with a live nuke on that damn boat. Take a platoon of Marines with you and the good doctor and secure that fucking package on the double!"

The master chief hurried a salute and ran off across the deck, screaming into his radio. By the time he was at the MH-53E Sea Dragon, a platoon of thirty Marines in full combat gear was hustling out to meet him. They were the same men that had been mustered earlier, but had never been dismissed pending the outcome of the operation. The master chief, Diane Peters and David Tompkins jumped into the helicopter first, followed by the Marines. The pilots had been on alert all day and were instantly ready to go.

As the helicopter slowly lifted off the deck, the master chief stood in the rear hold area and addressed the major and his platoon.

"Marines! We are landing aboard an Iranian cargo ship that is transporting an atomic bomb. There are enemy fighters aboard that ship, along with a SEAL team. We are to secure the ship and let the nuke doctors over here figure out how to disarm this weapon. Your mission is simple: Anything that moves that is not a U.S. Navy SEAL in battle dress uniform—or is not currently aboard this vessel—is meat, understood? You kill everything that moves!"

That was followed by thirty gung-ho *oooo-raahs* as the Marines slapped magazines into their weapons. The chopper sped out over the water, the beautiful red sunrise slowly starting in the east. Diane looked at the red fireball and prayed it was the only one that would be seen that day.

CHAPTER 43

D-Day, Sunrise

The MH-53E Sea Dragon was flying at a maximum speed of 150 knots toward the cargo ship, now visible in the distance. The master chief started grinning very uncharacteristically. Diane looked at him and shrugged.

"Hey, Doc, you ever jump off a moving helicopter?" he asked with a smile.

"Excuse me?" she said with very large eyes.

"Yeah, well, Doc, we ain't exactly at Dulles Airport. We may be taking fire when we try to land. We will hover above the containers and the pilot will stay as steady as he can, but we will be jumping off of this bird, under fire most likely. I just want you to prepare yourself mentally." He still had a grin on his face. He pulled out what looked like a large lipstick tube and smeared black grease paint all over his face, and then handed it to her. "I hate to see your pretty face get all dirty, but you might want to attract a little less attention to yourself. Give it to your buddy when you are finished."

She followed his example, and blackened her face like the master chief and the Marines aboard the helicopter. She hoped the black grease paint would hide how white her face had gotten at the thought of jumping off the rear ramp of the chopper. She finished and handed it to Tompkins, who looked equally thrilled to be jumping off the helicopter to disarm an atomic bomb. He smiled as best he could and leaned toward Diane. "Just like we practiced it—except for the part about being shot at."

A loudspeaker squawked and the pilot's voice announced that the ship was in sight and they were to prepare for assault. The rear ramp began to open, and the Marines began barking at each other and pounding each other's backs as they got their adrenaline rushing in anticipation of combat. With the ramp now fully lowered, the helicopter began slowly coming around in a circle as the pilot tried to maintain a complete stop while hovering about three feet above the containers. The containers were about six feet across, with a very far drop down to the deck below if you missed your landing. The swaying of the ship in the current and of the helicopter in the wind didn't make it any easier. The major leading the platoon was the first up and at the ramp.

He turned back to his men as he flipped his safety off, then yelled, "Okay Marines! This is what you get paid for! Watch for friendlies and make sure you pay attention to your landing! If you miss the container, you are dead! Now let's go get some!" With that, he took a slow jog to the end of the ramp and jumped down to the orange container below. The Marines followed him out, landing on the container and moving across the tops of the others, fanning out and making room for the next Marine to jump down. It was only about a three-foot jump, but with all of their gear on, holding a weapon above a swaying ship, it was horrifying enough. The master chief was last, behind the two doctors. He held their arms as they jogged toward the ramp.

"Just keep your eyes on the top of the container that you are landing on! Do not look anywhere else! Now jump!"

Dr. Tompkins jumped first and rolled when he landed, but a Marine grabbed his arm and kept him from rolling off to his death. Diane landed next, on her feet, without a problem. The master chief dropped their gear down to a waiting Marine, and then hopped down himself. As his feet hit the container, AK-47 fire erupted again, and was answered by thirty Marines. The master chief crawled over to Diane and Dave and used his body to shield them from the fire. He was screaming to them over the hundreds of outgoing rounds to keep down flat and not move until he told them.

The Marines kept returning fire until the major yelled to hold fire, and then the thirty men started scrambling down the containers and spread out all over the ship. There was occasional gunfire as the Marines mopped up whatever was left of the Hezbollah fighters, but the Marines made short work of them. When the ship went quiet, the master chief called to the chopper by radio. It came back around to the container and dropped a heavy winch, which was attached to the four corners of the container by Master Chief Parker and another Marine. The Sea Dragon slowly lifted the container and drifted toward midship where there was open deck, and then lowered it to the deck with the master chief, the two doctors and a lance corporal still on top of the container.

As soon as the container was on the deck, the master chief and lance corporal cleared the winch and the helicopter flew off to circle around and wait. Two Marines ran to the front of the container while the four people on top shimmied down the side. The master chief had Diane and Dave start taking out their equipment while he ordered a sergeant from the engineers to cut off the lock. The sergeant snapped off the heavy padlock and pulled it free. He and another Marine pulled the doors open slowly, looking for wires or detonation devices. As they slowly opened the doors, a Hezbollah fighter who had volunteered to guard the bomb with his life kicked the door open and continuously fired his AK-47 at everyone he could. The sergeant and PFC next to him were killed instantly, along with another Marine who was standing behind them. The rest of the Marines, even though they were taken by complete surprise, reacted instinctively and returned fire. The man inside was by himself, and was shot to pieces. Marines swarmed forward to grab their fallen comrades and check the inside of the container. Diane screamed at them as they entered.

"No one touch anything!" she yelled as she ran after them. They all froze, except those that were pulling the injured Marines away from the container to see if they could be saved. Diane had them all back out slowly, and she walked in herself, followed by Dr. Tompkins. The inside of the metal container was lined with a heavy wooden frame, and in the center of it was the large black metal bomb, held securely in place by the multiple latticework of beams. On the floor, also bolted to a beam, was a laptop computer with the screen showing a firing sequence and a clock. The large numbers on the screen were running backward from a little over a hundred minutes. Apparently, the bomb had a preset of two hours from activation, and the Hezbollah fighter inside had hit the arming sequence when the gunfire started.

She called the master chief over and pointed to the screen of the laptop.

"That can't be good," he said quietly.

"Sir, I would tell you to clear the ship, but quite frankly, unless you have enough planes to evacuate the entire fleet in less than an hour at supersonic speed, it won't really matter. We either manage to turn this thing off, or it's going to be uncomfortable around here for a spilt second or two."

"Don't bullshit me, Doc. Can you and your buddy turn this thing off or not?"

"I guess we're going to find out," she said, half to herself. "Dave! Bring our tools in here."

The master chief grabbed the major and had him set up a secure perimeter around the container, while the SEALs and half the Marines started at the bow and went through the ship room by room, deck by deck, to make sure there were no more terrorists aboard. A Navy corpsman had put Hernandez in a body bag, and a few Marines helped move him midship with the dead Marines, who would be removed when everyone else dusted off, assuming there was no mushroom cloud. Diane and Dave sat on the deck looking at the device, having a conversation about what kind of detonation system it had, whether or not they could simply unplug the computer without instantly triggering the bomb, how many rads they would absorb if they opened the nose to get inside, et cetera. The master chief listened for five minutes, then had to walk away.

He walked to the rail and called the captain on a direct radio. The captain answered quickly, and Parker just barked at him, "We are seriously fucked here, Captain."

"Talk to me, Master Chief," said Bennett.

"Sir, I am thinking that you and every pilot and person that will fit on a plane should get aboard something and get your ass out of this area. At least you can save the aircraft and some of the crew. I think the whole fleet is gonna get cooked."

"Hold on there, Master Chief, what exactly is your situation? Did the nuke docs take a look at the bomb?"

"Yeah, they're sitting there having tea and crumpets and discussing the next Nobel Prize in physics and shit while the clock timer is telling me I have less than an hour and a half to make peace with the Almighty."

"Jesus Christ. They don't think they can disarm it?"

"They ain't saying shit to me. They're talking brainiac shit, and in the meantime, the counter is whizzing by. What if we scuttle the ship and let it detonate under water? It might save the fleet. Or, fuck it, teach me to fly a chopper and I'll pick up the damn thing and drop it back in Iran. Just give me a fighter escort."

"You aren't dropping it in Iran, Parker. Sinking the ship may be the only option though, to minimize damage. I need to speak to the doctor."

Master Chief Parker walked back over to the Diane, who was now working with Dave to unscrew the front nose section of the bomb. "Hey, Doc, it's the Skipper. He needs to talk to you."

"I'm a little busy!" she snapped at him.

"Look, lady, the captain of the largest fleet in the world needs a moment of your time to make some serious fucking decisions. Now take the damn phone!"

She grabbed the phone from Parker and said, "Doctor Peters here, we are opening the nose cone assembly to see if we can disarm this thing. Do you really need me right now?"

"As a matter of fact, I do. Take a deep breath, Doc. I have

over ten thousand of my sailors, marines and airmen inside the kill zone of your little bomb, plus a few million civilians in the general vicinity. I need some probabilities and statistics here. If we sink the ship, it's in three hundred feet of water. How much will that shield the explosion? Can it save the fleet?"

"I don't think so, sir. We don't know how powerful this thing is yet. My guess is, it's fairly primitive, and maybe only as strong as a couple of Hiroshima-sized nukes. But even that would take out your fleet, sunk or not. You're just too close. Now, with all due respect, sir, can I get back to work?"

"Can you turn it off, Doc? Yes or no. I need something to go on."

"Sir, I have no fucking idea." With that, she handed the phone to Master Chief Parker.

He spoke into the handset. "You still here, Skipper?"

"Yeah, I'm here."

"Remember that cigar you gave me? Well, I'm gonna smoke it now and watch the sun rise. Gonna enjoy every last puff of this fucking thing. Maybe you got another one over there for yourself."

"Roger that, Master Chief. Keep the phone with you. Hey, how did the SEALs do?"

"One KIA—Hernandez. They did real good, Skipper. Took down almost the whole boat. The Marines did the rest when they got here, but there were three KIA, two wounded. There was a rag head hiding in the crate with the bomb. Caught us off-guard. My fault, Skipper. I should have thought of that."

"Smoke your cigar, Parker. And keep your fingers crossed. I'll check back."

CHAPTER 44

Tehran

The cameras and microphones were on, and the crowd was huge. News had already made it across town that Ali bin-Oman had been assassinated, along with many of Azed's followers. The crowd continued to build as the news was already showing central Tehran and shots of Grand Ayatollah Kamala. There was all kinds of speculation about how he had survived, but Kamala had been smart enough to enlist the help of the police and a few soldiers by making them feel important. They guarded him like he was the new president, adding to his perceived importance.

The sun was up now. Grand Ayatollah Kamala looked out at the new dawn and smiled. He hadn't felt so at peace since he was a child. He flashed to his loving parents, murdered by Islamic extremists that looked and sounded just like the fictional Grand Ayatollah Kamala—the old one. The new one was about to speak.

He approached the podium that had been set up for his speech. Loudspeakers had been brought in by the press, who would be recording his speech and transmitting it all over the Arab world. One of the imam's newfound supporters from the apartment complex had been chosen to introduce the famed cleric. He tapped the microphone and called for everyone's attention.

"God is great!" he cried, to resounding responses of the same from the huge crowd, now waving banners with Kamala's picture on them. "God has saved our Grand Ayatollah Kamala from destruction—blessed be his name! The Grand Ayatollah has had a vision—he has seen the way to a new Iran! Welcome him! Welcome him back from the dust and destruction. Grand Ayatollah Kamala will speak to you now!"

As the imam walked to the podium, the cheering from the crowd grew louder. For many Iranians gathered in the streets, this imam was the only thing keeping the country from falling into total anarchy and chaos. They had seen what had happened in Iraq as the war ended, and feared looting and rioting of their own. With Grand Ayatollah Kamala emerging as a new leader, there was the hope for maintaining order. As the imam held up his hands and asked for quiet, the crowd slowly calmed, until all was still and quiet. Hundreds of thousands of Iranians all over the country waited for news or direction from this man, now the apparent successor to their fallen leadership.

The Grand Ayatollah began.

"Allah Akbar! Allah Akbar! Allah Akbar!" For each of these shouts of "God is great," the crowd responded. Then the imam added, *"A salaam aleikum . . ."* and the crowd quieted down again. The imam, used to speaking to large crowds and being the center of attention, waited just long enough before speaking, allowing the silence to add to the drama. "It is the dawn of a new day, my brothers and sisters. Children of Islam, I have been given a vision from the Prophet Mohammed, blessed be his name, that I share with you today."

The crowd began cheering again, but the Imam cut them off and demanded quiet.

"That message was brought forth in a thunderclap and flash of white light. My mosque lies in dust as proof of what I have been shown. The Almighty has worked miracles before, throughout the ages, and is working one now. You are all witnesses to a miracle.

"I had a vision a few days ago. I was commanded by Allah the Merciful to call upon the president and our leaders, both political and religious, and to bring them here to my mosque. Never before in my life have I heard the voice of Allah come to me directly as it did that day."

The crowd hung on his every word. Many of them dropped to their knees as if praying to the imam.

"I was commanded to bring this gathering of Iranian power to my mosque, and so I did. And in a flash of white light and screaming of Allah's voice like thunderclaps, my mosque disappeared all around me, taking our leaders with it. Allah the Merciful wrapped me in his protective arms, picked me up from the destruction, and placed me back upon the earth away from the fire and death, and gave me instructions and a warning."

Cameras clicked photographs of the imam, but that was the only sound other than his voice.

"I have been shown a new path for our country. I am to take us on a journey that will bring Iran back as one of the great nations of the world, God willing. The old ways of Iran are over, removed from our soil by the will of God. It is a new day—a new age—a new history in the making. So much of what you have all been taught as the truth, so much of what we have all believed—it was all lies!"

Thousands of Iranians inhaling deeply at the same time in horror and disbelief made an ominous sound, like a ghost breathing.

"That's right—*lies*! Somehow, we have strayed from the Prophet's path and been told great lies. Lies that politicians and holy men have used to manipulate you, the true believers. It is outrageous and destructive and has been ended once and for all with the removal of liars and cheats from our midst! Nowhere in the Koran does it say that we must kill every human who does not follow the ways of Allah or his prophet Mohammed. Nowhere does it say that it is honorable to turn our children into walking bombs to kill the children of nonbelievers. Nowhere does it say that we should live in war and poverty and hate and violence—and yet look at the world in which the true believers are forced to live! Why is it that the Jews have turned worthless desert into vast farmlands and have grown industry, and yet our Arab brothers cannot? Why is it that the Jews in the world, such a small number of people, can have such a huge impact on in science, medicine, learning and business, and our Arab brothers on the West Bank and Gaza cannot feed themselves?"

A few people in the crowd screamed, "Death to the Jews!" and were silenced by the imam.

"*No! That* is the lie! *That* was my message from Allah, himself, blessed be His name! The Jews, the Christians, the nonbelievers, they are blamed for all of our problems—and it is *wrong*!"

The crowd was loud and screaming all kinds of protests to this outrageous commentary. The imam raised his hands and called for silence.

"We have killed each other for two thousand years! For *what*? A piece of desert that we do not want? Mecca is our holy place, not Jerusalem! The Jews and Christians are not our concern. Our own people are our concern, and yet we blame everyone except those that lead us and are responsible for helping our own people! The time to blame others is *over*! It is time for Iran to educate its people—all of them, including our women! It is time for the people to elect leaders who will govern responsibly and help rebuild our nation! Why do we spend millions to build an atomic bomb when we cannot feed our own children? It is nobody's fault but ours, and it is time we took responsibility!

"Hezbollah and Hamas tell you they are your heroes. They tell you to give them your children to become martyrs, to ensure generation after generation of hate and violence. Why? For what purpose? Their only purpose is to serve themselves. They do not serve God and they do not serve you!"

That was the last straw for many of the onlookers in the crowd, some of whom were Hezbollah themselves and had always looked up to the Grand Ayatollah Kamala as one of their great leaders. Pushing and screaming began in the crowd, but the imam continued, shouting over the noise.

"You see? They hear words they don't like and their answer is instant violence! They don't want peace, they don't want to help you, and they don't care about Iran! All they want is another two thousand years of death and destruction! It is *over*! Allah the Merciful has seen enough blood, and, God willing, we will build a new Iran that will be respected in the world. We can be a great nation, and I will lead you there with God's help! Who will help me build a new Iran for our children?"

The number of people cheering for the imam drowned out those who screamed in protest. The general near the imam was getting nervous. The crowd could turn at any moment, and he wasn't sure he liked what he heard coming out of the imam's mouth. As if reading his mind, the Grand Ayatollah took the general by the arm and pulled him closer.

"Iran is strong nation. We have fearless soldiers and brave citizens. We can work together! We will protect our country from outside forces, and we will protect our country from internal violence as well. General—will the Army keep the people of Tehran safe and help us rebuild?"

The general, stunned and on the spot, but realizing the potential to become a very important person in the next few seconds, leapt at the opportunity.

"Grand Ayatollah Kamala, citizens of Iran—you will be safe! There will be no looting, there will be no more violence. The Army of Iran will maintain order!"

The imam stepped back to the podium, still holding the arm of the general.

"We will not be a country of lawlessness! There will be *order*! There will be *elections*, and there will be a new government in Iran. A government that will serve its people and help them to help themselves."

The huge ovation that followed was deafening.

Al Jazeera reporters who had been hanging on every word began shouting questions, asking who was responsible for the bomb blast that destroyed the imam's mosque and killed most of the government leadership, who killed Ali bin-Oman, and who was in charge of the government now. The imam was brief in his answers.

"Article sixty-four of our Constitution states that there are to be at least two hundred and seventy members of the Islamic Consultative Assembly. Almost two hundred died yesterday. The president is dead, Grand Ayatollah Azed is dead. There needs to be immediate plans for new elections—perhaps even for changes to our Constitution! The people of Iran have voices that deserve to be heard."

Another reporter held a microphone to the imam and shouted his question. "Grand Ayatollah, who will claim responsibility for the assassinations and destruction of your mosque?"

"It was God's will. It doesn't matter who claims responsibility! We have an opportunity to rebuild our nation, and we mustn't lose this chance!"

"And will you seek to replace Grand Ayatollah Azed as Grand Cleric to the new president?"

"No, I will not," said the Imam. "I will seek to replace President Mowad Asmunjaniwal, and lead our nation into the future, God willing!"

With that, he turned and walked away into the crowd, surrounded by soldiers and police, ignoring the dozens of questions being fired at him simultaneously following his bombshell announcement that he would seek the presidency.

CHAPTER 45

FOP Iron Mountain, Hours Earlier

Jerry woke up Chris Mackey, who had crashed for almost five hours on a small cot. Mackey woke up disoriented and groggy and looked at his watch.

"Holy crap, I really crashed out, huh?"

"Yeah, well I hope it felt good, because you have about ten minutes to shit, shave and catch your helicopter."

"Where am I going now?"

"You are off to the *Kitty Hawk*. The NEST team found the bomb, thank God. You are being flown to Camp Eagle where an F-14 is going to supersonic your ass over to the *Kitty Hawk*. Once you get there, you'll get new orders about what to do with your package, assuming it hasn't blown up already."

"Gee, thanks," said Mackey as he stood and stretched. "Where is everybody?"

"The boys headed out a few hours ago with a ranger platoon to see if they can pick up Mike at the border. He should be showing up in the next few days. While you were sleeping, the shit was hitting the fan across the border."

Mackey pulled on clothes and grabbed his mess kit. He used the electric razor while Jerry briefed him.

"Grand Ayatollah Kamala has been organizing a huge crowd and may be the current favorite to replace the dead president. Ali bin-Oman was assassinated a few hours ago as well."

That got a look from Mackey. Jerry smiled and shrugged his shoulders.

"Accidents happen. The SEALs took over the boat with the nuke. That's the latest I have on that. They will transport the nuke to the *Kitty Hawk* I suppose, where you will fly it out of here. I have no idea where you're going with it. That's all I have. Be outside in five minutes with your gear. I hate long good-byes, anyway." He smacked Mackey on the shoulder and walked out.

Mackey was transported from Iron Mountain to Camp Eagle in forty-five minutes, where, as promised, an F-14 Tomcat sat waiting for him. Mackey climbed in the second seat after being suited up in his flight suit to prevent passing out at supersonic speed. Although an excellent pilot himself, Mackey had never flown in an F-14, and was actually excited to get a supersonic ride to the carrier. Traveling at over Mach one, they covered the twelve hundred miles and were on board the carrier *Kitty Hawk* in less than two hours. They landed with the usual bounce and yank of arresting cables grabbing a rocket-propelled aircraft.

Mackey thanked the pilot for the lift and climbed down onto the hot deck of the *Kitty Hawk*, where he was immediately greeted by an excited lieutenant commander, who rushed him up into the island's control tower. Mackey jogged after the sailor, sweaty in his orange flight suit. The lieutenant commander entered the busy bridge and introduced Chris Mackey to the commander of the battle group, the *Kitty Hawk*'s Captain Bennett.

Bennett dismissed the lieutenant commander and pulled Mackey aside to a quieter corner of the bridge.

"I understand that we have never met and you don't exist on any military payroll," grumbled the captain.

"Something like that, sir. I am just here to take a package from point A to point B. I have no further instructions."

"Yeah, well, if it were up to me, you wouldn't be here at all. You being here may just be adding one more casualty to this fleet. They tell you anything about what's going on out here?"

"Just that the SEALs took over the ship and I am here to move the package," said Mackey.

"Yeah, well somebody left out some minor fucking details, like you may have just been invited to the world's largest barbeque. You stay on my ass until I tell you otherwise. We're a little busy right now. The NEST team has two people on that rag head tub trying to disassemble the nuke, which is operational, armed and counting down to the big barbeque."

"Counting down, as in ready to detonate?"

"That is *affirmative*. Apparently, one of the little fuckers was hiding inside the container with the thing, and when he heard our guys getting close, he hit the trigger. It had two or three hours on it I guess. We are at about forty-something minutes right now, so our time together may be very short."

Mackey felt the blood drain from his face as he mentally tried to catch up to what the captain was saying to him.

An ensign double-timed over to the captain. "Sir, we have the White House on the phone. It's the commander in chief, sir."

The captain walked briskly to his phone on the bridge, Mackey tagging along behind him.

"Mr. President, this is Captain Bennett, USS *Kitty Hawk*."

The president of the United States was surrounded by the Joint Chiefs of Staff in the situation room. It was almost eleven P.M. back in the States, nine hours earlier than in the Strait of Hormuz.

"Captain, I want you to know that we are praying for you and all of our men and women in the fleet over there. What is the current situation?"

"The NEST team is working as fast as they can, Mr. President. My master chief is aboard the ship with them and he has been in radio contact with me every ten minutes or so, but it has been slow going. We had discussed sinking the ship now to minimize the radiation, but the ship is only in three hundred feet of water, and the NEST doc tells me it won't make much difference for a warhead this size. I have had the SEALs set the mines aboard the ship's hull anyway. When we get within five minutes of the detonation, we will sink her, sir. I will give that order myself, with all of my men aboard her. I am not a nuclear expert, but I have to think that the detonation at the bottom of the ocean will offer some protection to the rest of my fleet. Shall I order all aircraft to Saudi Arabia, Mr. President? We could at least save the aircraft, our pilots, and some of our personnel."

The phone was silent for a moment, as the president consulted with his joint chiefs. "Captain, we have to hope for the best, but prepare for the worst. I believe it would be prudent to evacuate all aircraft, with as many crewmen as possible. I'm sorry there isn't a way to get you all out of there," he said, his voice trailing off.

"Yes, sir. Thank you, sir. I will give the order to send out all aircraft. Sailors and Marines with families will be given priority for any room aboard the aircraft. I will, of course, be staying with my ship, sir."

There was silence for a second, and then the president's voice. "I understand, Captain. Do the best you can. That's all we can ask. Godspeed, Captain."

"Thank you, sir. My apologies for losing the fleet, sir. It will be the greatest disaster in U.S. Naval history."

"It isn't your fault, Captain. Go attend to your aircraft. We will be here watching and praying for you."

The captain lit his cigar, something he rarely did inside the bridge, and called his XO. "Sawyer! Put our nose into the wind and execute Desert Run. Sound assembly on the deck."

The night before, the officers had put a backup plan—Desert Run—in place to evacuate the ship's eighty aircraft. With five thousand sailors, marines and airmen aboard, less than twenty percent could be flown off the *Kitty Hawk*. The other ships in the fleet had a few helicopters, but no fixed-wing aircraft, and very few of their crew could be flown out. The XO and a ranking NCO had gone over a list of personnel, and pulled a thousand names of crew and air wing that had spouses and children. It wasn't anywhere near all of them, but it was the best they could do. Those personnel to be evacuated hadn't been told much, just that they were to assemble on deck if the order came. They had each been given an orange sheet with their name on it.

As the ship's announcement system called for all pilots to assemble, another order came announcing that any person with an orange sheet was to assemble on deck immediately. As those personnel double-timed it to the deck, they had no idea they had been given a ticket out of an impending mushroom cloud.

Mackey had heard every word and caught up to the situation. "Excuse me, sir. I have an idea."

"Make it fast," barked the captain as he watched the aircraft being rolled into position as the deck area sprang to life.

"I can fly helos and fixed wing. I can take a heavy helo and pick up the package, and fly as far away from the fleet as possible. In forty minutes, I could probably get far enough away to give you a fighting chance. Give me a fighter escort and I'll take the fucking bomb back to Iran."

The captain was laughing out loud.

"Excuse me, sir, I didn't think it was funny."

"I am laughing because I already had this conversation, almost verbatim. I appreciate your balls. There isn't time, however." He picked up his radio and called back over to Master Chief Parker.

"Master Chief, you copy?"

"Hey, Skipper. I am smoking a very fine cigar, thank you, while I watch these two psychos playing with a five-megaton warhead. The computer shows forty-two minutes until my cigar gets ruined. The only good news I can tell you is that the Marines and SEALs got to kill all the rag heads before the nuke does."

"You seem to be in fine spirits, Parker."

"Yes, sir, Captain. I should have brought a bottle of rum with me, however. These fucking Moslems don't drink. I looked everywhere—not one damn bottle of booze anywhere on this rust bucket."

"I have started evacuating all the aircraft. We may get as many as a thousand of our people off."

The master chief sighed heavily, and lost his jocular attitude. "That's good news, Captain. At least we can save some of them. It's not looking that great over here, John."

It was maybe the third time the master chief had used the captain's first name in as many years.

"Okay, Grant. Stay in touch, over."

"I hope not," said Master Chief Parker as he heard the word "over."

Diane and Dave had opened the nose cone of the bomb, exposing the computer boards and wires that surrounded the nuclear weapon.

Master Chief Parker walked up behind them. He thought about yelling *boom*, and then decided against it.

"How's it going, Doc?"

"I don't know. We are inside, but there are so many possibilities. This is a primitive device, but has a damn big warhead. We figure three to five megatons."

"So why not just cut the damn wires and call it a day?" asked Parker.

"Believe it or not, we had discussed that. If we cut the leads from the laptop to the device, it might just shut the whole thing down. On the other hand, it could set it off."

"That's great, Doc. Any other ideas, or should I flip a coin?"

"Yes, actually, we have started taking apart the primary explosive devices. If we can get enough of them off the warhead, we can sink it before it explodes."

"I thought you said sinking it won't help because the bomb was too big?"

"I said a nuclear detonation in three hundred feet of water would still hit the fleet. If we can disarm enough of the primary device, it will explode, but not with enough symmetrical force to cause the chain reaction for an atomic energy release. Now, with all due respect, I need to work."

"Anything I can do to help?"

"Yeah, get that nasty cigar away from me. I am getting enough radiation from this piece of shit, I don't need any more help getting cancer."

"Tell ya what, Doc. If you keep us all from getting blown to hell, maybe I'll quit."

The master chief puffed his cigar and looked out at his men with pride. He was surrounded by the best of the best with the SEALs and Marines, and it was a beautiful sunny morning. If it was to be his last, at least it was at sea with his warriors.

CHAPTER 46

Iran-Iraq Border

Duce, Tee and Still were embedded with the platoon of rangers that had been living on Iron Mountain for over six months. They had six of the best snipers in the Army with them, and the rangers knew the mountain passes like the back of their hands. They made the arduous journey in good time. Only Still had a hard time keeping up, but he was almost twice the age of the rest of the men. Once they were at the rendezvous point, they set up a small camp on the Iraqi side of the border and took shifts being on guard and monitoring the radios. When they had set up and had their first real break of the day, Still, Tee and Duce sat together and drank some coffee.

"Is this where you came back across?" Still asked Duce.

"No," he answered quietly, still picturing his friends covered with blood. "We were farther south. It was more wide open. I guess the boss figured we'd get lost trying to cross over here."

Tee looked around at the mountains and cliffs that surrounded them. "Yeah, probably a good move. If the rangers left me out here, you would never see my ass again."

"I hear ya, man," said Still. "And that fucking walk just

about killed me. I couldn't bitch out loud near those poor sons of bitches carrying eighty-pound packs, but Jesus Christ, I'm whooped. When I get back home, I am driving *everywhere*—I mean, like, from the kitchen to the bathroom, know what I'm sayin'? My walking days are done!"

Tee and Duce chuckled. They felt it in their legs as well, but sure weren't going to admit it to Still.

Tee asked Still, "You think he'll make it out? All hell is breaking loose over the border."

"Yeah, he'll make it out. He's a crafty sumbitch, and he's lived in that shithole this long without being caught, I'm sure he'll find a way to get back. The bigger question is what happens *after*."

"After what?" asked Tee.

"After *everything*. If everything goes just the way it's supposed to—what then? Even if our guy gets elected, or holds a major power position in Iran, what next? You think one man can turn a few million raving lunatics into rational citizens? I'll be amazed if Hezbollah doesn't kill him in one week."

Duce frowned his crooked frown. "Remember how you were saying Mike was a crafty sumbitch? I think this guy is the shit. He's lived under a fake identity for most of his life! Can you imagine? I'd be in the fucking loony bin. If anyone can pull this off, it's gotta be him."

"Yeah, well, I sure hope you're right, 'cause this has been the most miserable two weeks of my life outside of Vietnam, and I'd hate to have walked all this way for nothing."

And so they sipped coffee, shot the breeze, and waited.

CHAPTER 47

Strait of Hormuz

Master Chief Parker was pacing around the deck, finishing his cigar, when Diane called him over to the container. When he heard her voice, he tossed the cigar and double-timed it over.

"Whaddya got for me, Doc?" he asked.

She pointed to the device, which was partly disassembled on one side. Her partner, Dr. Tompkins, was on a phone with other NEST team members back on the *Kitty Hawk*. The NEST team on the *Kitty Hawk* was logged on to their computer systems and comparing diagrams and schematics to Tompkins's descriptions of the device to get the best advice. The screen on the computer read eleven minutes, eleven seconds, and counting.

"Sir, according to the best information available to us, I believe we have damaged the shell sufficiently enough to prevent the chain reaction. We also believe that cutting the computer timer off from the device will instantly set it off, so that's not an option. It is our opinion—Dr. Tompkins's, mine and the NEST team members on the *Kitty Hawk*—that if we sink this ship and allow it to detonate underwater, it will provide the safest possible outcome."

"That outcome, Doc—does that mean we have a chance to live through this?"

"A very good chance, but only if we can get everyone off and sink this ship in ten minutes."

"Say no more, Doc. Just get ready to move." He turned and pulled a whistle from his pocket and gave an ear-splitting shrill call. "Now hear this! We are getting off of this vessel immediately! Prepare for immediate evacuation! Officers, account for your men and assemble on me!" He grabbed his radio and called back to Captain Bennett, who was anxiously awaiting word. "Sir, we have high probability of surviving this thing if we get off this ship immediately and sink her in the next nine and a half minutes. I am requesting immediate evacuation of all personnel."

"Thank God, Master Chief. Evacuate immediately and return to the *Kitty Hawk*."

The master chief recalled the large Sea Dragon, which was circling the ship. With some very fancy flying, the pilot held his position just over the railing of the ship and lowered the rear ramp. The sea was fairly calm, and the ramp stayed within a few inches of the deck. As the Marines prepared to load their wounded and dead, and then evacuate, CPO Cascaes ran over to the master chief.

"Master Chief, do you have room for my men on your chopper?"

"I have room for all of you, Cascaes, and I suggest you get your team on board pronto, including whoever is still down in the sub."

"Negative, Master Chief. I cannot abandon that submarine. Besides, we may need it to recover whatever is left of the package."

"Cascaes, my guess is that there will be nothing left of anything down there, including your sub, but if you cannot scuttle your ship, then good luck and get moving. I'll take whoever you don't need to operate your vessel."

CPO Cascaes extended his hand. "Thank you, Master Chief. Hope to see you with dry feet real soon." They shook hands. Cascaes ordered all of his team to leave by helicopter, which was met with great protest when they realized Cascaes was heading back to the sub without them. He had three men on board the sub, plus himself, which was enough to operate it. There was no sense risking anyone else. He saluted his men and ran off to the side of the rail, where he jumped into the water feet first—a long way down to the surf. He recovered and swam back to the sub, climbed up the side to the sub's top hatch, opened it and disappeared inside. The SCUBA team was back inside with his second in command, and followed instructions immediately as they cut the power to the electromagnetic tethers and proceeded to maximum speed at periscope depth.

As soon as they were under way, Cascaes alerted his men to what was happening topside as he looked through the periscope. "We will stay full speed ahead, as far away from that ship as we can get. By my watch we have six minutes to maximize our distance. Our mines will detonate in two minutes, followed by the device in another four or so . . ."

Aboard the ship, the Marines were evacuating. Doctors Tompkins and Peters were using every last second to continue disassembling as much of the exterior shell as possible. Master Chief Parker ran up to them and yelled, "That's it! We are loaded and ready to go! This ship is going down in two minutes! Come on!"

The two of them dropped their tools and followed the master chief to the chopper. Parker picked up the two of them like they were weightless and tossed them up to the ramp. He screamed at the Marine major who was standing at the ramp, "Are we all present and accounted for, Major?"

"Aye, aye, Master Chief, including our casualties."

Parker jumped up into the ramp and hit the control that closed the door. He grabbed the phone off the wall that connected to the cockpit. "This is Master Chief Parker! Get us the hell out of here!"

The chopper was moving forward instantly, and they were at 150 knots within a minute. The sound of the three mines going off under the ship made everyone look out the porthole windows of the Sea Dragon. They were heavy charges, and they split the hull in two like a cracker. As the center collapsed, the bow and stern almost met in the middle. The containers all slid into the middle, falling like giant dominoes as the white foam blew over the top of the rails. Dozens of containers rolled, some of them covering the orange container that housed the atomic bomb. The ship sank quickly, in under four minutes, giving rise to some cheers and expletives from the Marines watching through the windows.

A few moments later, the device detonated, but only partially, sending a dull *thump* as the shock wave rolled through the ocean. Cascaes and his SEALs where tossed around slightly underwater, but the sub held together.

Cascaes, who had watched the ship sink off of his stern, turned to his crew. "That noise, gentlemen, is the sound of our fleet living to fight another day." The SEALs didn't cheer, they just let their heads rest back against the cold walls of the sub, and said quiet thank-yous to the Almighty.

CPO Cascaes turned to the other three SEALs on board the sub. "Hernandez didn't make it, fellas. He did real well out there. They all did. Everyone else evac'ed with the chopper. SEAL Team Six may have just saved the entire carrier fleet and prevented World War Three. Hernandez didn't die for nothing up there. I'm putting him in for the Navy Cross."

Cascaes turned around and peered through the periscope, not so much to see above the water, but to hide his own watering eyes.

He called back to the *Kitty Hawk*, where Captain Bennett was nervously waiting to find out whether or not he still had a submarine in the water. Hearing that they had survived the blast, he requested that they return and use their cameras to record the wreck and find out if there was anything that should be salvaged from the bomb, however unlikely. Cascaes turned the sub around and descended to almost three hundred feet, back to the location of the destroyed ship. With a few hundred destroyed containers and a shipwreck of twisted metal, it would be a long chore to find anything that resembled a nuclear weapon.

CHAPTER 48

Iran-Iraq Border

Mike had followed the same route he used the last time he left Iran, although this time it was a little more difficult. He had been stopped twice outside of Tehran and forced out of his car. His papers passed quick inspection, and his car had nothing in it to raise any suspicion. There were mobs everywhere in Tehran, some protesting and carrying signs for whomever they supported to replace their fallen leaders, some just out looking for the latest news and gossip. There hadn't been any looting because of a large Army and police presence, but the Army generals themselves were still debating as to whom was running the country. So far, the country had not slipped into civil war, but the demonstrations were getting larger and louder, and for the first time in a generation, there were groups calling for real elections and denouncing violence.

The Grand Ayatollah Kamala was all over the news, with hardliners reeling in shock, and moderates, who had long opposed his views, now coming to his support. The power vacuum was obvious, especially now with the assassination of Ali bin-Oman. Whether people suspected Kamala and his supporters or not, no one had accused him yet, most likely out of fear of making an enemy out of him. Kamala did his best to keep Army brass around him whenever on TV, giving the appearance of having national support and the strength of the armed forces, although not every general necessarily supported Kamala or liked his new view on the world.

It took two days for Mike to get back to the tribal lands of the Lur people. At the same village where he had traded his car the last time for a camel, he again saw the chief and sold the same vehicle. It cost him some extra cash this time around, since the car was fairly trashed, albeit by *them*. He purchased another nasty camel and some local food and told them he would see them soon, although in his own mind, he was saying *adios* forever.

With Iran's government in chaos, the borders had gotten busier. Hezbollah terrorists and other groups that had been infiltrating into Iraq were now returning to Iran to make sure the outrageous commentary of the traitor Grand Ayatollah Kamala could be crushed. While it was good for Iraq to have the terror organizations refocusing their efforts, it turned the border towns into the Wild West. As Mike neared the border, activity picked up both with Iranian Army patrols and small groups of militia from any one of a number of terrorist groups. He hid many times and was forced to wait until danger passed, being unarmed and without any kind of help available. What had been a half-day trip from the Lur village to Iraq last time now took two full days. When he finally arrived at the border, Iranian Army patrols were everywhere. Mike sat in the rocks and watched as the patrols completely ignored the militia groups that were crossing back and forth. Apparently, they were there to warn of any large-scale invasion from the U.S. or Iraq, but could care less about Hezbollah or the like. Still, Mike waited until near dark before he made his move to cross the invisible line that separated the two countries.

Mike had no compass, no radio, no equipment of any kind other than his brain, which had memorized maps of the emergency rendezvous point. This was the place where he had crossed many times before over the years, and he knew the narrow trails well. When he was fairly confident that he was not being watched, he crossed quickly into Iraq—as quickly as his camel would move, anyway. The Lur head wrap covered his face and hid his broad smile as he thought to himself that this would be his last camel ride—an experience he wouldn't miss.

He entered Iraq without incident and spent almost an entire day snaking through the mountain passes to his rendezvous point. Army Rangers stepping out in front of his camel with weapons out signaled that he was finally on his way home. He removed his head wrap and smiled broadly.

In English, he said loudly, "I am an American citizen, and I would very much appreciate it if you folks could get me the fuck out of here."

The sergeant laughed out loud, and Tee and Still stepped out of the woods with Duce walking out from the other side of the trail. "You've been a busy boy," said Tee.

"I *was* busy but I am officially *retired* just as soon as you can get me back to the good ol' U.S. of A."

Duce walked over and held the camel reins so Mike could dismount. Mike kicked the camel, and it knelt down on the ground with a loud protest. Mike hopped down and took the reins from Duce, then slapped the smelly beast in the ass and sent it on its way.

"Betcha a hundred bucks that nasty thing walks right back home to that Lur village. The chief will be thanking Allah for another three months. I will *not* miss sitting on that thing." Mike threw off the Lur garb and turned to Duce.

"You got a hot shower and something to eat anywhere close to here?" he asked with a smile.

"Fresh out of hot showers, but we can hook you up with some MREs. I hear there are plenty of hot showers back in the States, though. Okay boys, let's bounce!" announced Duce.

The rangers returned to their small camp and pulled down their tents to begin the long walk back to Iron Mountain, where Mike would debrief Jerry and catch the first ride back home.

CHAPTER 49

USS *Kitty Hawk*

C hris Mackey was standing with Captain Bennett on the deck of the carrier, near the island, when the Marine helicopter landed. They had called ahead, and Navy corpsmen were on hand when the rear ramp opened. The dead and wounded were escorted to sick bay, and the Marines assembled on the deck in formation, with the SEALs and NEST team alongside. Captain Bennett walked over to where the marine major and ranking SEAL saluted.

"Casualties have been taken to sick bay, and all Marines are present and accounted for, sir," snapped the major. The SEAL repeated the same report.

"At ease, gentlemen—and lady," said the captain, looking at Diane. "You have completed a dangerous and important assignment. While we did not recover the device, I still consider this mission an overall success. I will expect full reports by this afternoon, at which time all members of all teams will each receive two weeks liberty to the port of your choice. Outstanding job, people. You are dismissed, and I want you off this flight deck. I have a hell of a lot of aircraft returning to this carrier in the next few minutes. Dr. Peters, come with me. You too, Major."

Mackey followed them back into the island, where they hopped on an elevator to the bridge. The captain introduced Mackey to Diane and the major. They went back to the captain's office and sat down at his conference table.

"You did one hell of a job out there, Doc. Your NEST team here was a busy bunch of beavers. They took over this office with their computers and were running schematics and theories back and forth between you and Nevada. I guess your training paid off big-time."

"Training and some guessing, sir. Quite honestly, we were in way over our heads. We were trained extensively in search and identification, along with emergency evacuation procedures. We never trained to actually disassemble a nuclear device— that was only classroom theory mixed with desperation."

"And guts, Doc. Don't forget guts," added the major.

"Amen to that. In any case, I have been in contact with our SEAL team leader aboard our submarine. They have searched the wreck site, but it is the opinion of our officer that there isn't anything recoverable down there. I was just curious about your assessment, if you have one. I need to call the commander in chief and tell him whether or not there is a loose nuke down at the bottom of the strait."

Diane nodded her head. "I understand, sir. We wouldn't want anything recovered that could be reused by these groups. I suppose if someone had the right equipment—a sub with radiological detection equipment, and a way to pick through tons of scrap metal—they might be able to salvage some tiny pieces of radioactive material, but realistically, the warhead would have been blown to a million pieces under water, and scattered in that wreckage. I am confident that whatever is left down there will stay down there."

"Just don't eat the crabs from around here for another hundred thousand years or so, right Doc?" the major said.

"Actually, I think very little will be contaminated. The pieces will be buried under heavy steel, and in another few months, probably a few hundred tons of sand. All things considered, I think we came out pretty well." She sat back and exhaled, and let the reality of her day sink in. She was somewhat ashen looking.

"You think we 'came out pretty well,' Doc? I had ordered all of my aircraft off of this float along with whatever person- nel I could save from being incinerated. Forget the few billion dollars you saved the U.S. taxpayers, you saved most of my sailors and Marines. I am not sure if you even qualify, not be- ing actual military personnel, but I am putting you and your buddy—what's his name?"

"Dr. Tompkins."

"Dr. Tompkins—I am putting both of your names in for the Medal of Honor."

She smiled. "I am honored to be considered, sir, but actu- ally, you are correct—I work for the Energy Department. I am not a soldier. I'd settle for a few days off on a beach some- where."

"Funny you should mention it," said Mackey.

They all turned and looked at him. He shrugged and smiled. "I was flown out here on a virtual suicide mission to fly that bomb somewhere. Turns out, I get to live after all and I have no mission currently. The beach sounds perfect. I'll buy the first round. Maybe the second and third, too."

She laughed, but he didn't take his eyes away from hers. She realized he probably wasn't kidding, and she blushed, which wasn't missed by the captain.

"Dr. Peters, you have two weeks liberty just like everyone else. You want to spend it with this man, it's fine with me. If you'd like me to throw him in the brig, that's fine with me, too."

Diane smiled and looked right at Mackey. "Thank you, Captain. I'll see what he can do to sweeten up the offer, and get back to you on that."

"Fair enough." He gave a rare smile. "Major, I'll need a full briefing as soon as you can put it together. In the meantime, I wanted both of you here in the room when I call the com- mander in chief. I am sure he'll want to thank you personally."

CHAPTER 50

FOP Iron Mountain

Jerry was sitting on his ammo crate lounge chair drinking lousy coffee and waiting for Langley to call him back. He had called in, and both Davis and Murphy were in with the joint chiefs and would get back to him. He had just gotten word from the rangers that Mike was safe and they were on the way back to the forward observation post. There were still two large pieces of the mess that weren't finished yet. Bijon needed to secure power in Iran, and a few hundred suicide bombers with chemical weapons were running around in Lebanon, Gaza and the West Bank.

He had worked some big cases in his career, but this was the topper. Although he was more of a manager than a field operative this time around, it had been a stressful few weeks. He was thinking about Mike coming out of Iran for good. Might be a good time for a long break for himself, too. Maybe do some fishing. He was enjoying his fishing fantasy when the radiophone beeped.

"Iron Mountain, here."

"Hey, Jerry, it's Dex." Murphy was so tired his speech was

slurred. "Stay awake" pills could only go so far before you needed to actually sleep. "What have you got for me?"

"Our boy should be safe on the mountain in a few hours. He is in Iraq."

"Great news. Any word from inside?"

"Negative, and I don't expect any. Maybe ever. At some point, he may be running the show, and might have open relations with the U.S. Might get a chance to catch up on old times then, but I doubt he'd be able to do it before then. He'll have a lot of eyeballs on him now."

"Yeah, I would expect so. Word is Hezbollah has already put a price on his head. They are supremely pissed at his new enlightenment, and they aren't alone. I hope your boy can stay alive for the next few days."

"Me, too. What's the word on your side?"

"All good news so far. SEALs and Marines took down the ship. The NEST team neutralized the bomb and saved the entire fleet. One last piece of this sticky wicket to deal with, which POTUS will take care of with a phone call."

"Phone call?" asked Jerry.

"Yeah, he is going to brief the Israeli prime minister in a few minutes. He is going to give him the whole story. Should be an interesting conversation. I would imagine the Israelis won't be pleased to find out they were out of the loop for this long with a nuke potentially going off on their soil. We are rattling every cage and shaking every tree we can to get some hard intelligence on the whereabouts of these chemical weapons, but preliminary reports aren't good."

"How so?"

"Typical terrorist warfare. Early reports have the weapons stockpiled in hospitals, mosques, schools—civilian areas. If the Israelis hit them, the civilian casualties will be enormous."

"So what are they going to do?"

"What would *you* do?" asked Dex sadly. "They have no choice. By the time the Arabs get done spinning the tale, it will have the Israelis dropping chemical weapons on the Palestinians and Lebanese."

"Jesus. Same shit, different day. Let me know how it goes. I will advise you when I have everyone back on the mountain. Call me if anything changes."

"If anything changes," said Dex, "you'll be watching it on Fox News."

CHAPTER 51

USS *Kitty Hawk*

The USS *Pigeon* secured the USS *Intruder* and the hatch opened. CPO Cascaes climbed out, followed by his three men, who then climbed the ladder back up to the ship. Cascaes would later be flown by helicopter over to the *Kitty Hawk*, where he would report to Captain Bennett and be reunited with his men. His actions that day would later earn him a Navy Cross and promotion to Senior Chief Petty Officer.

Aboard the *Kitty Hawk*, Master Chief Parker stood outside on the bridge balcony with Captain Bennett and watched as the last of their aircraft returned to the *Kitty Hawk*. They stood in silence, smoking cigars, and thinking that it had been a pretty good day after all. They had come within a hair of losing their entire flotilla—thousands of servicemen and -women and a few hundred billion dollars worth of equipment. An event like that stays with a person for a while. Both men wished they could just unleash the power of their fleet on some responsible target somewhere, but, unfortunately, those decisions were above their pay grade.

Inside the wardroom, what had started as a joke between Mackey and Diane had boiled over into a serious conversation about sharing their two-week liberty. Mackey was up front about his plans for retirement from "government service," as he put it. Diane wasn't an idiot—she knew he was CIA or something, and found him intriguing, although a bit older than her. She had come pretty close to being part of a mushroom cloud that morning, and the idea of being on the beach with a handsome man was sounding pretty good. They walked the ship and got to know each other for a few hours. By mid-afternoon, they had decided that two weeks in Hawaii, very far from where they were right now, sounded like a pretty good plan.

Mike, Tee, Still and Duce arrived at Iron Mountain late the following morning. By the time they arrived, Still had come to the conclusion he was officially done. Tee and Duce, on the other hand, were as gung-ho as ever, and figured they were far from finished. Depending on what happened in the next week or so, they might be getting started on their next assignment. Mike listened quietly to their discussions the whole trip back, but said very little. He was torn. He worried about Bijon and the future of a country that had been his home for so many years—although he was somewhat a prisoner all those years. He was finished with all of this now himself, but it would be a long time before he knew what it was like to be normal again. All he wanted was a beach that had a bar and lots of women, all speaking English while wearing very small bathing suits.

When they arrived at the FOP, Jerry was there to greet them, and called them into the cave, where a small TV was turned on. Their satellite dish enabled them to pick up Fox News back in the States, and as soon as they walked to the TV, they all sat and listened.

And now for this special report—Crisis in the Middle East.

Israel invaded southern Lebanon, Gaza and the West Bank today after dropping leaflets warning residents to evacuate before they were attacked. The Israeli Air Force and IDF artillery began pounding targets, and there are scattered rumors of chemical weapons being used in Lebanon. Similar stories are being heard in Gaza and the West Bank, where several dozen explosions have occurred, sending clouds of unknown poison gas throughout several refugee camps. While Israel vehemently denies ever using any chemical or biological weapons, reports of tens of thousands of Palestinian deaths are beginning to be heard all over Gaza and the West Bank. Israel's prime minister has called a press conference, and has promised to deliver news that will shock all civilized nations of the world.

The president of the United States and the British prime minister, who had just arrived in Washington, also said they would be holding a joint press conference following the Israeli prime minister's address. They, too, say that their press conference will send shock waves throughout the world that will reverberate for a long time, and prove the need to continue the war on terror that has grown unpopular in recent months.

Meanwhile, in Tehran, radical Moslem leader Grand Ayatollah Kamala has stunned conservative Iranians with a break from his previous position against Israel and the West. In excerpts from speeches he delivered all over the Middle East via Al Jazeera and Iranian television, the Grand Ayatollah was shown speaking to huge crowds in Tehran. He claims that a divine vision has caused him to change his world-view. He no longer demands the destruction of Israel and all infidels, and has proposed opening relations with the West if elected to replace assassinated President Mowad Asmunjaniwal. In comments that were nothing less than shocking to his supporters, the Grand Ayatollah has admitted that many teachings of Islamic leaders in Iran and elsewhere have been gross distortions of the Koran meant to distract Moslems in the Middle East from the failed governments of those countries. He pointed to poverty levels in oil-rich nations, the lack of education, and increasing violence as proof of the government's inability to lead. If elected, the imam claims he will rebuild Iran to a modern nation that will encourage a more open society, tolerant of non-Moslems.

Several Hezbollah militants have been arrested after attempting to assassinate Grand Ayatollah Kamala, who was unhurt in the plot. Iranian Army officials foiled the attack and killed the militants. Kamala wasted no time in saying that Hezbollah again proves his point, that too many Moslems resort to violence when they are challenged on any political or religious viewpoint. Kamala claims he will lay the foundation for a peaceful Iran that will be a partner in the global village. Huge demonstrations continue all over Iran as political forces fight for seats in the new government to be elected in two weeks. While half of the Iranians polled object to Ayatollah Kamala's new views, it is doubtful that any single political opponent can garner enough votes to beat him in the upcoming elections . . .

Jerry turned off the television and looked at the four exhausted men in front of him. "Mike and the rest of you, I have been saving these for a long time. It is the rest of your six-pack, Mike. I gave you the first two the last time you came out of Iran. You have to share these."

He threw each of them warm, rusty cans of beer from his pack.

"You guys earned these. The world may never know what you guys did, but you'll know for the rest of your lives. I think I can say, on behalf of every citizen of the United States, thank you."

From the classics
to the cutting edge
Don't miss the intrigue and the
action from these internationally
bestselling authors...
Tom Clancy
Clive Cussler
Jack Higgins
Your favorite international thrillers
come from Berkley.
penguin.com

Don't miss the page-turning suspense, intriguing characters, and unstoppable action that keep readers coming back for more from these bestselling authors...

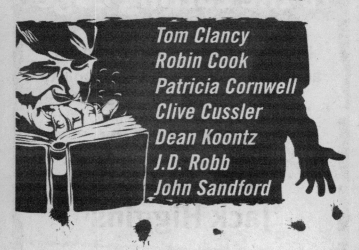

Tom Clancy
Robin Cook
Patricia Cornwell
Clive Cussler
Dean Koontz
J.D. Robb
John Sandford

Your favorite thrillers and suspense novels come from Berkley.